DARK ANGEL'S SEDUCTION

THE CHILDREN OF THE GODS BOOK 15

I. T. LUCAS

Also by I. T. Lucas

THE CHILDREN OF THE GODS ORIGINS

THE CHILDREN OF THE GODS

DARK STRANGER

DARK ENEMY

KRI & MICHAEL'S STORY

DARK WARRIOR

DARK GUARDIAN

DARK ANGEL

DARK OPERATIVE

PERFECT MATCH

PERFECT MATCH 1: VAMPIRE'S CONSORT
PERFECT MATCH 2: KING'S CHOSEN
PERFECT MATCH 3: CAPTAIN'S CONQUEST

SETS

THE CHILDREN OF THE GODS BOOKS 1-3: DARK STRANGER TRILOGY—INCLUDES A BONUS SHORT STORY: THE FATES TAKE A VACATION

THE CHILDREN OF THE GODS: BOOKS 1-6—INCLUDES CHARACTER LISTS

THE CHILDREN OF THE GODS: BOOKS 6.5-10 —INCLUDES CHARACTER LISTS

TRY THE CHILDREN OF THE GODS SERIES ON **AUDIBLE**

2 FREE audiobooks with your new Audible subscription!

NOTE FROM THE AUTHOR:

This is a work of fiction!

Names, characters, places and incidents are products of the author's imagination or are used fictitiously and are not to be construed as real. Any similarity to actual persons, organizations and/or events is purely coincidental.

CONTENTS

CHAPTER 1: BRUNDAR

Faith.

Brundar had lost his so long ago, he couldn't remember ever believing that there was any good in people.

Betrayal by someone you considered a brother, someone you loved and trusted with not only your heart but your very life, would do that to a guy.

He'd learned his lesson the hard way.

He trusted no one, depended on no one, except himself and his sword arm and his aim.

Deadly.

It was more than a description, it was his essence.

He was the Grim Reaper.

Or at least he had been until Calypso had turned his world upside down. The sense of vertigo was disturbing, destructive, dangerous to a warrior who depended on a quiet mind to maintain the focus crucial to his survival.

The only antidote was distance.

Not his resolve because his was worth shit, and not his logical mind because it barely functioned in Calypso's presence.

The further away from her he got, the more time that passed since he'd been with her, the clearer his thoughts became.

One would think that he would utilize the one remedy available to him and stay the hell away from her. But no, apparently he was a glutton for the fucking vertigo because time and again he returned for more.

If Brundar had had any faith left in him, he would have prayed to the Fates for guidance. But the bitches were a myth, existing only in the minds of fools. As to those made of flesh and blood, he had no friends, and the only one even remotely close to him was his brother, who was the equivalent of an old yenta and the last person Brundar wanted to confide in or ask for help. Anandur would do anything for him, he never doubted it, but he would exact a payment in the form of information to feed his insatiable hunger for fresh gossip he could spread around.

With a sigh, Brundar filled the carafe with water from the filter and poured it into the coffeemaker.

"What's that grim face for?" Anandur asked as he entered the kitchen.

Brundar ignored him.

But naturally, Anandur wouldn't let it go. "You seem gloomier than usual. What's the matter, no food?" He pulled the fridge door open. "Do not despair, bro. We have leftover Italian." He took out the container.

Brundar regarded his brother with a grimace. "Only you can eat pasta for breakfast."

"You're welcome to cook. I would like an omelet with a side of hash and four pieces of toast," Anandur teased. "But since you won't..." he shrugged. Forking a swirl of cold spaghetti straight from the container, he stuffed it into his mouth.

The guy could eat anything, including a week-old moldy pizza and food leftovers on other people's plates.

Charming and easygoing, Anandur had the capacity to feel for his partners and yet never get attached or possessive. No woman ever harbored ill feelings toward him, and not because he made sure they didn't remember him. The guy's thrall was so pathetically weak that he could barely erase the memory of his bite.

How the hell did he manage to keep his heart open while protecting it from emotional attachment?

"Let me ask you something." Brundar poured himself coffee.

"Ask," Anandur said with a mouthful of pasta.

"You were fond of that Russian you pumped for information, right?"

Out of all the Guardians, Anandur was the only one who would take on a mission like that. He had no qualms about pretending to be a lowly deck boy or seducing one of Alex's all-female Russian yacht crew.

Acting the bum was one thing. Anandur probably had fun with that. But agreeing to whore himself out was another.

Thankfully, Kian had never asked Brundar to do anything even remotely of that nature. He was a lousy actor, and using sex as a tool was abhorrent to him. Give him a weapon, point out an enemy to kill, and he'd deal with it.

Even if he hadn't had issues with the morality of such underhanded acts, he was too rigid for subterfuge.

"Yeah, she was a fine piece of ass. Not the sharpest brain, but the shapeliest legs. Beautiful and strong." Anandur flexed his biceps. "I mean muscle strong. When she wrapped those around me and squeezed, believe me, I felt it." Anandur shifted himself in his pants.

Evidently, he remembered Lana quite fondly.

"But even though you liked her and spent a few weeks with her, you had no problem saying goodbye."

Anandur grabbed a mug and filled it from the carafe. "Not entirely true. I was worried about how she would take it. But Lana is a tough cookie and life-smart. She said she didn't feel it either. It wasn't love. We parted as good friends." He took a sip of coffee.

"What would you have done if she'd clung to you?"

"Then it would have been a bitch. I don't like hurting people. Not unless they earned it, that is. Alex, for example, I had no problem hurting. The scumbag got off easy with entombment. I would have flayed his skin off first."

"I would have helped."

They nodded to each other in agreement.

It warmed Brundar's cold heart that his brother wasn't all that different from him. On the outside, the guy might have appeared the charming and good-natured one; on the inside, though, he was just as bloodthirsty and cruel as Brundar.

But unlike those they hunted, he and his brother reserved their wrath for those who'd earned it. Alex and other scum like him who kidnapped people and sold them into slavery didn't deserve mercy. They deserved eternal damnation in the deepest, most fiery pits of hell, in the company of other soulless creatures who preyed on the weak.

Anandur put the mug on the counter and lifted the box of leftovers, taking another forkful. "Why all the questions? Do you need advice on how to dump someone?"

"No."

Anandur's smile turned into a frown. "When you actually want to talk, come find me." He stood up and threw the empty container in the trash.

If Brundar wanted advice, he needed to keep talking. "Did you ever feel like you wanted to keep one of the human women you hooked up with?"

Anandur shook his head. "No. Do you want to keep yours?"

Brundar should have known better than to turn to his brother. He needed answers, not more questions. Anandur was as blunt as ever, but not helpful in the least.

"As what? A pet? Keep her locked up until she gets old and dies?"

With a sigh, Anandur patted his shoulder. "It's tough to have feelings for a human. I can't believe I'm saying that to you, not when I've been waiting for centuries to hear your heart beating again, but you need to get rid of the girl sooner rather than later. It's a shame because I'm glad to see you finally thawing, but the longer you wait, the harder it's going to be. I don't want to see you break."

Regrettably, Anandur had no magical solution. His words echoed Brundar's thoughts to the letter.

"Can I trust you not to breathe a word of this to anyone?"

"All you have to do is ask, and it's done. Did you ever know me to reveal a secret I was asked to keep?"

Brundar thought back to Anandur's many years of gossiping, and the truth was that he'd never betrayed the confidence of anyone who'd asked him to keep a secret.

He dipped his head in a slight bow. "My apologies for insinuating a flaw of character. The insult was unwarranted."

Anandur rolled his eyes. "Sheesh, so formal. Apology accepted." He clapped Brundar on the shoulder. "Good luck with your lady friend. Whatever you decide to do, you can count on me to back you up."

"I know."

"Good. Sometimes I'm not sure you remember that."

CHAPTER 2: CALLIE

*W*aking up alone wasn't a big surprise. But it was disappointing nonetheless. Callie hadn't expected Brundar to stay the night, but a tiny part of her had wished he would.

This morning, her heart and her mind were in an even greater state of sensory overload than the day before. Probably because she'd had time to process. She needed to talk about what had happened between them. She needed to feel connected to the man with whom she'd shared so many firsts.

The girl who had married the first guy she'd had sex with had celebrated her divorce by seducing a dangerous man who was so far from the norm he was practically an alien. And she wasn't referring to Brundar's sexual proclivities, which were strange to say the least.

Look who's talking.

As if she'd been an innocent lamb who had no idea what she was getting herself into. Brundar had been honest and upfront about everything, and yet, fully informed of his preferences, Callie had pursued him with a single-minded determination. On his side, he had done everything he could to deter her.

Was that why she'd gone after him like she'd never gone after any guy before?

Perhaps she'd subconsciously considered his reluctance a challenge?

Or was it something else?

What did it say about her that she'd chosen a bondage aficionado as her first after Shawn?

Way to come out with a bang, Callie.

It had been amazing.

She hadn't known such heights of sensory pleasure were even possible. And she hadn't expected a guy who kept his heart locked in an impenetrable box to be so completely self-less either.

Knowing that without a condom he couldn't take it any further, he'd pleasured her into oblivion and then refused her offer to reciprocate orally because she'd been exhausted by the experience.

On the other hand, had the lack of a condom been an excuse? And if yes, why?

Callie had no plausible answer for that.

Why would a guy deliberately choose to go home with a giant case of blue balls? And it wasn't as if Brundar hadn't been affected. She'd seen the evidence of his arousal even though he'd never taken off his pants.

One thing Callie knew for sure, as soon as she made it to a pharmacy, she was going to buy a bunch of them.

The thing was, it wasn't all about sex, and emotionally Callie had been left bereft. She needed more from a relation-ship, even a casual one. But then, she should've been prepared for that. What had she expected from a guy whose range of emotions spanned between indifferent to margin-ally interested, or from stoic to mildly amused?

Nevertheless, Brundar's quiet presence had been reassuring. She loved having him around even though she was the one doing all the talking and his responses were limited to an occasional nod or a single word.

It was strange how this man who seemed as cold as a marble statue had managed to fill the apartment with warmth. In his absence, the place felt like the temporary shelter it was and not a home.

Maybe she could call Brundar and invite him to stop by and have lunch with her. They could talk, or rather she would talk and Brundar would do his statue impersonation. It was better than the silence, better than the vacuum in which her thoughts ran in circles with no anchor.

She had his number, but he'd given it with explicit instructions to use only in emergencies. Was there a way she could claim her need to see him was an emergency?

For her it was.

Right. The last thing she should do was to appear clingy and needy, not unless she wanted to see him run leaving skid marks on the sidewalk.

He would be at the club tonight. She could hold out until then.

A cup of coffee in hand, Callie sat down at her dining table and opened a book, ready to put in her two hours of studying.

After half an hour she gave up. At the rate she'd been going, it would've taken her double the time to go over the same material. She couldn't concentrate, reading the same paragraph over and over again and still not getting what she was reading because thoughts of Brundar kept interfering.

Crap. She needed someone to talk to before her head exploded.

Calling Brundar was out, and calling Dawn was still dangerous, which left only one person.

Miriam. Or Miri as the barmaid liked to be called.

They'd exchanged numbers with the vague promise to hang out sometimes. Maybe she should take her new friend up on that offer.

With spiked blue hair, arms that were covered in tattoos starting at the wrist and going all the way up to her shoulders, a nose stud, and a dirty mouth, Miri wasn't the type Callie would've normally befriended.

But that was the old Callie who for the past two years had been living under a rock. The new Callie was all about grabbing life by the horns, which translated into taking chances, experimenting with new sensations, and getting to know new people.

Pulling her phone out of her purse, she rang Miri.

"Yeah."

"Hi, it's Callie. Do you want to hang out before work?"

"I do, but I have a nail appointment."

Miri's nails were tiny works of arts, and she changed the designs on a weekly basis.

"How about after your appointment?"

"I have a better idea. Come with me."

"To the nail place?"

"Yeah. Yours could use some decorations."

Callie had had her nails done exactly once. For her wedding. "Don't I need an appointment?"

"Nah. You're with me. Get ready. I'll come get you in half an hour. And wear flip-flops if you want your toes done too."

"Thanks. You're awesome." Not having a car was a drag. She was lucky Miri didn't mind picking her up.

Dressed in a pair of old faded jeans, a plain T-shirt, and flip-flops, Callie waited for Miri's call. She was excited. Since Dawn had left for MIT, Callie hadn't done anything fun with a friend.

When the call came, she ran down the stairs taking two at

a time, her flip-flops making a ruckus that echoed through the stairwell.

"Are you going to get acrylics?" Miri asked as Callie got in. "They are durable." She wiggled her fingers, tapping the steering wheel to demonstrate how tough her nails were. This week it was butterflies—a different one for each nail.

"I think I'll start with a manicure and a clear nail polish."

Miri smirked. "A nail virgin, eh?"

"No, but almost. I had them done once. For my wedding."

"You're married?"

"Not anymore."

"High five, sister."

They clapped palms.

"What about you?"

Miri shrugged. "I dumped my boyfriend's sorry ass after three years of living together. Got tired of watching him sit around the apartment and do nothing, while I worked and paid the bills and did everything else. Supposedly, he was pursuing his true calling." She rolled her eyes, making air quotes with her fingers while holding the steering wheel with her thumbs.

"What was it?" Callie asked.

"His true calling? He claimed it was music. But the only thing he excelled at was bumming, while I was the idiot enabling him. Took me three fucking years to get smart and realize that the motherfucker was using me."

With a screech of tires, Miri turned into a parking spot that had just been vacated.

The *salon* occupied a corner of a tattoo shop and had only one beautician, a woman who was covered in even more tattoos than Miri, displaying them proudly by wearing a muscle shirt and shorts.

"Hey, Lisa, can you squeeze in a manicure for Callie here before your next appointment?"

"What's up, Callie?" Lisa smiled before turning back to Miri. "Depends on what you have in mind for today. If it's something elaborate then no."

Miri plopped down on a chair and pointed for Callie to sit next to her. "I'm in a patriotic mood. Stars and stripes. That shouldn't take too long."

"Then yeah." Lisa put a folded towel over her workstation.

Sitting sideways and facing Callie, Miri offered Lisa her hand. "So, what's the story with you and Donnie?"

What? That came out of nowhere.

"Donnie the bouncer? Nothing."

"You spend all your breaks outside with him. And I know that he walks you home sometimes. I was wondering if you guys had something going on."

"I go outside to give my eardrums a break from the hellish sound levels in the club, not to hang out with Donnie, although he is a nice guy and I enjoy his company. But he is only a friend. Nothing more."

Miri narrowed her eyes at Callie. "What about when he walks you home? Do you ever invite him to come in?"

"No, I don't."

The girl wasn't buying it. Her eyes were still full of suspicion. "Why not? You're single, and you think he is cool. Not too shabby to look at either."

Aha. So that was the reason Miri had invited her to come have her nails done. Not because she wanted to be friends, but because she wanted to grill Callie about Donnie.

Barely stifling a laugh, Callie crossed her arms over her chest and returned Miri's glower. "I think someone has a crush on our hunky bouncer."

Miri waved her free hand. "Your lingo is so high school. No one over eighteen calls it a crush."

"What do they call it then?"

"Doesn't matter. I think he's hot. Don't you think?" Miri was still fishing.

"I think he is a great guy, and he is all yours. The only reason he walks me home is that Brun... I mean Brad asked him to. Franco walks me home too. Do you think I have something going on with him as well?"

Miri shrugged. "Some girls like variety. I don't judge."

Yeah, right. "Well, I don't. One is more than enough for me."

"And who's that one?"

Wasn't it obvious? Or was Miri playing dumb to have Callie admit it?

Whatever, she had no reason to hide their involvement. Brundar hadn't told her to keep whatever was going on between them a secret. He might have implied it by ignoring her at the club, but she could play dumb as well as the next girl. The bottom line was that she needed someone to talk to, and Miri was the only one available. Even if she had her own agenda.

"Brad."

Miri's eyes widened. "I heard rumors, but I didn't believe them. You have the hots for the Grim Reaper?"

Ouch, what a nasty nickname. "You know how it goes. The heart wants what the heart wants. It might not make sense to anyone else, but he is the only one I'm interested in."

"Poor girl." Miri reached with her free hand and patted Callie's knee. "He is a looker, I'll give him that. And I hear he is good with the whip. So I guess he appeals to a certain type. I just didn't think you were into that stuff. You sure don't look it with your innocent girl-next-door looks."

"Kinky," Lisa butted in, which earned her a hard stare from Miri.

Callie felt her cheeks heat up. "I'm not." She shivered just thinking about it. "Not whips and stuff like that."

Miri smirked. "I don't judge, girl." She lifted her tattoo-covered arm. "It's not like I don't get it. I don't do tats just for the ink."

"You don't?"

Lisa snorted. "Nope."

They were both weird. "I have no idea what you're trying to say, but whatever. Brad helped me a lot while expecting nothing in return. In my book, it makes him a good guy. He might appear cold and indifferent, but I think it's only a mask to hide who he really is inside."

Miri lifted a pierced brow. "And what if it isn't? What if what you see is what you get? Would you still want him?"

Callie didn't need to think about it. The answer was instantaneous. "Yes."

Lisa shook her head, while Miri made a show of mock crossing herself. "May God have mercy on your soul, my child."

CHAPTER 3: RONI

"Goodnight, Roni." Mildred kissed his forehead. "Are you sure you don't want us to stay with you?"

She was such a sweetheart.

His handler and his wife had spent all day sitting in Roni's hospital room. Barty was there to keep an eye on him, making sure he didn't get his hands on a computer, but Mildred was there because she cared.

What did his bosses think he could do? Hack the Pentagon from his hospital bed?

Maybe. If he had a reason to.

Even feverish with pneumonia and weak like a newborn, Roni could still wreak havoc if allowed access to the Internet.

The paranoia was justified.

After all, the government had been holding Roni captive for years and he had a score to settle. But even if he had the opportunity, he wouldn't hack the system with malicious intent. To use the backdoor he'd programmed, he needed the system up and working fine.

Roni patted her hand. "I'm sure. Besides, you have to go. Visiting hours are over."

The bossy bird of a nurse had informed them that everyone needed to leave. Sylvia was allowed to stay only because Roni had told everyone who cared to listen that she was his fiancée.

Rising to his feet, Barty hiked his pants up. "I'll be back tomorrow morning, kid. If you need anything, you can call me. Jerome is just outside your door. You can ask him to make the call." He clapped Roni on the shoulder, so gently that it was almost a pat.

God, he was going to miss the old jerk and his kindly wife.

"Yeah, okay. See you tomorrow morning," Roni said, his voice quivering a little.

The fever was making him mushy. That's what it was. Because no way in hell would he shed a tear because that old asshole and his wife, who really was a sweetheart, were leaving and he wasn't going to see them ever again.

Once they were finally gone, Sylvia's crew would arrive and spring him free.

In the long hours he'd been waiting for Barty and Mildred to leave, Roni had made up his mind. It was a no-brainer. To stay meant that he would keep doing what he loved doing but have no life. To go with Sylvia, even with no chance of ever turning immortal, still meant doing what he loved doing, but with perks.

Either way, he would be a prisoner.

As long as the immortals kept him pampered and Sylvia warmed his bed, he didn't mind never leaving their lair, or whatever they called their home. As it was, he spent most of his days in front of monitors, and it didn't really matter to him where he was doing it.

"Thank the merciful Fates." Sylvia let out a breath. "I thought they would never leave."

"Yeah. I'm ready to get going."

"I'm glad you decided to take the chance." Sylvia sounded relieved.

Good, it meant she wanted him even as a human, but he needed to make sure. "What happens if I don't turn?"

She looked away. "I'm not sure. Normally, someone who is really good at thralling would get into your head and make you forget everything you've learned about us. But I'm hoping our regent would allow you to stay. First of all, because we need you, and second of all because I doubt anyone would dare mess with that brilliant brain of yours—it's too valuable. And if that's not enough to convince him to let you stay, I'm going to plead and beg and do whatever I can until he does."

Roni took her hand. "You really care about me."

"Of course, I do, dummy."

He smirked. "Hey, a minute ago you called me brilliant."

"You're both. But seriously, you know that if you stay with us as a human, it's like a life sentence. You can never leave."

"As long as I have you, I don't mind. It's not like I want to go anywhere without you."

A tear slid down Sylvia's cheek. "Don't give up yet. I'm not. I'm going to implore the Fates every day all day long until they get sick of hearing my prayers and turn you. I don't want to watch you get old and die. I can't."

He squeezed her hand. "I'm not giving up. I don't care if I have to let all the males of your clan take turns beating me up and biting me until it happens."

It wasn't an idle promise. For Sylvia, Roni would even face that Brundar dude Andrew thought was so mean and scary. One of the males must have the right venom composition to turn him. Because there was no way Roni wasn't a Dormant. Not with his grandma surfacing decades after her supposed death by drowning, looking not a day older than she did at twenty-five.

Sylvia nodded and squeezed his hand back. "That's the spirit. Never give up, never surrender."

"I'm with you, baby. Call your posse."

Pulling out her phone, Sylvia sent the text.

"What about Jerome?" Roni asked.

The guy knew him well, which meant it wouldn't be easy to thrall him to forget why he was there, and who he was guarding.

"We will take care of him."

"You're not going to do anything to him? Right? I like the guy."

With a smile, Sylvia leaned and kissed his cheek. "I wish everyone got to see this side of you. Underneath that prickly exterior, you're a nice guy."

Roni shifted up, making himself more comfortable. "Don't read too much into it. I don't want to see Jerome hurt, but that doesn't make me a good guy. I'm not violent, that's all."

Sylvia patted his arm. "Yeah, yeah, keep telling yourself that. Anyway, one of the guys is going to thrall him to believe that his shift is over and someone is coming to replace him."

"He is not going to leave his post until his replacement arrives."

"Don't worry about it. He'll be convinced it's okay to leave. Let me just send them a text with instructions." Her fingers flew over the screen.

"Why does it have to be one of the guys? Can't you do it?"

Sylvia shrugged. "I can, but I don't have as much practice. The guys do it all the time. Once they bite a woman, which they do almost every time they have sex, they have to make her forget the fangs. Immortal females don't have such problems. We don't bite. Much." She winked.

"Good. Because I don't think I would've liked being a pincushion, even for your cute little fangs. Those fuckers hurt."

"I don't know about that. Supposedly, the ladies enjoy it very much." Her eyes lit up the way they did when she was turned on.

Good. Because for some reason, being the one doing the biting sounded way more sexy than being the one bitten. If Sylvia didn't share his opinion, Roni would've felt guilty about having such seemingly misogynistic thoughts. "I hope you'll find out soon."

"I do too. But even if you turn tonight, it will take up to six months for your fangs to become fully operational."

"Bummer."

She waved a hand. "I can wait."

Hopefully, she wouldn't end up waiting for nothing.

"Tell me more about where I'm going. If I'm to spend the rest of my life locked up, at least I hope to spend it in luxury."

Her smile wilted, but then she put a brave face on. "You will. And the lockup is only temporary. We are building a new place that has large open areas. It's going to be ready in a couple of months. You won't have to spend all of your time indoors."

He chuckled. "You forget who you're talking to. Hackers are like vampires. We shun the sun and lurk in our lairs."

"I'm not going to let you do that."

"Oh, yeah?"

"Yeah. You're going to eat right, move your ass every couple of hours, and spend at least an hour a day outdoors. Even if you don't turn, I'm going to make sure you live long and prosper."

He loved when Sylvia made *Star Trek* references, and more than that he loved that she cared. Still, he had an image to protect.

Roni glowered at her, pretending to be mad. "I'm not even there yet, and you're already bossing me around?"

"Trouble in paradise?" Anandur sauntered into the room accompanied by a freaky looking dude who was more handsome than humanly possible.

"Yamanu at your service." He offered Roni his hand.

"Roni." He shook it, hypnotized by the guy's pale blue eyes and singsong voice. "You're the thrall master, right?"

"Very astute observation," Anandur replied. "Get dressed. We are moving out." He handed Roni a plastic bag.

Glancing at the various tubes and monitoring wires sticking to him, Roni wondered how he was supposed to manage that.

"I'll unhook you," Yamanu offered.

With fingers that were much gentler than their size implied, Yamanu had Roni unplugged from everything, while Sylvia took care of the equipment with her special magic, so none of it sounded the alert.

His girlfriend had some impressive skills.

A few minutes later, they left the hospital room. Yamanu and Sylvia stepped out first, with Yamanu making sure no one spared them a second glance, while Roni and Anandur trailed behind with him leaning heavily on the big guy.

Roni would've felt better about starting this new phase of his life walking unaided, but in a way, it was symbolic of the future awaiting him. As a hacker he'd always worked alone, and as a prisoner he'd lived alone.

But from this day onward, he'd have to learn to work with others while living with an entire clan.

CHAPTER 4: CALLIE

*W*hile waiting for Miri to fill her drink order, Callie leaned on the bar and observed the crowd. Another couple had just disappeared into the side corridor, on their way to the basement. Something was going on down there tonight.

Were they having a party?

"There is a lot of traffic today." She pointed her chin in their direction.

Miri put two drinks on Callie's tray. "It's Wednesday."

"So?"

"Demonstration day. Must be something super interesting to attract so many."

"I wonder what it's about." Callie lifted the tray.

"Who knows?" Miri leaned closer, her chest almost touching the bar. "Maybe your boyfriend is demonstrating whipping techniques?"

"Ha, ha," Callie chuckled while nervously glancing around. "He is not my boyfriend," she whispered.

"Right."

After delivering the drinks, Callie stopped by a couple of

tables and collected new orders.

"I'm dying of curiosity." She handed Miri the tickets. "Do you think they will let me watch during my break?"

Miri shrugged. "You can ask your boyfriend. He is the boss and what he says goes."

Good idea. If she could find him. When she'd gotten to work, Brundar was already down in the basement, and he hadn't surfaced yet.

Was he busy?

Or was he avoiding her?

She had a strong suspicion it was the second one.

Coward.

If he didn't want to hook up with her anymore, all he had to do was say so. This hide and seek game was ridiculous.

Callie felt her cheeks heating up, but this time it was anger and not awkwardness that was causing the blush. She'd give him another hour, and if he didn't come up by then, she would call him, using the emergency number he'd given her.

The hour was almost up when Callie spotted Franco emerging from the side corridor. Pushing people out of her way, she rushed over to him.

"Franco! Wait up!" she called as he opened the door to the supply room.

On the other side of it was the employee entrance, and if she didn't stop him, he would leave before she had a chance to talk to him.

Holding the door opened, Franco turned and scanned the crowd for his caller.

She waved at him.

He lifted a brow.

"Do you have a moment? Or are you in a super hurry to get out of here?"

He smiled. "For you, I can spare a moment." He opened

the door wider. "Please, step into my office." He waved her on into the supply room.

"I heard you guys are holding a class down there. Can I watch? I mean, during my break."

He shook his head and patted her shoulder. "I'm sorry, Callie, but I have a policy about keeping the nightclub's personnel and that of the lower level separate. If you worked downstairs, it would have been a different story. But you're not old enough."

Disappointing to say the least. "Any chance you'd change your mind about the age limit? I know that until recently it used to be twenty-one."

He shook his head again. "It works better this way. Most of the members are older. And we want to make sure no one gets in with a fake ID. Other nightclubs have gotten in trouble because of nonsense like that, and those were just regular clubs."

"But you know me. You know I'm over twenty-one."

"That's enough, Callie." Franco used his drill sergeant's tone. "I don't have time for this."

That commanding tone and that stern look might have scared most people into compliance, but not Callie. Not while she was mad and on a mission.

Another day? Maybe?

"Can you at least tell Brad to call me? Or come up and see me?"

He cast her a curious look. "I will when I come back."

"Thank you. And sorry for bothering you, sir."

The formal address seemed to mollify him. "It's okay."

The thing was, Franco didn't come back. Or if he had, Callie had missed him.

She'd waited and watched people leave from that freaking side corridor all night, but there had been no sign of Brundar or Franco.

"Come on, Callie." Donnie looked impatient. He'd been waiting outside and then came in looking for her.

She buttoned up her light jacket. "Let's go."

"Finally."

It was after closing time, and she was taking her sweet time getting ready to head home, just in case Brundar finally showed up. But it wasn't fair to Donnie. With both Franco and Brundar busy elsewhere, he was stuck with walking her home.

"You can drive me home. It will take less time." It wasn't fair of her to take more of Donnie's time than necessary, but after the noise and the smells of the nightclub, Callie preferred walking. The ten minutes' stroll in the crisp night air was relaxing, and listening to Donnie talk about his latest comic starring Bud, the mighty slayer of rogue vampires, was fun.

Most nights Donnie seemed to enjoy it too.

He wrapped his arm around her shoulders. "Are you kidding me? Walking you home is the best part of the night for me."

Talk about awkward. Maybe Miri was right.

Had Callie been too preoccupied with her own problems to notice that Donnie wanted to be more than a friend?

"I want to ask you something, Donnie. What do you think of Miri?"

He shrugged. "I'm thinking of a comic she could star in. She'd make the visuals stand out. But I can't think of a story for her."

That wasn't what Callie had in mind. But maybe she could steer him in the right direction. "She could be Bud's girlfriend."

Donnie shook his head. "Nah. They don't fit. A comic needs contrast. The strange looking guy with an ordinary

23

looking girl or the other way around. You can be Bud's girl-friend in the story."

She lifted her hand. "Please, don't. I need my privacy."

"Don't worry, I'll change the way you look. But I can base a character on you."

"I can live with that. Who would you cast as Miri's boyfriend?"

"Let me think…"

Donnie looked up to the sky for inspiration, which meant he didn't see himself in that role. A pity.

"I know. A computer nerd. Maybe a hacker."

A more direct approach was needed. "How about a comic book nerd?"

It took him a moment to catch her meaning. He laughed, his big body shaking. "Me? No way. Miri is cool, but she is too cool for me."

"What's your type?"

"Someone like you, or Fran." The way his voice got all soft when he said Fran's name said it all.

"Fran is cute." The girl was a student and worked only on weekends.

"Yeah. But she ignores me. Probably thinks I'm a dumb bouncer. All muscle and no brains."

"She doesn't know you. You need to talk to her. Show her that you're much more than muscle."

"How can I do it when she barely says hi to me?"

"Easy, give her one of your comics. With a dedication."

"What, just shove it in her hand?"

"Yeah. Bring a few to give to other employees too if it makes you feel less awkward."

Donnie nodded. "It wouldn't hurt to do some PR."

"Exactly. That way everyone will know how extremely talented you are. Just don't bring the ones starring Brad."

"No way. Even I wouldn't want to mess with your boyfriend."

And just like that her good mood vanished. "Stop saying that. He is not my boyfriend."

"Then what is he to you?"

"I wish I knew. For a few days, I was stupid enough to think he was. But how can he be when he spends nearly all his evenings and nights downstairs? Playing with other women? That's not my definition of a boyfriend. I have no wish to become one of his many whatever he calls them. His playmates or scene partners or whatever."

Donnie stopped and turned to face her. "He owns half of the club, and he is into that shit. A guy like that can't be monogamous. Part of his job is to teach and demonstrate, and he can't do that while keeping his hands off. What did you expect? That he would quit everything because he likes you?"

"Yeah, I kind of did. Silly me."

"Come here." Donnie pulled her into a bear hug. "You can either accept Brad the way he is or find someone else. Those are your only two options. You can't change him into who you want him to be."

"I know."

CHAPTER 5: BRUNDAR

*B*rundar collected his equipment and put everything into a large gym bag. His demonstrations always drew a crowd, and this evening was no different. He liked that part. Teaching others how to do it right. Hopefully, this time Gloria's husband was paying attention to what Brundar had been doing to his wife and would be able to replicate the intricate knots in their private play. Next class would be a hands-on for the participants, with the couples experimenting and Brundar only supervising.

It would be interesting to see how much they remembered. Worst case scenario, if they messed it up so badly that the knots couldn't be untied and they couldn't get their partners free, the ropes could be cut off.

"Brad, can you come into my office? I need to run a couple of things by you."

Brundar lifted his head and regarded Franco. "About?"

"Your expansion plans."

"You said you didn't want the hassle."

"I changed my mind."

"Good." Brundar's ideas would bring much needed additional profit to the club. Franco's reluctance hadn't made sense. Just because they were finally breaking even didn't mean that everything was going great. In business, not moving forward didn't mean staying in place—it meant going backwards.

Besides, if Brundar stayed to talk to Franco after closing, he couldn't see Calypso as he'd intended, which was a good thing. He needed time to think, and if he went home with her, thinking would be the last thing he'd do.

It was shameful that he needed outside help to stay away from her. He had no willpower when it came to Calypso.

Gym bag in hand, Brundar followed Franco into his cramped office. The memory of Calypso sitting in the same chair he now took was playing a number on him. Franco said something, but Brundar wasn't with him. All he could think of was Calypso's lips as she worried them while going through the paperwork, and what they'd done after that.

"Callie asked me to tell you to call her, but you were busy. So I'm telling you now."

"Did she tell you why?"

Franco smirked. "She tried to convince me to let her see the demonstration. I told her no. Obviously, she is going to try you next. Tenacious little thing."

"You have no idea."

Franco shook his head. "Pretty girl, but too mouthy for my taste."

Brundar stifled a growl. "You have nothing to worry about. She is not after you."

"Didn't think she was, my friend." Franco smirked. "Not for a moment. I'm just commenting on the fact that she is mouthy and far from submissive. I saw that you had her fill out paperwork."

Damnation. He'd forgotten to destroy that file. "Shred it.

She was curious. The paperwork was meant as a scare tactic. I had no intention of making her a member. Too young."

"And too vanilla," Franco added.

Brundar closed his eyes and counted to five, waiting for his fury to subside. Franco read Calypso's file. It was worse than if he'd seen her naked. Her soul was bared on that questionnaire. But it wasn't Franco's fault. It was Brundar's.

"Give me her file."

When Franco just looked at him, Brundar felt like baring his fangs. Instead, he repeated, "Now, Franco."

His tone must've penetrated Franco's momentary stupor, and the man scrambled to riffle through the files in his filing cabinet.

"Here." He threw the file to Brundar as if it was about to catch fire.

Franco was an ex-Marine, not a guy who spooked easily. Brundar must have looked terrifying.

"Thank you," he said, his speech sounding like something between a slur and a hiss.

"Your eyes are glowing." Franco pointed at Brundar's face.

"Contact lenses reflecting the light."

"Don't give me that bullshit. Your eyes fucking glow. What are you?"

Hell and damnation.

Brundar leaned closer. "Look at them now. Do they look like they are glowing?"

"Yes."

But it was too late for Franco. Brundar had him in a thrall. Justified this time. But as long as he was already in the guy's head, he might as well erase the memory of that fucking file. In fact, he was going to erase this entire conversation.

In the time it took Franco's eyes to regain focus, Brundar stashed the file in his gym bag.

Franco rubbed his temples. "Where were we?"

"Expansion plans."

"Right. The liquor store next door is willing to let us have their basement. They are not using it, and we can connect ours to theirs by cutting out a doorway."

"How much do they want for it?"

"That's not a problem. A few hundred bucks a month. The remodeling is. I don't have the funds for that, you know that. Are you willing to invest more?"

"I will invest my share and lend you enough for yours. I don't want to own more than half of the club. But first, let me crunch the numbers again."

Franco nodded, then rubbed his temples. "I know there was something else I wanted to talk to you about, but I can't remember what it was. I must be getting old."

"Are we done?"

"Yeah. We can talk about the other thing tomorrow if I remember what it is."

"Goodnight, Franco." Brundar lifted his gym bag and walked out.

Pulling out of the club's parking lot, Brundar had every intention of going home. Instead, he drove to Calypso's.

Not wanting to wake the girl, he let himself in using the spare set of keys the landlady had given him.

His careful steps were soundless as he entered Calypso's bedroom. For a few moments, he just looked at her, but then the compulsion to get closer animated his feet. He took a few steps and stood by the bed, watching her beautiful sleeping face for a few moments longer.

But that wasn't enough either.

Defeated, Brundar took off his boots and his socks and climbed on the bed next to Calypso, lying on top of the comforter while she was bundled underneath it.

Better.

Some of the tightness in his chest eased. Brundar inhaled Calypso's scent, feeling as if he was drawing his first full breath of the day. The thing was, he hadn't been aware of the tightness and the shallow breathing until he came home to her.

A moment later, she turned in her sleep and threw an arm over him, then sighed as if until now she hadn't been able to take a full breath either.

CHAPTER 6: CALLIE

*C*allie had slept better than she had in years. There had been no tossing and turning, no disturbing dreams about running away from monsters, no impossible puzzles to solve, only complete relaxation.

If not for the sudden loss of warmth, she would have kept sleeping, refusing to wake up and lose that peaceful feeling.

As it was, she reached her hand for the spot beside her, searching for the source of warmth. There was no one there, but there had been. The top of the comforter wasn't cold.

She popped her eyes open to see Brundar's back. Holding his boots in one hand and his socks in the other, he was trying to sneak soundlessly out of her room.

I knew it! He has an extra set of keys.

The thought should have bothered her, but it didn't.

How could it?

To come in the middle of the night and just lie in bed next to her meant that he couldn't stay away. Callie felt like pumping her fist in victory.

The change in her breathing pattern must have alerted

him to the fact that she was awake, and he turned his head. "Did I wake you?"

"I guess you did. But I don't mind. Why are you leaving?"

"I need to be at work."

"Guarding your big shot cousin?"

He nodded.

"Can you at least stay for breakfast?"

"I don't have time."

"Coffee?"

He glanced at his watch, then nodded.

"Great. Give me two minutes to get ready. Do you know how to work the coffee machine?"

A small smile pulled on one corner of his lips. "That's the only thing I know how to make. I'll get on it."

If she hurried, she could make him a quick breakfast, and not send him on his way with an empty stomach.

After a quick visit to the bathroom, Callie pulled on a pair of leggings and an oversized T-shirt, ran a brush through her hair and padded to the kitchen.

The coffee machine was just starting to make hissing sounds, which meant she had a couple more minutes before it was ready. Plenty of time to stick a few bread slices into the toaster and scramble some eggs.

Passing him by, she kissed Brundar's cheek. "Thank you for coming and keeping my bed warm." She loaded the toaster first, then grabbed a frying pan.

"You're not mad that I let myself in?"

"No. I figured you had another set of keys. You're welcome to come in anytime you want. It's not like I'm afraid you'll catch me naked." She winked at him.

If Callie hadn't been so attuned to the slightest change in Brundar's expression, she wouldn't have noticed the impact that what she'd said had had on him.

He looked stunned, though to anyone else he would've

looked as impassive as always. The guy wasn't as unfeeling as he pretended to be. A lot was going on underneath that stoic exterior. She just wished he would lower his guard around her, just a little, and let her glimpse the man inside.

"You're too trusting, Calypso. The world is full of evildoers, and it's difficult to tell the good guys from the bad."

Callie cracked two eggs into the pan, then reached for two more. "I know. But you're not one of them. If you wanted to hurt me, you could've done it anytime. Besides, I seriously doubt that this building's security system or the locks on my door would've posed much of a challenge for you. Right?"

Getting up to tend to the coffee, Brundar nodded. "You happen to be right about me. But promise me you'll be much more careful with everyone else. Don't let anyone in here without telling me first."

Callie lifted a brow. "Now, that sounds creepy, Brundar. Don't you think?" That was something Callie would have expected Shawn to say. She loaded Brundar's plate with most of the scrambled eggs and added three pieces of toast. "Butter?"

He nodded. "It's not what you think. You live alone, and anyone who comes in here knows it. You'll be safer if they hear you call a friend and tell him or her who you're with. Right now I'm the only one you can call."

That made sense. But there was one problem with that. "You told me to call you only in case of emergencies. If I invite Miri over does that count as an emergency? Or Donnie?" She cast him a sidelong glance, checking his reaction to her mention of the hunky bouncer.

Bingo!

Brundar's jaw tightened. "Why would you invite Donnie?"

She shrugged. "He walks me home. I feel like I should at least offer him coffee." Callie stifled a smile. She was willing to bet that from now on Brundar would be the only one walking her home.

"I can't always answer calls. But you can text me anytime. Just make sure that whoever you let in knows you're texting me about them."

Well, well, wasn't that a major breakthrough? He was allowing her to text him.

"How are the eggs?" she asked.

"Excellent. Everything you make is."

Callie waved a hand. "You've seen nothing yet. All you've had until now were quick impromptu meals. How about I invite you to dinner this evening and show you what I can really do?"

Brundar barely managed to keep his stoic mask on. But Callie caught the excited gleam in his eyes.

"That is an offer I can't refuse. What time?"

A point for Brundar, even though she was a little disappointed. At least the guy was honest, admitting that he was excited about the meal and not about seeing her. "Is five too early? I want us to have plenty of time before I have to leave for my shift at the club."

"I can be here at four if you want. I'll ask to be released from duty earlier."

Again with the military lingo. She wondered where he'd served and in what capacity.

"Perfect. Now eat your eggs before they get cold."

While Brundar got busy cleaning his plate, Callie went through a mental list of her best recipes. She didn't dare try something new in case it didn't work out. Not all recipes were as good as they looked on the screen.

The same applied to plans. Not all worked out as well as anticipated. An idea that seemed great in theory could crash and burn when implemented.

Her seduction plans aside, Callie still owed Brundar a

huge debt of gratitude, and the only way she knew how to repay even a fraction of what he'd done for her was to cook him dinners every night from now until about forever.

It wasn't as if she had much else to offer him.

She would've gladly done his laundry and picked up his dry cleaning too, but she knew he would be offended if she offered.

Brundar would refuse any attempt on her part to repay his kindness.

Callie didn't like being in his debt or anyone else's. But there were several factors at work forcing her to swallow her pride and just say thank you.

One was that she couldn't have done it without Brundar's help, and that cooking him dinners would never come close to repaying that debt.

But more importantly, Brundar deserved to feel good about what he'd done and was still doing for her. To look for convoluted ways to repay him was like telling him she felt bad about accepting his help, and therefore taking away from his pleasure of providing it.

Oftentimes, the giver got more out of the giving than the receiver got from the receiving.

CHAPTER 7: KIAN

$\mathcal{K}$ian tapped his hand on the conference table to get everyone's attention.

When they quieted down, he began. "We have two topics on the agenda for this meeting. One is the progress with the autonomous cars, and the other is the continuing murders. Let's start with the easy one. The cars."

William pushed his glasses up his nose. "They sent a rep to the factory in Sweden. The prototype should arrive here the day after tomorrow."

The guy's face had gotten so gaunt that it no longer fit the frame, and the glasses kept sliding down. William needed a new pair. But more than that he needed a change of pace.

"We will test the prototype as soon as it arrives. Once we know what changes are needed, I want you to book a flight to Stockholm and supervise the production line. At least until the first batch is ready to ship."

William looked uncomfortable. "I hate flying."

Bhathian clapped William on the shoulder. "Then load up on Snake's Venom before you board and sleep throughout the entire trip. First class has seats that recline all the way. They turn into very comfortable beds."

William shook his head. "I don't like getting drunk either. I'll figure something out."

Kian nodded. Council members and Guardians alike could not afford to have quirks like aversion to flying. They had a job to do. "Good. Let's move on to the murders. Onegus?"

"Our men are all clear, thank the merciful Fates. All have alibis for the time of at least one of the murders. I think it's safe to assume that we don't have a madman in our midst, let alone two who went on a simultaneous killing spree. Which leaves either a Doomer or a random, unaffiliated immortal."

Kian raked his fingers through his hair. "True, now that we know there are more than two players in this game, we need to take it into account. It can be a lone immortal, unaffiliated with any group, maybe a member of Kalugal's crew."

Onegus reclined in his chair and crossed his arms over his chest. "I wish we could find him, see if we could work together. Think how much stronger we could be with an additional group of highly trained warriors. We could continue their training until they reached Guardian level. A lot easier than starting with newbies who have no prior training or combat experience."

Kian leaned forward. "You would trust ex-Doomers?"

Onegus shrugged. "We have two who've proved themselves quite helpful."

"Not the same, Onegus. If Kalugal indeed managed to defect with an entire platoon, he and his men can take us on with ease. Are you willing to risk it? Because I'm not."

Onegus let his arms drop. "Of course not. It was just wishful thinking on my part. I'm tired of trying to manage with only six Guardians. That's more than enough when nothing is going on, but not nearly enough in time of trouble."

"Which is the big conundrum." Kian sighed. "Most of the time Guardians have little to do. But when you are needed there are not enough of you to do the job. I want to start patrolling the areas where the murders occurred."

"Can't do it." Onegus shook his head. "They were spread out, and the way Los Angeles is built, it's not like there is a center where everything happens. You need a lot of men to do that."

"Hey!" Kri called out. "Chauvinist much?"

Onegus pinned her with a hard stare. "We are talking about an immortal male gone rogue. I would never send a female Guardian after him. And if it makes me a chauvinist, I can live with that."

Kri humphed. "I can take on most immortal males."

"Civilians," Kian said. "If this is an ex or active Doomer, he is not a civilian. Do you think you can take on Dalhu? Or Robert?"

"Not Dalhu, I've seen him fight. But maybe I can take on Robert."

"Match! Match! Match! I want to see a match," Yamanu singsonged while drumming his hand on the table and making the whole thing shake.

Kian groaned. Sometimes his Guardians behaved like high schoolers. Correction. Kindergarteners. "You're welcome to invite him to spar with you in the gym. I'm sure he would love it. I'm just not sure what Michael would think of you getting physical with an immortal bachelor who is not a relative of yours."

"I don't care what he thinks. He can watch if he wants."

Yamanu rubbed his palms together. "That would be one hell of a show. I call dibs on a first-row seat."

"Enough!" Kian raised his voice.

Everyone quieted instantly.

"This is an official meeting, not a social gathering. I need suggestions for patrolling the murder areas. If we believe this is the work of an immortal male, it is our responsibility to deal with him. The human authorities can't and should not have to take care of it."

The door opened, and Okidu walked in with a tray. "I brewed fresh coffee, master."

"Thank you, Okidu." Kian waited while the butler put a porcelain cup in front of each person and then poured them coffee from the two thermal carafes he'd brought.

When he was done, Okidu bowed and retreated from the room.

"Any ideas?" Kian glanced at Brundar who hadn't spoken a word yet.

The Guardian who was the master of stoic expressions looked perturbed, his forehead creased and his eyes focused somewhere on his knees. His body was sitting at the conference table, but his mind was miles away.

If Anandur's remark hadn't been a joke, then Brundar had gotten himself a woman. Not a hookup, but someone he saw on a regular basis. Which would explain his peculiar mood. Getting involved with a human was a bad idea, and Brundar was well aware of that.

"I could tap into the surveillance cameras in the area." William brought Kian's attention back to where it needed to be.

"To what end?" Onegus asked. "Someone would have to watch the feed. If something suspicious came up, even if we had men on standby in the area, they wouldn't get there in time to catch the bastard."

"True," Kian conceded. "But they can make it in time to save the woman from bleeding to death. Besides, we will at least have a visual. We can continue the search using the facial recognition program."

"I wonder why the police are not doing that," Kri said.

She had a point, but Kian doubted they had. The police only looked at the feed after they found a victim, not as a prevention method. But William's suggestion gave him an idea.

"Here is what I think we should do. William, go ahead and hack the surveillance cameras. I'll contact Turner and have him find us a contractor to monitor the feed. They will contact us and call an ambulance if needed. We can take up the investigation from there."

William lifted a hand. "It will have to wait until I come back from Sweden. I can't do it all in one day, which is all the time I have before the prototype car arrives and I have to get busy with that."

Anandur snapped his fingers. "Not a problem. We have a new hacker on board."

Kian lifted a brow. "The kid? I understand that he is in the clinic, sick with pneumonia."

"He is. But knowing Roni, he could handle this even sick as a dog." Anandur turned to William. "If you can show him what you need and provide him with the equipment he needs, he can probably do everything from his sickbed."

William shook his head. "That's a lot of equipment."

"Then we move his sickbed to your lab, together with Bridget to keep an eye on him." Kian looked at William for approval.

The computer lab was the guy's whole world. He wouldn't be thrilled about letting the kid in there unsupervised.

"Let me talk with him first. See how good he really is."

Anandur chuckled. "He is good."

CHAPTER 8: RONI

*B*eing sick sucked.

Roni was bored out of his mind, and lying in bed all day was getting on his nerves. The trouble was that walking around unaided was still a no-no. Hell, even going to the bathroom required leaning on Sylvia or one of the nurses for support.

He vehemently refused a catheter, which meant no intravenous either.

His pneumonia was viral, so there wasn't much the hot little doctor could do with medications other than fever reducers.

It still bugged the hell out of him that he was younger than the hot-looking doctor's grown son. He had to remember that looks were deceptive as far as immortals went, and some of these people were ancient.

Anandur, who was a major goofball, was fucking one thousand years old. How was it possible?

Roni got the biological explanation, but that was just a small part of the equation. The amount of information the guy must've absorbed over his long life should have made

41

him a genius. But he wasn't. Mentally, he was just an ordinary dude who acted like any twenty-something-year-old.

Well, not exactly. There were a few tells.

Like, forget politically correct. The way the guy talked, every other sentence had something that would offend an average millennial.

And his jokes. Come on, Anandur needed major help in that department. He was almost as bad as Barty.

Fuck. He hoped the guy was okay. Barty was either worried sick or spitting mad and cursing Roni with every vile thing he could think of.

Both Barty and Jerome would get in shitloads of trouble because of him. Mostly Jerome. Barty had done his part in guarding Roni, but Jerome had abandoned his post. No one would believe him that he'd somehow gotten hypnotized.

Guilt was an unfamiliar and unpleasant sensation.

What he wouldn't have given for a laptop right now. There was nothing that could take Roni's mind off life's stinky nuggets like a good hacking session that required his total concentration.

"I brought you soup." Sylvia entered his room with a tray.

"I don't want soup."

"Well, tough, Mr. Grumpy, soup is what you get. Bridget said you need plenty of liquids."

Sylvia pressed the foot pedal, lifting the back of his bed to a sitting position. "Open wide." She brought a spoon to his mouth.

He shook his head.

"Do you want a catheter?"

"No."

"Then open up."

Resistance was futile.

Sylvia smiled. "That's a good boy. Now let's try another."

"Yes, Mommy."

She fed him another spoonful, and another until the bowl was empty.

"All done. See? It wasn't so bad."

Roni grunted in response.

The soup wasn't bad, he was just sick and tired of hospitals, and of bland food, and of nothing to do.

"I need a laptop. Can you get me one?"

Sylvia put the bowl on the tray and hopped on the bed to sit next to him. "I have to ask around who has a laptop to spare."

"Don't you have one?"

"I do. At home. I don't live here."

He glanced at the soup. "Then where did you get that from?" As far as he knew, he was the only occupant of the clinic, and it had no dedicated food service.

"Nathalie, Andrew's wife made it. She sends her love and apologizes for not coming to visit. It's because of the baby. She and Andrew can't get infected, but they are afraid of an airborne virus clinging to their clothes and then attacking little baby Phoenix."

Roni frowned. "When is that baby going to turn immortal?"

Sylvia shrugged. "I don't know," she said while looking away.

He knew exactly why she felt uncomfortable. Did she think he was stupid and wouldn't figure it out?

In case he didn't transition, which seemed most likely at the moment, Sylvia didn't want him to know more than he already did. Fewer memories to wipe away.

"Did anyone talk to Kian about me?" At least they'd finally told him the name of the guy who was in charge of Roni's future. He was sick of calling him the big boss, or the dude on top.

"I'm sure someone did. But we are all waiting to see what

happens. If you transition, then there is nothing to talk about."

"Bridget said that the pneumonia might be the reason I'm not transitioning. My body needs to get healthy first." Chances were the doctor was just being nice and trying to give him hope. It made sense, though. Like the way certain diseases stalled the onset of puberty.

"She is absolutely right."

Someone knocked on the door.

"Come in," Roni called out in his sick guy's barely there voice. But for the immortals it should be enough.

"The room is soundproofed. I'll go see who it is." Sylvia hopped down and went to open the door.

"William. What are you doing here?"

"I came to see my new partner."

Partner?

The clan's famous science genius was calling Roni a partner? That must mean that they had decided to let him stay no matter what.

"Sure, come in." Sylvia moved aside to let William in.

He was tall, though not as tall as Anandur, more like Andrew's height. But he didn't look so good. The dark circles under his eyes were so deep that even his glasses couldn't hide them.

"Hi, Roni, I'm William." He offered Roni a hand.

Roni shook it. "Usually my handshake is more manly than the limp noodle I can offer you now."

"No worries. How are you feeling?"

"Like shit."

William pulled up a chair and put it next to Roni's bed. "Yeah, me too. I have trouble sleeping lately."

"I can see that."

William looked up at Sylvia who was leaning against the wall. "I'm sorry. Did I take your chair?" He started to get up.

"No, keep it. I usually sit on Roni's bed."

"Oh." William dropped his butt back and pushed his glasses up his nose. "So I hear you have some mad skills?"

"I do."

"I have a job for you."

Roni felt like William had just thrown him a lifeline. "Yes, thank you. I'm going insane with nothing to do."

William smiled. "You came in last night, and it's not even midday yet. Do you always work around the clock?"

"Every moment I can."

"Same here."

Roni liked the guy. A kindred spirit. "High five, dude."

William obliged him, lifting a palm up and holding it close to Roni's so he didn't have to lift his own too high to reach it.

"What's the job?"

"Hacking into surveillance cameras."

"Child's play."

"Hundreds of them. Spread over fifty square miles of densely populated urban area."

"Still child's play, but time-consuming."

"Right. Time that I don't have because I have another project I need to take care of. Anandur suggested I check with you. Are you up to it in your current state?"

"Yes, yes, and yes. Where do I work?"

"Wait a moment." Sylvia pushed off the wall and came to sit on Roni's bed. "You're so sick I have to spoon feed you. And you think you can work?"

"My body is weak. Not my brain."

"You need your hands to type on the keyboard."

"I can manage that."

She shook her head. "Not unless Bridget says it's okay. Even Kian can't go over her head where her patients are involved."

45

"Then call her in."

Sylvia turned to William. "Can't it wait a few days until Roni feels better?"

William sighed. "Did you read about the string of murders?"

"Of course. They think it's some satanic cult."

"We think it's an immortal male gone insane. Not one of ours, Onegus checked everyone's alibi. It's either a Doomer or an unaffiliated immortal. We have to help catch him. Every day that passes without us doing anything could mean another victim's life."

Well, that put things in a different perspective. Roni's mind went to work.

Sylvia looked like she wanted to say something, then shook her head and got off the bed. "Let me find Bridget." She turned to William. "Should I tell her what's at stake? Or do you want to do it?"

"Makes no difference to me."

"Then I'll tell her."

"Thank you."

When Sylvia left the room, Roni asked the most pertinent question. "Tell me about your equipment. I need to know what I got to work with."

William's face brightened with the first real smile since he'd gotten there. "You're in for a real treat, Roni. I have the best setup in the world."

"I highly doubt it. Until yesterday, I worked with the finest setup the government of the United States of America can put together. I'm sure it's the best in the world. You can't possibly have anything even remotely as powerful."

"You'll be singing a different tune once I tell you what I got."

CHAPTER 9: BRUNDAR

*B*rundar knocked on Onegus's door.

"Come in."

"I'm leaving early today," he said as he walked in, stopping a couple of feet away from Onegus's desk.

"Again? What about your evening classes?"

"Taken care of."

Instead of the reprimand Brundar had been expecting, the chief Guardian smirked. "So it's true. You've got yourself a woman."

Out of respect for his superior, Brundar didn't tell him to fuck off. Instead, he lifted a brow then turned on his heel and walked out.

What a bunch of juvenile busybodies. Given the respect the Guardians were regarded with by the rest of the clan, they should at least behave like the warriors they were supposed to be. In war and in peacetime.

Besides, Brundar didn't have a woman. Calypso wasn't his. She was a temporary distraction he needed to get out of his system. Maybe his obsession with her would end once he finally bedded her.

If he was lucky, it would be the same for her. Once she satisfied her curiosity, she might realize he wasn't the right guy for her. Because he wasn't. He wasn't the right guy for any woman.

It would be best if she pushed him away.

Hell, he had a feeling that as long as it was up to him to break them up, it was not going to happen anytime soon. When Calypso pushed his buttons, he responded. She controlled him as if he had no mind of his own.

Brundar shook his head. It boiled down to two options. Either Calypso stopped pushing those buttons of her own volition, or he ensured she had no access to them.

To prove his newfound resolve or rather lack thereof, he stopped by a liquor store to get the wine and cocktail fixings he'd promised her because he was a man of his word, and not because he felt as if Calypso's dinner invitation was a date and it would be rude to arrive empty-handed. Leaving everything in the cardboard box the cashier had given him would send the right message—no fancy wrapping paper and no sappy cards to give her the wrong idea.

As Brundar let himself into the building using the extra set of keys and took the stairs up to her apartment, the smell of delicious food made him salivate in anticipation.

He rapped his knuckles on her door.

A moment later, Calypso opened the way, rendering him breathless and speechless.

"Hi." She looked at the box tucked under his arm.

It took him a moment to respond. "You look beautiful." He couldn't stop his eyes from roaming up and down her body.

Her hair was done in big fat waves, her green eyes were emphasized by long lashes painted black, and her perfect body was encased in a knee-length, strapless black dress that had no visible zipper, which meant it could be pulled down or up with a single tug.

A pair of small, gold earrings was all the jewelry she had on, but then Calypso didn't need any decorations to accentuate her beauty. Dressed in that curve-hugging dress, a pair of tall, spiky heels making her legs look amazing, she was sure to cause men to drool and stutter, which meant she was never leaving her apartment in that getup unless escorted by him.

The woman was beautiful in jeans and sneakers, with no makeup and her hair gathered in a ponytail. All decked out she was a stunner.

A smile brightened Calypso's face. "Thank you. You look amazing. But then you always do." She motioned for him to come in.

Brundar had put on the grey slacks and the blue button-down shirt not because this was a date, but out of respect for all the trouble Calypso had gone to in preparing this special dinner.

Damnation. Who was he fooling? It was a date, and they'd both dressed up for the occasion.

Putting the box on the kitchen counter, Brundar started pulling out the assortment of wines, liqueurs, and vodkas he'd bought. "Where do you want me to put these?"

She looked at the number of bottles and shook her head. "One could go on the table, and the rest wherever you find space. I guess the vodka can go into the freezer."

When he was done, Calypso showed him to the dining table. "Please, take a seat."

He remained standing. "Do you need help bringing things from the kitchen?"

"I've got it. You can uncork the wine. Other than that just sit down and prepare to get pampered."

Why did that sound so good?

Had he ever been pampered?

Not even as a boy. His mother was a lovely woman, but she'd been a scatter-brained mother who'd often forgotten to prepare meals for him. Anandur would bring something he'd killed, skinning and roasting it over an open fire, and Brundar had done the same to the fish he'd occasionally caught.

Though after Lachlann's betrayal, he'd never fished or eaten fish again.

Even the smell of anything fishy brought on nausea.

Brundar reached for the wine bottle. This was not the time to bring up bothersome memories. This was a time to enjoy getting pampered by a beautiful woman.

Probably the only time he would, so he'd better enjoy it.

Uncorking the wine, Brundar poured it into the two wine glasses, then sat down and admired the table.

A white tablecloth, two candlesticks, a vase with several cut flowers, and cutlery for two.

He wondered how meals were served in other human households. Was dinner a formal affair like this one? Did families gather around a dining table or eat at the kitchen counter? Did it make a difference?

After all, food was food and how it was served wasn't important. Or was it?

Calypso walked in with a bowl in each hand. "Onion soup with cheese crostini." She placed one in front of Brundar, then sat across from him with the other. "*Bon appetit.*"

"Thank you." Brundar dipped his spoon in the soup and brought it to his mouth. "Delicious," he said after taking two more spoonfuls.

Calypso beamed with pride. "Thank you. This is just a simple dish. Wait until I bring out the next one: spicy grilled shrimp over shaved fennel slaw."

Before he could think better of it, Brundar grimaced.

Calypso's smile wilted. "What's the matter? You don't like fennel? Or shrimps?"

If he could stomach it without getting nauseated, Brundar would have shut up and eaten. But barfing over Calypso's masterpiece was worse than admitting he didn't eat shrimp.

"I don't like seafood. Can you serve the slaw without the shrimp?"

"Certainly. I'm sorry. I should've asked you beforehand if you were allergic to anything, or if there was anything you didn't like. It's just that Shawn ate everything, so it didn't cross my mind."

"I don't like to hear about your ex while eating."

Calypso flushed red. "Oops. Sorry. I don't like it either. It's an appetite spoiler."

Brundar lifted his wine glass. "To a new life. Let the old one be forgotten."

Calypso lifted hers and leaned closer to clink glasses with him. "To a new life."

As they drank the wine, Brundar had a passing thought that he should do as he preached. It was hypocritical of him to ask Calypso to forget about her unfortunate marriage while he still clung to old hurts, letting them define who he was and how he lived his life.

CHAPTER 10: CALLIE

Embarrassing, Callie thought as she collected the bowls. A good hostess would have checked with her guest about likes and dislikes. She'd been so busy planning the perfect dinner, it hadn't crossed her mind that Brundar might have a problem with any of it.

At least he'd enjoyed the onion soup as evidenced by his empty bowl.

The slaw wasn't really a big deal either. The shrimp and the slaw were stored in separate containers in the fridge, so she could just omit the shrimp. If Brundar didn't like seafood, the smell would probably bother him. She could have them for lunch the next day.

But the slaw on its own was more of a side dish than an appetizer. Serving it as a separate course wouldn't look right. Instead, she decided to go straight to the main course and add the slaw to the plates.

Taking her time to arrange everything the way she'd seen chefs do it on television, Callie looked at her creation with satisfaction. Not perfect, but pretty damn good for a home cook who'd learned her stuff from searching recipes on the Internet and watching YouTube to see how it was done.

"Fennel and rosemary-crusted rack of lamb, with spicy-sweet pepper medley, and fennel slaw," Callie announced as she carried the two plates to the dining room table.

"Sounds fancy." Brundar stood up and took one of the plates off her hands. "Smells good too."

She sat down and pulled a napkin over her knees. *"Bon appetit."*

The look of bliss on Brundar's face was worth the hours of effort Callie had put into preparing this meal.

Would he look as blissed out during sex?

Regrettably, she wasn't going to find out anytime soon. Brundar had made it clear that the blindfold wasn't coming off. Ever.

We'll see about that.

After finishing almost everything on his plate, Brundar lifted his head and glanced at her. "Aren't you eating?"

"I'm full."

He looked at her plate. "You've barely touched anything."

"I kept tasting what I was making while cooking it, and I was already quite full when we sat down to eat. The soup finished the job."

She smiled when Brundar glanced at her plate longingly. "Would you like to finish it for me?" She hoped he wasn't grossed out by her offer. Shawn had had no problem polishing her plate clean. But Brundar wasn't Shawn, and thank God for that.

"Are you sure? You could save it for later."

"I'm sure." Callie pushed her plate toward him. "I have plenty left over."

That settled it for him. In a matter of minutes, he cleaned her plate as well.

"Can I get you more?"

He shook his head and leaned back in his chair. "I'm more than full. Thank you. This was the best meal I ever had."

Callie chuckled. "Thank you for the compliment, but I guess you've never eaten in a gourmet restaurant. Not that I ever had the pleasure, but I'm sure I can't compare."

"On the contrary. One of my cousins is a gourmet chef, and until today I considered his cooking the best."

Obviously, he was exaggerating. All she did was find interesting recipes to make. That didn't make her a chef. Those people invented the recipes.

"Thank you." Then the other part of what he'd said registered and she lifted a brow. "Another cousin? How many cousins do you have?"

"Many."

"It must be nice having such a big family."

"In some ways it is. In others, it is not."

"Like what?"

He shrugged. "It's good to have a safety net. As annoying as my family can get, I know they will catch me if I fall. But when those busybodies, who don't understand the concept of privacy and boundaries, meddle in my life, I'm not sure the net is worth it. It can be suffocating."

Callie heard little of what Brundar had said after his first sentence. She was taken by the idea of having a safety net comprised of family members who cared.

It was a rarity in the modern world.

How different would life have been if she'd had that? Not that she would have asked for help. But knowing it was there and available if she needed it desperately enough would've made her life a lot less stressful.

Would her father have recovered sooner after losing her mom if he'd had help?

He might not have sunk into depression if he'd had a support system in place. Brothers, sisters, and cousins who would have taken turns making sure he was okay and helped him raise his daughter.

"I wish I had a large family that actually cares. You should be grateful for yours."

"I am. Defending the clan is my job, and I regard it as both a duty and a privilege."

"A whole clan? And what about your cousin the big shot with the butler whom you guard, isn't he your priority?"

"That's part of my job too. He manages the family business for all of us. My brother and I make sure no harm comes to him."

Fascinating. It almost sounded like a mob organization. But Brundar was too honorable of a man to take part in something illegal.

"I think so too. I mean about it being a duty and a privilege."

Brundar dipped his head. "I'm glad you see it my way."

"I wish I could be part of your clan." She regretted the words the moment they'd left her mouth. The meaning he could attach to them could be very different from what she meant by them. Callie felt her cheeks get hot. "I mean to be under the protective umbrella of it, I didn't mean to say that I wish you'd marry me or anything like that."

A sad smile tugged on Brundar's thin lips. "Of course, not. You're too young to be thinking of marriage. The first one robbed you of your youth. You need to attend college, get your degree, and then get a job doing what you love doing. Not to mention the partying a young woman like you should partake in. All those things need to happen before you settle down again."

All true, except for the partying. The train had left the station on that a long time ago. What the heck did she have in common with a bunch of college kids? They might be the same age as her, but that didn't put them on an equal footing. Life had made her older than her years.

"Speaking of college. I'll take you up on your offer to produce a fake ID for me. I hope you're right about the administration accommodating my situation. It's not like I have a restraining order against Shawn I can show them as proof."

"Don't worry about it. I'll take care of the fake papers, and I'll make sure they don't give you any problems over the name change."

"Don't tell me. You have another cousin working at UCLA."

That got a real smile out of him. "Not as far as I know. But my government contacts can come in handy again."

Callie shook her head. "Amazing. I still can't believe how lucky I am to have you as a friend. Fate must've prompted me to go to your club that night."

Brundar shifted in his chair. "Are we friends, Calypso?"

She winked. "With benefits."

Brundar ignored the suggestive remark, pretending as if he didn't know its meaning. Not his usual style, true, Brundar was quite direct. But she couldn't believe a handsome young guy like him didn't know what the phrase friends with benefits meant.

CHAPTER 11: BRUNDAR

*C*alypso rose to her feet and collected their plates. "Are you ready for dessert?"

"There is dessert?"

"Cinnamon-orange crème brûlée."

Brundar's eyes almost rolled back in his head. "I can't wait to taste it."

Talk about pampering. If she were an immortal, he would've proposed right there—the whole ridiculous thing of dropping to one knee and begging her to become his. Not really, he wasn't husband material, but the thought felt good. Evidently, Anandur was rubbing off on him because that was something his brother would have done.

He should help. Calypso had worked hard to prepare this amazing dinner, and that was pampering enough.

Pushing his chair back, Brundar got up and followed Calypso to the kitchen. "Can I make coffee?"

She smiled up at him. "Sure. You're good with that machine. I liked my coffee this morning."

Yeah, as if putting a pod into the coffeemaker and filling it with water was rocket science.

"I'm good with a lot of things. Anything kitchen related is not one of them."

"Good. Otherwise, there would've been nothing left for me to do for you, which would've bothered me. You did so much for me. You still do."

Brundar wanted to tell her that there was no need but stopped himself in time. For Calypso, it wasn't just about gratitude. She seemed to genuinely like cooking. The right thing to do was to thank her and tell her how much he'd enjoyed himself.

"I need to keep coming up with things I can do for you, just so you keep feeding me."

"It's my pleasure. You're welcome anytime." Calypso removed the foil from two small serving dishes and sprinkled sugar over them. "This should be done at the dinner table, but I'm afraid I'll set the place on fire." She pulled out a gas torch from a drawer.

"I suggest you stand back." She waved the torch.

"What are you going to do?" He stepped back, his eyes following the device in her hand.

"Just watch."

Switching the torch on, Calypso aimed the flame down at one of the dishes. The sugar caught fire, browned, and a moment later the flames died out. She repeated the process with the other one.

"Yay! I did it!" Grabbing her creations, she carried them to the dining room.

Brundar waited until the coffee maker finished brewing, filled two cups and brought them to the table. "I didn't know cooking involved such risks."

"That's only risky in the hands of an amateur, like me. Professional cooks have it down."

She didn't seem like a novice to him.

"How many of those did you make?"

She smiled sheepishly. "That's my second time. Let's see how well they turned out."

Brundar picked up the little spoon and scooped some of the crème into his mouth.

Bliss.

"What do you think? Is it any good?"

"It's excellent."

"I'm so glad to hear you say it. That's the only part of the meal I was worried about."

"Everything tasted amazing. Thank you."

"You're welcome."

As he finished the last spoonful, Brundar noticed that Calypso had barely touched her dessert. Perhaps she was saving it for him? After he'd finished everything she'd left on her dinner plate, she might have thought she hadn't made enough.

"Eat your dessert, Calypso." He pointed at her dish.

She shook her head. "I'm full. Do you want to finish it?"

He would've loved to, but he wanted her to have it. "I'm full too. Eat!" To emphasize, he pushed his chair back and rubbed his stomach as if it was overstuffed.

"Sheesh, you're so bossy." She crossed her arms over her chest. "There are like a thousand calories in this. I'm watching my weight."

He cast her an incredulous glance. "You don't need to lose anything. In fact, you could use a few more pounds."

Calypso shook her head. "I'm starting to believe that you really haven't had any girlfriends. For future reference, avoid mentioning weight even if asked. Never tell a woman she needs to gain or lose any pounds. Consider it a taboo subject."

"What should I say, then?"

"That you think she is perfect the way she is."

"You are perfect. And that's not a polite lie."

59

Her smug smirk and the naughty gleam in her eyes had seduction written all over them. Calypso quickly polished off her dessert and a moment later she pushed to her feet and sauntered over to him.

"You're perfect the way you are too." She sat on his lap and leaned against his chest while tucking her hands between her thighs.

He appreciated that she hadn't tried to get away with touching him and was making sure not to forget by keeping her hands entrapped.

Lifting her head, she kissed the underside of his jaw, then whispered, "I bought lots and lots of condoms."

Brundar's cock surged against the thin fabric of his slacks, poking Calypso's sweet ass.

"You've been a naughty girl, haven't you?" His hand closed on her nape, caging her in place.

She licked at his jaw, sending a bolt of fire straight to his balls. "A well prepared, naughty girl," she breathed.

So it seemed.

The lady wasn't going to take no for an answer, and frankly, he was tired of playing hard to get. With one arm under her thighs and the other wrapped around her waist, holding her tight against his chest, he pushed off the chair and strode to her bedroom.

Taking in the scene before him, Brundar stopped at the doorway.

When Calypso had told him she was well prepared, she'd meant more than the condoms. Four scarves were tied to four corners of the bed's iron scrollwork, and a fifth one was lying on the bed, its bright colors in stark relief on the white bedding.

She'd thought of everything.

Sitting on the bed with Calypso still wrapped in his arms, Brundar wanted to flip her over his knees, expose that beautiful ass of hers, and give her a few teasing spanks. Except, he was swimming in uncharted waters. This wasn't a scene at the club.

Should he thank her for dinner with tenderness?

Or should he give her what he knew she craved?

He didn't know her well enough to choose for her. It would be best to ask.

"Now, what should I do?" He reached behind himself for the scarf and handed it to her. "Should I reward you for an amazing dinner, or punish you for your presumptuousness?"

The scent of her arousal intensifying, Calypso obediently wrapped the scarf over her eyes, tying the ends in a loose knot at the back of her head. "Both."

Brundar smiled. With the blindfold in place, he no longer feared his fangs showing. For some reason, his fangs tended to react sooner and with less stimulation than those of other immortal males, reacting to the slightest provocation, aggression, or conversely arousal. He kissed her tenderly, going for slow and sweet instead of rough and intense.

She moaned, wiggling on his lap, impatient for her funishment.

Taking his time, he caressed her silky face, the long column of her neck, and the tops of her breasts, all while exploring the sweetness of her mouth, tasting the crème brûlée on her tongue.

When he was done with her mouth, he guided her gently to lie belly down over his knees, her cheek resting comfortably on the bed.

Her contented sigh erased the last of his doubts about what Calypso wanted him to do to her next.

This felt very different from any scene he'd ever participated in. Holding Calypso snugly against his middle was all about intimacy and closeness. Not about keeping his partner at a safe distance. Surprisingly, it felt good.

More than good, it felt right.

But only with Calypso.

Somehow, she'd managed to penetrate the shields around his heart and make a home for herself inside it. When he left her, and he didn't kid himself that he could stay, he would have to tear that piece of his heart out and leave it behind because it belonged to her and always would.

Right now, though, he was hers, and she was his, and the future or the past didn't exist at this moment.

Holding the bottom of Calypso's stretchy dress, he prolonged her anticipation by inching it up her thighs in slow motion. She had plenty of time to reconsider if she wanted to. But as with everything else, the lady knew precisely what she wanted and wasn't shy about asking for it.

When the dress finally cleared the bottom swell of her ass, Brundar let out a hiss. Not only did the tiny thong she had on leave her butt cheeks bare, but the gusset was soaked through.

Unable to resist, he snaked a finger under the scrap of fabric, dipping it in Calypso's arousal. The gentle touch had her jerk up, but he held on, keeping her tightly secure against his stomach.

She was in desperate need of relief, but he didn't want her orgasming yet. Still, he couldn't just leave her like that. He could ease her a little until she was primed for the big finale.

A strangled moan escaped her throat as he pushed a finger inside her scorching, tight sheath. Calypso managed to wiggle despite his tight hold. Tightening his arm around her middle, he added another finger, and then another, stretching her to where it must've bordered on discomfort.

Calypso stilled, absorbing the fullness, getting used to the sensation.

He withdrew his fingers and delivered the first smack.

"Oh, God," she hissed, her hands fisting the comforter.

The flare of her arousal was so potent, it wreaked havoc on his restraint. Brundar was a hair away from stripping her naked and entering her in one hard thrust.

But this was about Calypso and her needs. His would come later.

A few more smacks and she would orgasm just from the spanking.

Should he let her?

Yeah, this time he would. Calypso was too far gone to survive a drawn-out foreplay. She needed this one now.

"Put your hands behind your back, sweetling," he said as he caressed her perfect globes.

The pose would be less comfortable for her, but it would prevent her from instinctively reaching behind her. He didn't want to accidentally smack her hands. Besides, the confinement would further ratchet up the potency of her arousal.

And his.

CHAPTER 12: CALLIE

"*P*ut your hands behind your back, sweetling."

Callie responded to Brundar's command with a pained groan. Already turned on beyond belief, she was almost sent over by his stern tone and what he'd asked her to do.

Gritting her teeth, Callie held it off. There was so much more coming, and she wanted to savor it all. If she climaxed now, he would stop spanking, and she would miss out on it.

As soon as she obeyed, he gripped her wrists with one strong hand and started a steady beat on her upturned behind. The first few smacks were so light they almost felt like caresses, but soon his tempo increased and with it the sting. Still, it was far from painful. He was only teasing her. In the world of kink, this was like foreplay, and she was ready for the real thing.

Brundar stopped and massaged her warmed globes, his finger sliding down to her wet center. "How close are you, sweetling?"

"Close," she husked.

His grip on her wrists tightened, and he pulled her even

closer against his body, his warmth and his scent and the feel of his hard abs further scrambling her brain.

The next smack took her by surprise.

It delivered a real sting that had her jerking on Brundar's knees. This was what she imagined a punishment spanking would feel like. Then came another one, just as hard, on her other cheek.

Callie tensed in anticipation, but instead of a smack, Brundar's hand caressed and massaged the ache away.

"Okay? Too much?"

Was it? Callie wasn't sure. "Maybe a little."

His hand kept on caressing. "Remember. One word from you and everything stops. No fear."

"I'm not afraid."

"Good." He kept massaging and caressing, giving her time to process what she was feeling.

In retrospect, those two hard smacks had been more intense but not really painful. It was fear that had made her tense.

She wiggled as much as his iron hold on her allowed, signaling that she was ready for more.

"Words, Calypso."

"Please continue."

He gave her butt cheek an approving squeeze before resuming.

It was perfect. Not too hard and not too soft, it was exactly how she wanted it. Despite the rapid climb of arousal, Callie managed a brief moment of clarity. This had been a test of sorts. Brundar couldn't have known where her sweet spot was without stretching her limits. He was good at reading her responses, but he wasn't a mind reader. The important thing was that she could trust him.

The man was devoted to bringing her maximum pleasure.

With that realization, Callie let herself go in a way she hadn't before.

Complete surrender.

Her orgasm crested, washing over her in wave after wave of languid fire instead of one volcanic eruption.

"Oh, sweetling." Brundar lifted her off his lap as if she weighed no more than a pillow, turned her around and cradled her in his arms as if she was precious to him.

What a feeling.

His hand soft on her cheek, he turned her head toward him and kissed her as tenderly as he did before.

"Good?" he asked.

"Excellent."

His arms tightened around her. "There is no more beautiful and titillating sight than you in the throes of climax."

It was on the tip of her tongue to tell him it was unfair of him to deny her the same. Brundar would look magnificent as he reached his peak. But there was no point in bringing it up and ruining the sweet moment between them.

As it was, Brundar had already relaxed his own rules by not tying her up. Instead, he'd held her tightly against his body throughout.

Was it the first time he'd been that intimate with a woman?

Could she ask him that?

Her need to find out was so intense it was undeniable. "Am I the first? I mean like this. Close and personal."

"Yes."

Satisfaction, pure and sweet.

"Good."

Brundar didn't have a monopoly on one-word answers. In fact, she was starting to like them. He was right. It was a more efficient way to communicate if one didn't mind sounding like a Neanderthal.

Next thing she would be using grunts instead of words.

"What's that smug little smile about?"

Callie chuckled. "I was just thinking that we rub off on each other, and that pretty soon I'd be talking in grunts instead of words."

"I don't grunt."

"Yes, you do."

There was a moment of silence, during which Callie regretted not seeing Brundar's expression. It was one thing to have sex blindfolded; conducting a conversation was another. Without the facial cues, she was literally blind.

"Not a lot," he acquiesced.

Carefully, afraid she would bump her nose on his jaw, Callie lifted her head and kissed his cheek. "Thank you."

"For what?"

"Compromising." Callie meant about everything. About relaxing his rules and holding her close, and about agreeing with her on a silly thing like whether he tended to grunt a lot or not.

"Aha." He let go of his grip on her, allowing a few inches between their bodies, and tugged on her dress. "As sexy as this is, I think it's time to get rid of it."

"I agree." She lifted her arms.

He pulled it off with one tug. "I like this dress. You should always wear things that are easy to take off. But only when you're with me."

"Yes, sir." Even though the dress didn't show cleavage and reached down to her knees, the clingy fabric and how easy it was to pull off made it somewhat scandalous. She would've never dared to wear it while going out alone or with a girlfriend.

"I like it when you're so agreeable." Brundar chuckled. "Even though it's only when it suits you." He unclasped her strapless bra, baring her breasts.

Her nipples breathed a sigh of relief, figuratively speaking. The strapless bra had been tight and uncomfortable, especially when her poor little nipples had beaded with arousal but had nowhere to go.

Brundar traced his finger over the bra's compression lines. "Next time you wear this dress, don't wear this instrument of torture beneath it. Even bondage doesn't leave marks like that."

He lifted her and laid her on the bed. "Arms up, baby."

She stretched like a cat on a windowsill on a lazy afternoon.

Brundar tugged off her tiny thong and cupped her molten center. "I'm going to enjoy the hell out of lapping up all the nectar that you've made for me."

Hopefully, he would do more than that. She had no intention of letting him out of her bedroom until he joined them as one.

This strange and wonderful man belonged to her, and she needed to claim him. She would let him believe he was the one doing the claiming, but at the same time, she would be staking her claim on him.

CHAPTER 13: BRUNDAR

*I*t hadn't even crossed Brundar's mind to put Calypso face down as was his habit. Her ass was magnificent, but he liked the frontal view better. Taking a long moment to admire the woman sprawled before him, he started with her lush lips that were upturned in a little secretive smile, continued to her slender wrists and ankles that were secured to the bed frame, then back to her face and her beautiful green eyes that were regrettably covered by a silk scarf.

What would it be like to look into those eyes as he made love to her? To watch every expression?

Except, he had little choice in the matter. It wasn't about him seeing her, but the other way around. Besides, she already had him spellbound. Her eyes had the power to cement that spell in place for good.

"Calypso," Brundar uttered her name like a prayer.

No woman had ever looked as beautiful, as majestic, and as powerful as the one spread-eagled on the bed before him.

A goddess.

She had him wrapped around her little finger, and they

both knew it. He might have been the one who'd spanked her and tied her up, but there was no question as to who held the power in this exchange—not in his mind, and not in hers, judging by that victorious smile on her lips.

Were men fools for thinking they were ever really in charge?

He was reminded of a passage from the human Bible that had struck him as odd. As a whole, it was hard to claim the Bible as anything but patriarchal, and yet it said, "Therefore shall a man leave his father and his mother and shall cleave unto his wife; and they shall be one flesh."

The reality of the human world Brundar had grown up in was that the wife left her father and mother and followed her husband. Not the other way around. But he was starting to think that the Bible was spot on. For the right woman, a man would leave everything and everyone dear to him because she was the key to his happiness, his future, and without her there was nothing.

Or more accurately, nothing important.

Being a master swordsman and the clan's best fighter provided Brundar with a sense of worth and no small amount of pride, but only Calypso made him feel needed, wanted, and desired.

"Brundar?" There was a note of worry in her tone.

Did she think he'd left?

He would never leave her side after tying her up, but in a way she was right. He'd retreated inside his own head and had stayed there for far too long. "I'm here."

Her smile was back. "Why are you over there and not over here?"

"I had to take a moment to admire your beauty, sweetling."

The smile got wider.

As he started unbuttoning his dress shirt, Brundar

wondered if Calypso was listening for clues. Did she hear him shrugging it off and laying it on the dresser?

"Are you taking off your clothes?" She sounded so hopeful.

"Impatient?"

"You bet."

Kneeling beside her on the bed, he caressed her soft cheek.

"Kiss me," Calypso whispered.

He took her sweet lips, licking into her mouth and sliding his tongue along hers in lazy swipes. Even though his impudent cock strongly disagreed, there was no hurry. Brundar intended to take his time feasting on the beauty before him until he got her senseless with need and climaxing all over his face.

She was already panting restlessly, her nipples so stiff they must've ached.

He would be neglecting his duty if he didn't do something about it right away, providing the relief she needed.

Moving to kneel between her spread legs, Brundar lowered his torso and braced on his forearms.

In anticipation, Calypso arched her back.

Not wanting to prolong her torment, he dipped his head and closed his lips around one turgid peak, treating it to a few swipes of his tongue, then moved to the other and repeated.

The first sound Calypso made was a sigh of relief, the second was a throaty moan, and as his fingers gently tugged on one hard peak while he sucked on the other, her moans became louder.

He loved that she was uninhibited this way. Her moans and her cries of pleasure were his rewards, and she was just as generous with those as she was with everything else.

Kissing his way down her flat belly, Brundar closed his

eyes and inhaled the unique musk of her arousal. If he could bottle that scent, he would carry it with him everywhere and take whiffs every time he missed her. She was addictive.

Her belly quivered under him, the muscles contracting in anticipation. "Brundar," she whispered his name like a plea.

"I've got you, sweetling." He licked into her, touching the pad of his thumb to her sensitive nub. She bucked, and he pressed his hand to her belly, holding her down as his tongue rimmed her entrance and his thumb moved in slow circles around the second most erogenous part of her body.

What most men didn't realize was that the seat of a woman's pleasure resided between her ears. That was why sex games were more about altering perception than a specific touch, and why pain could in certain situations be interpreted as pleasure but not in others.

A true master manipulated body and mind.

He pushed a finger inside her, then added another and flattened his tongue over the needy button jutting from the top of her sex.

Her head thrashing from side to side, Calypso alternated between needy moans and impatient hisses. Hanging right on the edge, but unable to dive over it, she needed one final push.

Brundar curled his fingers inside her, pressing on that bundle of nerves that was sure to send her flying, and yet she didn't, her frustrated groans sounding pained.

Strange. Up until now, he'd marveled at how responsive Calypso was, how easily she reached her climaxes, but something seemed to bother her, preventing her from letting go.

Female orgasms were finicky.

Slightly too much or too little touch could make the difference between a woman's ability to orgasm or not. And a disturbing thought could have the same effect. Maybe the ties were too tight?

"What's the matter, baby? Are you uncomfortable? Do you need me to loosen the knots?"

Biting on her lower lip, she shook her head.

"Then what is it? You need to tell me."

"I'm afraid," she whispered.

He hadn't smelled fear on her, but then the scent of her arousal was quite overpowering.

"Of me?"

She shook her head again, her cheeks turning bright red. "I'm afraid that you will make me come with your fingers and your tongue and then leave again like you did before."

Poor girl. She was too anxious to climax.

"I have no plans of leaving without sinking my shaft all the way inside you and fucking you into oblivion like I promised. Where do you keep that stash of condoms you mentioned?"

"The nightstand drawer."

Brundar leaned over her and pulled the drawer open. Calypso hadn't been kidding. She must've emptied the store's entire supply of the brand she'd chosen.

He picked a packet up and chuckled. "Should I be flattered? Size extra-large?"

Worrying her lower lip, Calypso smiled. "What I felt through your pants seemed extra large."

Brundar shook his head, pressing his lips together to stifle his retort. What had she used as comparison? Was that jerk of a husband of hers an extra large? Or was he just a large, and Calypso expected Brundar to be larger?

To voice those thoughts would not only be a dicky thing to do, but it would most likely kill her mood. It was sure as hell killing his.

"Let's try it on and see if you were right."

"Like you don't know."

"Different brands have different sizes. Like shoes." Or so he assumed.

He had no need for them. Immortals didn't contract diseases, and the chances of him impregnating a mortal were slim. Besides, most were on the pill or some other form of contraceptive. The last time he'd used a condom was when a partner had handed it to him, insisting that he put it on before blindfolding her. He couldn't remember what size it was, only that it had felt uncomfortable.

Unbuckling his belt, Brundar hoped he remembered how to use the damned rubber. For his first time with Calypso, he would've preferred nothing between them.

Regrettably, it was not to be. Not unless he thralled her right now, which he didn't want to do either. Sober consent aside, he just wanted to be with the real Calypso, to feel her responses, to hear her moan and plead loudly and clearly with nothing to dilute her experience.

Except for the bloody rubber.

Calypso's belly quivered, and a moment later she erupted in giggles.

His pants and boxers hitting the floor, Brundar paused. "What's so funny?"

"I don't know. Maybe comparing condoms to shoes?" She erupted in a new wave of giggles.

It was anxiety. Calypso had been waiting and preparing for this moment, building up her anticipation, while all along fearing that he would back away. Now that he'd reassured her, her relief was coming out as laughter.

He didn't know what to say in response, but he knew how to stop the giggles.

Thankfully, as he carefully rolled down the condom, it wasn't as uncomfortable as the other one, which meant that Calypso's assessment of his size had been accurate.

Climbing back on the bed, he lowered himself on top of

her, bracing his weight on his forearms but letting his chest touch hers.

Calypso sighed in contentment, her body soft and giving under his.

"Are you ready for me, sweetling?" He nuzzled her neck.

"I've been ready since the first moment I saw you."

Reaching a hand between their bodies, he stroked along her wet slit, gathering moisture and dragging it up to tease her.

She arched her back. "Please, Brundar, I can't wait any longer. I need you inside me."

How could he refuse her? How could he refuse himself?

Positioning himself, Brundar breached her entrance with just the head and stilled, giving her time to adjust to the invasion.

She pushed her pelvis up, impaling herself on another inch. "More."

His control snapped, and he surged all the way inside her, filling her, stretching her in a way that must've been painful. And yet, Calypso didn't cry out and didn't drop back down. Instead, she kept her pelvis raised as if afraid he would withdraw before she was ready to let him.

He wasn't about to.

Not yet.

Even the rubber couldn't take away from this moment. Being inside Calypso felt like nothing he'd experienced before.

It was a true joining.

It was perfect.

Did it feel this way because he wasn't indifferent to Calypso like he'd been to all the others?

Or was it something else?

The Fates must really hate him for taunting him with the

perfect woman, sending him a human he couldn't have instead of a Dormant or an immortal.

Cupping Calypso's cheeks, he kissed her lips, licking inside her mouth, gently at first then with more fervor as holding still became too much.

He retreated and surged again, then again, ramming into her full force.

By the third thrust, her inner muscles fluttered around him, and she screamed her release into his mouth.

By the fifth pump, his own climax came barreling up his shaft, along with the undeniable need to sink his fangs into Calypso's neck. Clasping her head in an iron grip, he hissed and struck her soft flesh. She tensed as his sharp canines broke her skin, but she didn't jerk back, submitting beautifully to his claiming.

A moment later, Calypso's body went lax under him, and her facial muscles relaxed into an angelic, blissful expression.

Brundar retracted his fangs and licked the twin puncture wounds closed, then buried his face in that same spot he'd just bitten—where her neck met her shoulder.

In a little bit, he would enter her mind and erase the memory of his bite. But in the meantime, he would enjoy the incredible sense of connection for a little longer.

CHAPTER 14: CALLIE

*C*onfusion greeted Callie as her brain restarted after short-circuiting for several moments, or was it longer?

With her body languid, and her mind working in slow motion, it was hard to grasp the thoughts swirling around her head like croutons in a French onion soup, and concentrate on anything.

The previous time Brundar had worked her up into a mind-bending orgasm, she'd been out of it for nearly an hour, during which Brundar had removed her restraints, carried her to bed, and cleaned her up. She'd felt none of that, waking up wrapped in blankets with Brundar sitting next to her fresh out of the shower.

This time, however, she must've woken up earlier because she could feel him wiping her gently with a warm washcloth.

Was blacking out and passing out from powerful orgasms normal?

Or maybe it only happened to her twice in a row because both times were firsts.

At the club, Brundar had introduced her to bondage and

erotic spanking. The experience had been so intense that it was no wonder she'd passed out after orgasming. Heck, afterward, she'd been as exhausted as if she'd run a marathon.

This time had been just as intense or even more so because Brundar had finally joined them.

Had he felt the same thing she had?

The connection?

The indescribable awareness of finding her way home?

It had been so much more than sex. Then again, it could all have been in her head. The buildup of anticipation prompting her to assign meaning to what was nothing more than incredible sex.

One thing Callie was sure of, though. She wanted more of that. Heck, she wanted that every day, preferably more than once, for the rest of her life. But if it were too much to ask for, she would settle for one daily dose of a mind-blowing orgasm, please.

Brundar was turning her into a sex addict. But it was all good. Craving one man a lot couldn't be unhealthy, right?

She felt Brundar move the warm washcloth to her inner thigh.

Was tending to her privates part of the aftercare she'd read about?

The blindfold was still on, but her arms and legs were free. Callie reached for the washcloth. "You don't have to do this."

With a growl that sounded more animal than human, Brundar moved her hand aside and continued his ministrations. "Better get used to it because I'm always going to take care of you."

Oh, she could get used to him taking care of her, no problem.

The question was what he'd meant by that. Caring for her after sex?

For Callie it meant the whole kit and caboodle, like a commitment and a relationship, and all that jazz.

Except, there was something to be said for Brundar's cleaning routine too, especially when he pushed on her knee and spread her thighs wider. The combination of dominance and gentle care was like an erotic Molotov cocktail on Callie's arousal, igniting it and getting her wet all over again.

It hadn't gone unnoticed. The washcloth disappeared, replaced by Brundar's finger.

She chuckled. "Are you going to punish me for ruining all that careful cleanup work?"

His finger traced her slit. "On the contrary. I'm going to reward you." The finger kept doing wicked things to her.

Callie lifted up to get a little more, only to have Brundar's hand push down on her belly. "Arms over your head, Calypso. Grab onto the headboard and don't let go."

"Yes, sir."

She felt like giggling again. Brundar was trusting her to keep her hands away. Not that she minded him tying her up, not at all, it was hot as heck. But she wanted more than that. Eventually, she hoped he would allow her to touch him. In the meantime, leaving her unrestrained was a step in the right direction.

Getting between her upturned knees, he spread her thighs even wider and blew on her heated flesh. Imagining what he saw, Callie felt a blush creeping up her cheeks. She was completely exposed to his gaze, her lower lips spread so wide that she felt his cool breath all the way inside her.

A moment later his tongue speared into her, pulling a ragged moan from her throat. His strong hands holding her thighs spread wide, he licked and sucked like a man possessed.

It was too much. Callie forgot about keeping her hands up above her head and reached for his head, tugging on his hair.

His warning growl reminded her of her mistake.

Immediately, she reached back for the iron scrolls of the headboard, gripping on to them for dear life.

Brundar stopped his attack for a moment to lift her legs and drape them over his wide shoulders, exposing her even more. But at this point, Callie was beyond caring.

"Please."

She didn't have to wait long.

Penetrating her with two fingers, Brundar sucked her clit in.

Her moan sounding more like a strangled, pained cry, Callie exploded, the tightly wound coil inside her springing free.

Through the orgasmic haze, she heard a wrapper tear, and a moment later Brundar was inside her. He wasn't gentle, going hard and deep with one powerful thrust, then pulling almost all the way out only to ram back inside her full force.

Hanging on to the headboard for dear life, all she could do was spread wide and accept his hammering. It was exhilarating to feel Brundar lose control like that. There was nothing cold or reserved about the man on top of her.

Callie would've given anything to see his face lost to the passion. Grunting and growling, Brundar sounded like a rutting animal, and yet she couldn't imagine him as anything less than the beautiful angel he was.

Her dark angel.

It was a heady feeling to be the one who caused this powerful and proud man to lose control.

His grip on her hips was bruising, but Callie didn't care. He was claiming her, leaving his mark on her, and in turn, she was claiming him. As his shaft swelled inside her, stretching her to her limit, another climax rolled over her like a semitrailer going downhill with no brakes.

She screamed.

But this time she didn't black out.

CHAPTER 15: SHAWN

Staring at the divorce papers, Shawn couldn't believe that he'd signed them. Served him right for getting wasted. Weed on its own was harmless, and so was alcohol, but they sure as fuck didn't mix well.

When he'd sobered up, he'd found the signed divorce papers on his coffee table, and purple fingermarks on his neck.

Fuck, he must've attacked the delivery guy.

Shawn smiled. If he'd ended up looking the way he had, the other guy had probably ended up in the hospital. True, he hadn't wrestled since high school, but he was as strong as an ox.

Except, he would've expected the weasel to report him to the police. Maybe he didn't do it because of the damage he'd done to Shawn's neck. It would have been hard to prove who started the fight.

Shawn had been in enough brawls to know that. It was his word against the delivery dude. Maybe the guy had a record and couldn't afford to tangle with the police.

Whatever.

The thing that bothered Shawn the most was that until recently he'd been glad that the bitch had left, and couldn't understand why suddenly it had started making him angry again. After all, he got to keep the house, which was worth much more than the measly amount she'd taken by emptying half of their savings.

The ones she knew about.

The real money was in an account only Shawn had access to. The stupid bitch thought he was depositing all of his income into their joint account. Shawn was way too smart for that. Only the base salary went in there. His commissions and his bonuses and money from the deals he'd made on the side went into his private account.

In that regard, signing the divorce papers without a fight had been a smart move on his part. If lawyers had gotten involved, they might have discovered the money he'd hidden from her, and the fucking whore would have walked out with way more money than she'd ever imagined.

If he'd let her out.

She had been smart running off the way she had.

Nah, Callie was a dumb little cunt. She must've had help. Probably the guy who was screwing her. The one she left Shawn for.

Was it one of the waiters at Aussie?

He needed to go there again and talk with her friends. Get some more information out of them. Callie hadn't told anyone that she was running out on him. She hadn't even told her bosses that she was quitting.

But one of the other bitches must have known something. That slut, Kati, had looked at him funny like she suspected he'd been beating Callie up.

Fuck, maybe if he had, the little bitch would've had more respect for him. He'd been too easy on her because he wanted to get her pregnant. Every month he'd hoped she was, and every month he'd been disappointed.

The slut was probably taking some form of contraceptives. But if she was, she must've hidden it damn fucking well. He went through her things almost every day and checked all her credit card purchases. If she'd been seeing a doctor or buying pills, he would've known.

Sneaky little bitch must've found a way. Maybe her friends had gotten it for her?

He was not going to make the same mistake with the next woman he claimed as his. From the very start, he'd show her who was boss, and she would know her place—barefoot and pregnant and jumping to obey his every command.

CHAPTER 16: TESSA

*T*essa eyed the two guys standing next to Karen with identical conceited smirks on their handsome faces. Both were young, in their mid-twenties, with athletic builds and hair so short they looked practically bald.

"Good evening, ladies. I want to introduce my two friends, Yoram and Gadi." She pointed at each guy as she said his name. "They've graciously volunteered to be your punching dummies."

The one named Yoram flashed a smile, revealing perfectly straight white teeth. "We didn't volunteer. We've been drafted," he said, casting an accusing glance at Karen.

She shrugged. "I figured my generous hospitality deserved a little something in return." She turned to Yoram. "If you want to crash at my place while visiting Los Angeles, you can put in some work. Except for love, and you have mine, nothing in life is free."

At first glance, the guys seemed intimidating. Standing with their hands clasped behind their backs, their feet parted in a military stance, they looked dark and dangerous. But as soon as Yoram smiled and started his friendly banter with Karen, the knot in Tessa's stomach eased.

Sharon elbowed her. "Yum."

"Uh-huh." They were handsome, but neither could hold a candle to Jackson.

"Ladies, as I've said before, you need to practice your moves on real men in real situations," Karen continued. "Yoram and Gadi are both tough commando soldiers. I know because I trained them both. They can take whatever you dish out. They'll be wearing groin protectors, so that area is not off limits. The only thing you shouldn't do is the eye-gouging move I taught the class before last."

Tessa grimaced, and she wasn't the only one. Karen's no-nonsense fighting technique was brutal in the extreme.

"Both men are well trained, are in peak health, and weigh around two hundred pounds each. The odds are that you will never encounter a heavier or stronger assailant. Let's see if you can take them down."

Karen turned to the guys. "Suit up, boys, and protect those family jewels. I want to see babies from both of you."

Their tough Krav Maga instructor was an interesting cross between a drill sergeant and a pushy mother.

Sharon smirked. "I would like a go at those family jewels."

"Stop it," Tessa hissed in her ear. "They'll hear you."

"No, they won't."

"Whatever, it's not my problem. If you want to flirt with Karen's friends, it's your business.

"Sharon, darling, how about you go first?" Karen's mocking tone convinced Tessa that she'd overheard her friend.

"Sure." Sharon sauntered to the mat area.

The instructor took her by the shoulders and turned her around. "You just stand there, like you're waiting for a bus.

Gadi will come at you from behind and grab you. Try to get free."

"Got it." Sharon rotated her shoulders as if she was a fighter getting ready for a match.

Tessa rolled her eyes. Her co-worker was one of the worst students in the class. She was in for some major humiliation.

"Go!" Karen gave the command.

Gadi rushed toward Sharon's back. Catching her around her waist, he lifted her off the ground with one arm as if she weighed nothing and closed his other hand over her mouth to prevent her from screaming for help.

The knot in Tessa's stomach tightened, and she swallowed hard to stop bile from rising up her throat.

It's not real. It's not real, she kept repeating in her head as Sharon thrashed in a futile attempt to get free, pin-wheeling her legs as if she'd learned nothing.

Gadi pushed her face down to the mat and pounced on top of her, pinning her hands behind her back.

Karen clapped her hands. "Okay, Gadi, that's enough. Sharon, you can get up."

The guy sprang back to his feet and offered a hand up to Sharon, whose face was redder than a ripe tomato.

Addressing the class, Karen waved a hand in Sharon's direction. "See? This was an excellent example of what not to do when someone grabs you from behind."

Hands on her hips, Sharon hung her head in shame.

The instructor clapped her on her back. "Let's try this again. But this time you do what I taught you, eh?"

Sharon nodded.

"Do you need a moment?"

"I'm good."

Karen clapped her on her back again. "Good, good. This time I'll have Yoram come at you, so you won't know what to anticipate. Ready?"

Sharon nodded.

Yoram grabbed her the same way Gadi had, but used both arms around her middle, pinning her arms to her sides.

This time, Sharon didn't panic and dropped down before he had a chance to tighten his grip. From her squatting position, she straightened, elbowed him in his tummy and ran. Exactly like Karen had taught them to do.

After a few steps, she stopped and turned around. "You let me go. I know I couldn't have gotten away from you if you really held on."

Yoram flashed his cute smile again. "I'm stronger and better trained than the average man. So I allowed for that. But if you want, we can do it again."

With a wink, Sharon shook her head. "Maybe after everyone else has a go and you're tired."

He pointed a finger at her. "It's a date."

Sharon turned and sauntered back toward the group, sashaying her hips, then looked back to catch Yoram ogling her ass.

Someone was going to get lucky tonight.

Karen, being the insightful woman she was, kept Tessa for last. The guys were good sports. Even though they were tired and sweaty, they both kept smiling and encouraging the women to do their worst.

"Tessa, you're next." Karen beckoned her to the mat.

Tessa took a deep breath and got in position. After watching Yoram and Gadi with the other women, she was okay with one of them grabbing her.

Hopefully.

The last thing she needed was a panic attack in front of all these women.

Karen walked over to her and bent her knees, so they were eye to eye. "You're small, Tessa. But that's actually an advantage. First of all, no one expects you to fight. You look like easy prey. Use it to your advantage. The faster you respond, the better. The moment he grabs you from behind, make yourself limp as a noodle and drop to the ground. Take a step forward, and while you're getting up, use the momentum to kick him in the groin as hard as you can, then run while he's nursing his balls. Got it?"

"Got it." Tessa glanced at Gadi.

He cupped himself, tapping his knuckles on the rigid protection over his family jewels. "Don't be afraid to hurt me. Kick like your life depends on it. Your foot is probably going to hurt more than my nuts. "

She nodded and turned her back to him.

Gadi lunged at her, gripping her not too gently. But Tessa had practiced this move so many times, the response was instinctive. She didn't need to think what to do next, she didn't need to think at all. She just acted. Turning her body limp as a noodle, she dropped the second she felt him coming at her, not giving Gadi a chance to get a good grip. She turned exactly as Karen had told her to, delivering a roundhouse kick to Gadi's protected family jewels.

Somehow, her kick was powerful enough to send the two-hundred-pound man flying back to land on his butt, gripping his injured privates and writhing on the floor.

Shit, he'd lied to her. Her foot hurt only a little, while he looked like he was in real pain. Unless Gadi was pretending to boost her confidence. She eyed him suspiciously, but he was either a very good actor or hurting for real.

Nevertheless, it had been a commendable performance. Hers as well as his.

Karen was the first one to clap, followed by Yoram and then the rest of the class.

Poor Gadi was still on the mat. Had she really hurt him?

Tessa crouched next to him. "Are you okay? Is this for show, or are you really hurt?"

He winked at her. "A little bit of both. Good job, Tessa." He offered her his hand.

Not sure if he wanted her to help him up or shake it, she opted for the safer route and tried to pull him up.

If he hadn't helped, Gadi would still be down on the mat. His two hundred pounds were more than double her weight.

Karen pulled her away from the smiling Gadi, wrapping her arm around Tessa's shoulders.

"You see, ladies? This is what training can do for you if you practice the way you should. If Tessa can do it, so can you, eh?"

Sharon clapped again, and the rest of the class followed. "Way to go, badass!"

Tessa grinned. She was a badass.

Gadi came over and wrapped his arm around her middle, pulling her away from Karen.

"How about we celebrate? Can I interest you in a drink? Or a cup of coffee with a Danish?" He leaned to whisper in her ear. "I'm not much of a drinker. I'm more of a coffee and cake kind of guy."

Unbelievably, Tessa felt flattered by his flirting, and not anxious at all. "If I weren't engaged, I would've loved to. You're an awesome guy."

He made a pouty face, which looked adorable on his rugged face. "That's a shame. Do you have a friend you can hook me up with?"

She glanced at Sharon, who was all over Yoram. "I think your friend called dibs on mine."

Gadi followed her gaze. "I see. Well, it seems like I'm on my own. Do you know which of these ladies are single?"

"I do." Tessa spent the next five minutes giving Gadi a rundown on each one of the unattached women.

"Thanks," he said when she was done. "I'd better get to

work before they all scatter." He rubbed his hands, a predatory gleam shining in his eyes.

It seemed like another lady was going to get lucky tonight.

Karen clapped her hands. "Listen up, ladies. I promised you dangerous jewelry, and I brought samples. Come take a look. If there is anything you like, there is a stack of order forms next to the display you can fill out. When you're done, hand them to me."

Tessa had been waiting for that. After Karen had told them about the rings and bracelets that doubled as weapons, everyone had been looking forward to checking them out.

"This one is simple." She lifted a silver-toned ring with a pointy edge. "You use it as a knuckleduster." Karen demonstrated, making a fist and punching the air with the sharp triangle pointing out.

Tessa put it down on her order form.

"This one is special." Karen put on a heavy ring. "It has a retractable blade." She pressed on one of the fake jewels and a tiny blade popped out. "Now I know what you're thinking. What on earth can you do with such a small blade?"

With a secretive smirk, she looked around at her eager audience, waiting for someone to make a suggestion. When no one had, she turned to Gadi. "Can you give me a hand?"

He walked over, and Karen handed him duct tape. "Wrap it around my wrists."

When he was done, Karen used the tiny blade to cut through the tape. "This could also work on a rope. Or to gouge out an eye." She jabbed the blade in the air at eye level.

Tessa cringed again but added the blade ring to her order form.

"The bracelet." Karen lifted a plain looking metal cuff with several gaudy fake jewels glued to it. "This you can kill with." She tugged on one of the jewels, pulling out a metal wire so thin that it was barely visible.

Moving fast, she caught poor Gadi by surprise, holding the wire a few inches away from his throat.

Gadi froze. "Careful with that, Karen."

Gasps sounded from all around.

"I am, darling." Karen kissed his cheek and carefully withdrew the wire. "This is so thin, you don't need much force to cut someone's neck. Very useful. But there is a caveat. You need to act fast and catch your nemesis by surprise."

Tessa added the deadly bracelet to her order. "Anything else in your bag of tricks?" she asked Karen.

"Oh, there is plenty. But I didn't bring it all. You can have spiky heels that can kill, sneakers with retractable blades, pendants with tracking devices. You tell me what you want, and I'll bring a sample."

Tessa handed Karen the order form. "I don't know what else there is. So how can I ask for it if I don't know if it exists?"

"Good point. I'll bring the catalog next time."

"When will the stuff I ordered get here?"

"A few weeks. Everything is made in China. Slow shipping."

That was a shame. Tessa couldn't wait to have all those gadgets. She'd feel like a real 007.

Casting a quick glance at Sharon, she saw her friend was still busy flirting with Yoram. But it was okay.

After today's lesson, Tessa felt confident enough to go out into the dark street and walk to her car by herself.

CHAPTER 17: JACKSON

"All done," Gordon announced. "I'm ready to hit the sack."

Jackson glanced at his watch. "Dude, it's only eight-thirty." He needed to talk to his friends about their future.

Gordon was leaving at the beginning of the school year for the University of Arizona, and Vlad was starting Santa Monica College. At least he was staying in town.

"I'm tired. I just want to get in bed and watch a few episodes of *Rick and Morty* before I fall asleep."

Both Gordon and Vlad were obsessed with the cartoon. It had a few funny episodes, but Jackson didn't get their fascination with it.

"I want to talk to you guys."

Gordon sighed. "About?"

"What am I going to do when you guys are in college?"

Vlad emerged from the kitchen with a six pack of soda cans. "I'm still here."

"Yeah, but how many hours can you work?"

His friend folded his long and wiry frame into the front booth and popped the lid off one of the sodas. "I can still do the mornings, preparing the dough and doing the baking for the day, but I can't stay after that."

That was better than nothing, but not enough. Jackson pushed his bangs back and slid into the booth next to Vlad. "I'm thinking about closing the café."

Gordon sat across from them and grabbed one of the sodas. "That's extreme. Why don't you hire a couple of humans?"

"It's not going to be the same without you guys."

Gordon put a hand over his heart. "I'm touched. But really, man, life goes on. You can't expect things to stay the same."

"I know. It sucks. Vlad and I will need to find a new drummer for the band."

Jackson had known that one day they would need to part ways, but he'd hoped he had more time.

"What about the new place?" Vlad asked. "The village needs someone to run the café over there."

The thought had crossed his mind. Nathalie couldn't manage it for the foreseeable future, but Carol was doing fine without her.

"Kian will probably close the one in the keep and Carol will manage the new one."

Gordon shook his head. "I overheard Bhathian talking about her training for some secret mission."

Jackson's ears perked up. "And you kept it to yourself? Talk!"

Gordon shrugged. "I don't know what it's about. Bhathian was talking to Andrew about it, and both of them were shaking their heads like it was the dumbest idea ever."

Whatever it was, Carol leaving the café was news to Jackson. Without her, there would be no one to run the old or the new place, and people would be majorly bummed if that happened. Besides, it was a wasted business opportunity.

If he could figure out the logistics, maybe he could jump on it.

"I can't run the place by myself."

Vlad put his empty can on the table. "What about Onidu? He's doing a fine job."

"If Amanda agrees for him to continue, then I might be able to pull it off. But I still need you to bake."

"I said I would."

For a few moments, the three of them sat in silence, thinking.

Gordon lifted his head. "Maybe you could advertise a position on the clan's digital bulletin board. Not everyone works full time. Before Carol took over Nathalie's café, she was a bum. Does Sylvia work?"

Jackson shook his head. "I don't know."

The board was a good idea, though. Maybe some of those who had jobs would want to quit after moving to the village. The commute was going to be much longer. Besides, the place was so nice people would want to hang around.

"Tessa and I applied for a house."

Gordon grinned and lifted his palm for a high five. "Congratulations, man. Moving in together is a big step."

"We didn't hear from Kian yet. Maybe we need to be officially mated first."

Vlad toyed with his empty can, squeezing and bending it into different shapes. "That's an even bigger step. Are you sure about it? You're still a kid."

"I don't feel like a kid. And yes, I'm sure."

Vlad flipped his long bangs back. "Then you're lucky. I wish I could find a girl. I wouldn't even mind a human."

Jackson sighed. "Tessa is still one."

Vlad patted his shoulder. "Don't worry. She will turn. The Fates would not have brought her to you just to dangle happiness in your face and then take it away."

That was exactly what Jackson was afraid of. "The Fates are not always kind. Sometimes I think that they like to play with us. They get bored and look for poor saps like me to mess with."

It felt both good and bad to finally voice his fears. He'd been keeping them inside himself for too long, fronting optimism for Tessa's sake.

Vlad shook his head. "I don't think the Fates are capricious. I think they just have a bigger plan than we can see."

Gordon pushed to his feet. "All this talk about Fates is one big bullshit. I'm going to bed. You guys can discuss philosophy without me."

Jackson nodded. "Goodnight, Gordon."

The guy took a few steps then turned around. "I'm sorry, Jackson. I know that you're scared, and believing in some cosmic order makes you feel better. I shouldn't have said anything."

"No, that's okay. You're right. The moment I start relying on the Fates is the moment I start relying less on myself, which is not good. I will do what I can, and if the Fates want to help, that's great. But if they don't, it's fine too."

Gordon smiled. "That's the Jackson we all know and love. One hell of a cocky bastard who thinks he can take on the world and win."

"You betcha."

CHAPTER 18: RONI

*R*oni's new throne room left a lot to be desired, but considering that it started with a hospital bed and an assortment of medical equipment, he couldn't complain.

In fact, he was so comfortable he was considering adopting the same setup once the doctor cleared him to leave.

William's assistants, a bunch of super nerds Roni felt right at home with, were quite enterprising. They had rigged him up a contraption that suspended two large monitors over his bed, which he could move every which way he pleased. A regular hospital rolling table doubled as his keyboard desk, and the large towers were cooling behind the bed.

Bridget wasn't happy about the freezing temperature in the room; it wasn't the optimal environment for someone sick with pneumonia, but perfect for keeping the equipment running at optimum level.

Roni was used to working in a cold room.

Besides, Sylvia had brought him a sweater, a scarf, a knit

beanie, and fingerless cashmere gloves to keep him nice and warm. She was a keeper, just as Mildred had told him.

Damn, he missed Barty and his wife.

Working on and off all morning, Roni had been taking occasional naps when he'd gotten too tired. The fucking pneumonia was making him not only weak like a baby, but melancholy. Otherwise, he wouldn't be thinking about his old crusty handler and his wife, Mildred.

Being sick literally sucked the life out of him. It might have been his imagination, but Roni was convinced his hard-earned muscles were shriveling by the hour. Once he was back on his feet, he would be back to the scrawny scarecrow he was before a year of working out had filled him out a bit.

Fuck. He hated working out.

What a waste of time. The hour a day he spent working on improving his unimpressive physique could've been put to better use hacking and programming.

Someone knocked on the door.

"I'm busy!"

Another disadvantage of working from a hospital room was the doctor or one of her nurses interrupting him with their unnecessary checkups. He really didn't need his temperature and blood pressure taken once an hour every hour, day and night. It wasn't as if pneumonia was a deadly disease, at least he didn't think it was.

Ignoring Roni's clear dismissal, the knocker, a Lord of the Rings elf prince lookalike, opened the door and strode in as if he owned the place.

"I'll be brief," he said in a monotone voice. All that was missing was an Austrian accent, and it would've sounded a lot like the famous "I'll be back."

Roni gave the intruder a once-over. An intimidating dude. "And you are?"

"Brundar." The elf lookalike didn't offer his hand. Instead, he inclined his head in a gesture that looked more like a nod than an attempted introduction.

Wait a minute...

Brundar? The guy who gave Andrew the shivers?

It was good Roni was meeting the guy here, where he'd established his position as king, and not at the dojo. Otherwise, he would've felt intimidated as hell.

"I heard about you."

Brundar lifted a brow.

"Anandur threatened Andrew to bring you as my initiator if Andrew refused to do the honors."

Brundar regarded Roni as if he was an ant under a microscope. "Anandur should've done it."

Roni grimaced. "He couldn't get aggressive with me. I was not enough of a challenge."

Brundar nodded. "I can see how that could be a problem for him."

"But not for you?"

The guy affected a chilling smile. "Not for me."

He could see why Andrew didn't like the guy. From now on whenever Roni imagined a cold-hearted assassin, he would see this guy's face. And the fact that Brundar was enviously good-looking, like a fallen angel, only enhanced the chilling effect instead of softening it.

"What can I do for you?" It would be in Roni's best interest to have the guy indebted to him. If he ever needed anyone taken out, Roni would know who to turn to.

"William is not here, and you're supposedly one hell of a hacker."

"Not supposedly. I'm the best."

Brundar's lips twitched. "And modest, I see."

Roni shrugged. "It's not boasting when it's the truth."

"Can you hack into a university's computers and change

the name of a student? A friend of mine got accepted, but she needs to go under a different name."

"So you need me to change her records to reflect a different one?"

"Exactly."

"I will need a new social security number for the new name."

"I'm having them done. Birth certificate, social security, driver's license, passport, the works."

"Excellent. When do you need it done?"

"How soon can you do it?"

Roni had a lot on his plate, and hacking into hundreds of security camera feeds was time-consuming. If he waited until he was done with all of that to help Brundar's friend, it would be several days before he could get to it.

"William left a big project for me, but I'm willing to take a short break to help your friend. It will set me back a couple of hours." Let the guy think it was a bigger deal than it really was.

"Thanks. I owe you, kid."

Roni smirked. *Music to my ears.* "Get me her old and new papers."

"I'll come later when I have them. Does it matter to you what time?"

Roni shook his head. "Not really. I'm sick, as you can see, so I need to take short naps from time to time. If I'm sleeping when you come back, wake me up."

Brundar nodded, then smoothed his palm over his blond hair. "I don't know how it works with you being a human. Do I pay you? Can I get you something in return for the favor?"

"I'll take an unspecified IOU."

It was funny to watch the guy who was pale as a vampire to start with getting even paler. "That can be anything."

Roni chuckled. "Don't worry. I don't want your first-born or anything like that. I don't even know what kind of favor you're good for."

"I obey the law. So whatever you have in mind it can't be illegal."

Roni lifted a brow. "Says the guy who just asked me to falsify records."

Brundar shifted, putting his weight on his other foot. "That's different. Think of it as a witness protection program."

"What did she see?" Roni got excited. He was so bored with the project he was working on, he was hungry for a good story.

"It's not like that. Her ex-husband is dangerous. If he finds her, he will harm her."

The smile evaporated from Roni's face. "Say no more, my friend. It shall be done. No future favors required."

For the first time since he'd arrived, Brundar regarded Roni with real respect. Apparently, his hacking skills hadn't impressed the guy as much as his gallantry.

"I appreciate that. Whatever I can help you with, I will. Not as a favor, but as one warrior to another."

Roni snorted. "Warrior?" He looked down at himself. "Damn, this sweater must make me look good." He patted the sleeve. "But regrettably it's all false advertisement. There isn't much underneath."

Brundar didn't laugh at his joke. Hell, the guy looked like he never did.

"We utilize different weapons, but we fight on the same team."

Roni lifted his palm for a high five, but Brundar ignored it.

Strange dude.

He let his arm drop. "Thank you. I always thought of

myself as a cyber warrior, but you're the first one to acknowledge me as one."

Brundar inclined his head. "I'll be back with the papers." He turned on his heel and walked out without saying goodbye.

Kind of impolite, but then Roni often acted just as rude if not worse. The difference was that Roni was well aware of it and did it on purpose, while Brundar was just weird.

CHAPTER 19: CALLIE

allie's afternoon walk almost always ended at the neighborhood grocery store. With no car, she could only carry so much back home. The solution was to buy only what was necessary for whatever she planned on cooking for dinner and for breakfast the next day.

Her lunch was usually leftovers from dinner.

Unless Brundar came over, and then she had to stock up on more stuff.

Callie smiled. Feeding him was such a pleasure. The guy ate the way he made love, giving it his complete and undivided attention and savoring every little bite.

Absentmindedly, she rubbed a spot on her neck that held a ghost memory of a bite. She must've dreamt it because her neck was spotless. Brundar hadn't even left a hickey.

Probably a tiny bug bite she couldn't see or feel.

It had been two days since he'd made love to her. He'd said hi at the club, but that had been the extent of their interactions.

The logical part of her brain told her that he was busy. Guarding his cousin during the day and helping Franco run the club evenings and nights counted as two full-time jobs. It was a wonder Brundar had managed the little time he'd spent with her. In fact, he'd told her that he'd asked for a half a day off just so he could have an early dinner with her.

The other part of her brain, the one that was more emotional, felt neglected and unwanted.

He was avoiding her.

Today, Callie was once again eating dinner alone. It was no fun to cook for one, but she needed to eat, and there was no way she was going to stoop to sandwiches or frozen dinners. A simple dish of spaghetti with mushroom sauce that took about fifteen minutes to make was what she was planning for tonight. It was inexpensive, which was important since she was saving as much as she could to pay for school. Tomorrow, she'd eat the leftovers for lunch.

The only time Callie splurged on food was when cooking for Brundar.

Back at her building, she took the stairs up to her apartment. At her door, she put the grocery bag on the floor and shuffled through her purse looking for her keys.

The sound of the elevator doors opening had her turn around. Maybe it was her next door neighbor. The apartment adjacent to hers had been dark and quiet for the entire time Callie had lived there.

A woman was muscling a suitcase out of the elevator while pushing a carryon in front of her. Callie rushed over to hold the doors from closing on the suitcase.

"Thank you," the woman said, finally getting the heavy luggage past the metal sill. "I always over pack, forgetting I also need to schlep the thing around."

"Let me take this." Callie reached for the carryon.

"Thank you." The woman let go of the handle. "I'm right over here." She pointed at the door to the apartment next to Callie's.

"I thought no one lived there," Callie said as the woman pulled out her keys.

"I travel a lot." She offered her hand. "Hi, I'm Stacy."

Callie shook her hand. "I'm Callie."

Stacy opened her door. "Would you like to come in?"

Callie chuckled. "You just came back from what must've been a long trip. How about you come over to my place and eat dinner with me?"

Stacy looked tempted but shook her head. "Thank you. That's really nice of you, but I need to unpack, take a shower, etc."

It was quite obvious that the only reason Stacy had declined was that she was embarrassed about accepting a dinner invitation from a neighbor she'd just met.

"Come on. You can do it later. I hate eating alone. Besides, you probably have nothing edible in your fridge."

Stacy grimaced. "Don't remind me. I don't want to know what grew in there while I was gone."

"So, does it mean you're coming?"

"Yeah, you twisted my arm. Let me just push that monster inside."

Callie lent Stacy a hand. The suitcase had wheels, but it was so heavy they barely moved. "How much did you have to pay for excess weight?"

Stacy closed the door and followed Callie to her apartment. "The company I work for pays all of my travel expenses."

"Oh, yeah? What do you do, if you don't mind me asking?" Callie put the grocery bag on the counter and motioned for Stacy to take a seat.

"I'm a business consultant. I go in, talk to everyone, see what needs improvement, and sometimes even oversee the implementation."

Callie pulled out the box of spaghetti from the bag. "Sounds fascinating."

"It is."

"I'll brew us some coffee."

"Thank you. I need it."

Filling up a pot with water, Callie put it on the stove, then popped a pod into the machine. "I'm making spaghetti with mushroom sauce. I hope you're not allergic to mushrooms."

Stacy slapped a hand on her thigh. "Not counting the peculiar swelling of my hips, which is a reaction I get to any kind of food, I'm not allergic to anything."

Callie chuckled. "I have a similar allergy. Though in my case the swelling happens in my tummy."

Stacy cast her an incredulous glance. "What are you talking about, girl?"

"I'm a waitress. So I'm on my feet a lot. That's the only reason I don't gain weight."

Stacy frowned, making Callie uncomfortable. Was she one of those snobs who looked down at waiters and cashiers and the like?

"You must be getting excellent tips to afford this place."

Callie relaxed. The frown wasn't about what she'd thought. "I'm apartment sitting for the professor who lives here. He was kind enough not to charge me rent."

"Mike?"

She had no idea. "I guess so. The whole thing was brokered through a friend of his. I don't even know his name."

Stacy shook her head. "Mike moved out over a month ago. He got a job at Arizona State."

"I was under the impression that he was teaching a semester abroad."

"He did. Two years ago."

"Are you sure?"

"Positive."

What the hell?

What kind of a story had Brundar invented and why?

"Maybe we are not talking about the same person. Maybe another professor rented this apartment after Mike left and then got an offer to teach abroad."

Stacy crossed her legs. "I guess that's the only plausible explanation. After all, several professors live in this building because it's so close to USC. That's why the rent is so expensive."

Callie put on a smile. "Mystery solved. How do you like your coffee?" She changed the subject.

Frankly, she didn't believe for a moment the explanation she'd offered Stacy. Brundar had rented the apartment for her and concocted the story about the professor. The land-lady had probably told him about the previous tenant, and that was where he'd gotten the idea for his lie from.

The question was why?

And if he'd lied about that, what else had he lied about?

"Black, with stevia if you have it."

"Sorry. I only have regular sugar."

"Then one teaspoonful of sugar it is."

CHAPTER 20: BRUNDAR

*B*rundar had used his lunch hour to visit the document forger at his downtown studio. Francis's day job was artistic photography, and he was quite famous in the art community, but that didn't mean he was making money. For that he relied on his share in the clan profits, supplementing his income with superb forgeries.

"Did you get the name and social from the hacker? You're aware that I only make the documents, right?" Francis asked.

"I did."

Kian had another source for those. Though with Roni on board, Brundar didn't expect they would need that other hacker for much longer. Right now the kid was too busy with the assignment William had dropped on him, but once he was done with that, he'd be free for all the other things they needed a hacker for.

"I will have them ready for you tomorrow. Should I put it on Kian's tab, or are you paying for that yourself?"

"I'm paying."

"I'll give you the special clan discount. Seven hundred fifty instead of twelve hundred. Cash, of course."

"No problem."

Francis nodded, knowing not to offer a handshake.

Brundar glanced at his watch. He had less than twenty minutes to get back to the keep for Kian's emergency Guardian meeting, which meant he wouldn't have time to grab something to eat. Hopefully, Okidu would serve refreshments.

"Roni already has a wide area covered," Kian opened the meeting. "William's squad is going to monitor the feeds and alert the Guardian on duty if they see anything suspicious. I want you to start rotations. The murders have all happened after dark, so I'm not going to waste your time on that during the day. Onegus has prepared a schedule that requires each one of you to be on the alert five hours every other night."

Brundar groaned. Between his Guardian duty and managing the club, he was already stretched to capacity.

"Is there a problem, Brundar?" Kian asked.

"Could we suspend the self-defense classes until this is over?"

Kian nodded. "I don't like it, but I can't expect you guys to work sixteen hours a day."

Anandur snorted. "As if it ever stopped you before."

"In times of emergency, you bet your ass I expect you to give me everything you got. But this doesn't qualify as one."

Onegus tapped his pen on the conference table. "Should I inform all of our students that classes are suspended until further notice?"

"Carol and Kri can teach a few," Brundar offered.

Kri crossed her arms over her chest. "You guys are chauvinist pigs."

Kian glared at her. "As I said before, I'm not going to risk a female against a Doomer. These are all well trained immortal males."

"Yeah, yeah. The little lady will stay and teach the kids."

"You betcha. Onegus, talk with Carol and see what she can handle, then divide the classes between her and Kri."

Onegus nodded. "I'm going to email you the schedules with the area you should hang around. I also rented motorcycles for all of you so you can get to the scene of the crime faster. The helmets are also good to disguise your features."

Anandur rubbed his hands. "Which ones did you get?"

"BMWs."

"Sweet. Are they here already?"

"In the parking garage."

Anandur pushed his chair back. "Are we done? Can I go check out the new toys?"

"We are done." Kian rose to his feet. "I'll come with you. I need a crash course in riding one."

Anandur wrapped his arm around Kian's shoulder. "I'll teach you all you need to know."

Brundar parted ways with the gang at the elevators. The motorcycles would have to wait until after he'd had a couple of sandwiches from the vending machine in the lobby. At the rate his stomach was rumbling, even the powerful BMW engine wouldn't drown out the noise it was making.

At the café, he bought two readymade sandwiches and a muffin, then walked over to the counter.

"What can I get you, my absentee sensei?" Carol bowed her head in mock respect.

"Coffee. Large."

"Coming up, sir."

"Anandur was supposed to take over your training."

Carol shrugged. "He's busy too. Everyone is. We managed one session this week." She handed him a large paper cup.

"The Guardians are starting nightly rotations. You and Kri will have to take over the self-defense classes."

"Do I have to?" Carol grimaced. "We are seriously under-staffed in pretty much every department. I'm voting for employing humans. But of course, no one is asking for my vote."

"If you can figure out how to do it without revealing who we are, I'm sure Kian would love to hear it."

"Humans can run the café. We just need to be careful how we behave around them."

"That doesn't solve the shortage of Guardians problem."

She shook her head. "Kian needs to start using the reserves. Make it mandatory for all ex-Guardians to give one month a year. You know, like the National Guard. They are serving a few weeks every year, and if there is a war, they are called in to serve."

"I like your idea. "

Carol beamed. "Thank you. A compliment from you means a lot to me." She put a hand over her heart.

"But I think Kian had trouble convincing the retired Guardians to come in for training. Most are willing to come in case of emergency, but that's all."

Her face fell. "Oh."

Brundar allowed himself a small smile. "See you later, Carol. And don't give Anandur too hard of a time."

She saluted. "Do I ever?"

Not really. She was mouthy and didn't walk on eggshells around him like everyone else, but other than that Carol was a good person. Dedicated. Loyal.

Taking his coffee in one hand, Brundar tucked the two wrapped sandwiches under his other arm, grabbed the muffin, and turned to look for an empty table. There were a few, but on an impulse, he chose to join Robert at his.

"May I?"

Robert glanced at him over his newspaper, a surprised expression on his face. "Go ahead."

Brundar put down his lunch and pulled out a chair. "Any news on the murders?" he asked to start a conversation.

"Thank Mortdh, I mean the Fates, it was quiet for the past several days."

Brundar unwrapped his first sandwich. "We are starting nightly rotations."

"I overheard you talking with Carol. I'm glad. I hope you catch the bastard fast."

With a nod, Brundar bit into his sandwich and thought about what had motivated him to sit with the ex-Doomer.

The truth that he needed to talk to someone, and none of the males he worked with was a good candidate for a sounding board. Robert was still an outsider. Besides, the guy had an inventive mind. The ideas he'd come up with for the village were all excellent. Robert appeared to be a simple-minded fellow, but surprisingly he had the ability to think outside the box.

"Did you ever have a relationship with a human female?"

Robert frowned. "Aside from sex? No. Why do you ask?" He sounded offended.

Too late, Brundar realized his question might have implied suspicion on his part, somehow connecting Robert to the murders. Which prompted him to be more direct.

"I wondered how an immortal male who grew to care about a human female could end their relationship without hurting her feelings."

"Oh." Robert raked his fingers through his shortly cropped hair. "My only experience is with Carol." He leaned closer and lowered his voice. "Ending it wasn't my choice. Maybe you should ask her how to dump someone. Though I can't say my feelings weren't hurt."

Brave guy. Admitting to having been dumped took courage.

"I appreciate your honesty." Brundar unpacked his second sandwich.

"Sure." Robert smiled. "When Carol and I were in Vegas, I worked on a construction site with a crew of humans. They gave me good advice on how to pursue a woman, but not how to end things with one."

Brundar put the sandwich down on the wrapper. "Did it work? The advice?"

"Yeah, it did. But a man can only pretend for so long to be someone he is not. Carol wasn't interested in the real me."

CHAPTER 21: TESSA

*J*ackson eyed her. "You look different."

"How so?" Tessa patted her hair. Her hairdo hadn't changed since Eva had insisted on a total makeover. The color was still very blond, the cut very blunt, the length just a little longer.

"Your eyes sparkle. You seem upbeat, full of energy."

Her boyfriend, or should she start thinking of him as her fiancé? never missed anything.

"I kicked ass yesterday at Karen's class."

"Oh, yeah? Whose?"

"Karen brought two guys for us to practice on. They were both big, tough soldiers she'd trained herself."

Jackson frowned. "Did they frighten you?"

He knew men intimidated her, especially big ones. She shrugged. "At first, a little. But they were both so friendly. And flirty."

The creases between his brows deepened. "Who flirted with you?"

"His name was Gadi. But he was chill when I told him I'm engaged. He asked me to point out all the single ladies.

Sharon called dibs on the other one, Yoram." Tessa smirked. "I'm pretty sure she took him home with her."

Jackson was still glaring at her.

"Are you jealous, baby?"

"You're damn right, I'm jealous. I don't want any guys sniffing you up."

"Ugh, Jackson. That's gross. It sounds like you're talking about dogs."

"Men are dogs."

She lifted a brow. "Are you a dog?"

"Except for me. I'm a prince among men."

He was so cute. Tessa stretched up to her tiptoes and kissed his pouting lips. "Yes, you are."

That seemed to mollify him. But she felt like teasing him some more. "You keep saying that I'm hot. Do you expect no one to notice?"

For a moment, he seemed stumped, and she was ready to declare herself the winner of the teasing contest. But this was Jackson. He always had a comeback.

"Noticing you is a given, but not flirting. You don't go smiling at some guy who just had his hands all over you and expect him not to think of it as an invitation to flirt."

Tessa put her hands on her hips. "So what are you saying? That I can't even smile at anyone?"

"Not if they are male, between the age of seventeen to forty-five for humans, and no limit for immortals."

She lifted her chin. "I'm going to smile at whomever I want."

Jackson grinned wickedly as he dipped his head to look her straight in the eyes. "Is that so? What if I smile at whomever I want too?"

Crap. Jackson's smile could melt the panties off a librarian. Tessa didn't want him turning that charm on any woman, young or old.

She pointed a finger at him. "Don't you dare activate that pussy magnet of yours."

He almost choked on the snort that escaped his throat. "A pussy magnet? Where did that come from?"

She felt her cheeks get warm. Tessa made a point of never using language like that. "That's what Gordon calls you."

"I need to have a talk with Gordon about keeping his mouth clean around my fiancée."

Tessa slapped his bicep. "Oh, no you don't." Gordon and Vlad would never talk freely around her again. She liked that they treated her as one of the gang.

Jackson leaned in again, mirth dancing in his eyes. "Or what?"

Catching his chin between her thumb and forefinger, she mock glared back. "Or I'll kick your butt."

Instead of laughing or coming up with another teasing comeback, he got somber. "Yeah, you should. I should've thought of that sooner. You can practice on me." He patted his chest.

When she looked unsure, he flashed her his panty-melting smile. "Come on, kitten, show me your moves."

The effect of that smile combined with that seductive tone was that Tessa couldn't deny him anything. Besides, she was quite proud of herself and wanted to show off. The problem was that Jackson was way too strong and his reflexes were lightning fast. Her only chance was taking him by surprise.

"Okay. Let's clear some floor space." She lifted the folding tray they used as a coffee table.

Jackson took it out of her hands. "I'll clear the area, you bring the comforter from the couch and spread it on the floor."

She rolled her eyes. He was such a macho guy, never letting her lift anything.

Pushing the TV stand all the way under the window, Jackson cleared even more space.

Tessa took off her shoes and spread the comforter over the hardwood floor. "I'm going to stand here with my back to you as if I'm waiting for a bus. You sneak up behind me and grab me."

Jackson took off his sneakers and went to stand out in the hallway. "I'm very stealthy. Listen to the floor crack. That's how you'll know I'm coming at you."

"Thanks, Sherlock. I'm supposed to figure it out on my own."

"I don't make as much noise as a human because I pay attention to it. My hearing is much more acute."

"Okay." She turned her back to him, her whole body tensing in preparation for his attack. "I'm ready."

He was so fast, she felt the air move like a slight breeze a split second before his arms came around her.

Not giving him the opportunity to tighten them, Tessa twisted and dropped down, slipping through his loose grip. Bracing her crouching form with a hand on the floor, she turned her hips and delivered a roundhouse kick to his groin.

Jackson cupped his injured equipment and crumpled to the floor, his face twisted in pain.

"Oh, my God! I'm so sorry! I didn't think. Crap!" She kneeled next to him. "I should have told you to stuff a pillow in your pants."

It took him a moment until he was able to speak. "It's okay. You're amazing. I didn't expect you to get free, let alone kick me in the nuts."

Tessa winced. "Is there anything I can do?"

"Ice would help."

"Got it."

She rushed downstairs, filled a Ziploc bag with ice cubes, and rushed back, taking the stairs two at a time.

She handed him the ice bag.

"Thank you, baby." Jackson pushed his pants down and held the ice bag over his injured parts with only the thin fabric of his briefs as a barrier. After a few moments, his face relaxed.

"I'm so sorry." Tessa caressed his arm.

"Don't be. You can't harm me. Knowing you can kick ass for real is worth getting my equipment temporarily out of commission. I should come with you to your next class and thank Karen in person for teaching you to fight like that."

"I'm her best student." Tessa felt like she was allowed a little boasting. She was so damn proud of excelling at something she never believed she would.

"I bet you are. Just don't tell the guys that you've taken me down. Instead of a pussy magnet, I'll be called pussy whipped, or just a pussy." He groaned and kicked his pants all the way off. Lying down on the comforter, he lifted his knees so he could apply the ice pack to where he needed it most.

Ogling his powerful thighs and calves, Tessa felt like a lecher. He was in pain, because of what she'd done, and all she could think about was how sexy his body was. Then again, it wasn't her fault that Jackson was built like an Adonis. It was impossible not to ogle.

If she could only find an excuse for him to remove his T-shirt. And his briefs.

CHAPTER 22: JACKSON

*N*ursing his bruised kahunas, Jackson didn't immediately notice Tessa's expression turn from remorseful and concerned to horny and wistful. But luckily for him, he didn't have to rely solely on sight to figure out what his girl was in the mood for.

The faint aroma of her nascent arousal was affecting him even before he'd become aware of it. An immortal male couldn't ignore his female's arousal even if he wanted to. Especially while she was so close, kneeling next to him on the floor, so his nose was mere inches away from that intoxicating smell.

"How are you feeling?" Tessa asked, her voice turning husky. "Do you want me to kiss it all better?"

And just like that Jackson's shaft surged up, forgetting all about the pain and readying for action. "Do you think it would help?" he teased.

"I'm sure it would." Tessa licked her lips. "But for it to work, you need to take off all of your clothes."

He liked the game she was playing. "I heard that for the

healing to commence, both the healer and the injured need to get naked."

Tessa stifled a smile, going for a serious face. "Well, if it's in the name of healing, then all right. Should I help you with your briefs? It looks as if it would be difficult to get them past that impressive bulge."

"By all means." Tossing the Ziploc with the semi-melted ice cubes aside, Jackson lifted his torso off the floor, pulled his T-shirt over his head, then lay back down. "At your service, miss."

Tessa hooked her fingers in the elastic band of his boxer briefs and tugged down just a little, then reached inside and freed his aching cock before pulling them all the way down.

Staring, she licked her lips again. Could it be that she really enjoyed taking him in her mouth? He knew plenty of girls who did, but given Tessa's past, he would've never expected her to enjoy this. Especially when it was one-sided giving of pleasure.

"Nah-ah, kitten. You don't get to lick before you take your clothes off. A deal is a deal."

"True."

Jackson crossed his arms under his head, lifting it so he could watch Tessa strip for him.

Holding his eyes, she pulled her shirt over her head and tossed it on the couch, then unhooked her bra and aimed at the couch but missed. "Basketball is not in my future." She smiled sheepishly.

Jackson had a hard time focusing on anything other than her perky breasts. To keep from reaching for them, he laced the fingers behind his head and held on tight.

Her jeans and panties were next, tossed unceremoniously toward the couch, this time making the target.

"Score!" Tessa pumped her little fist in the air.

She was so fucking adorable, Jackson wanted to lick her

all over. Which he planned on doing very soon. There was no way he was allowing a repeat of what had happened last time. He would make sure this was as different from any oral she'd experienced in the past as it could get.

"Okay, Mr. Patient, may I proceed with my therapy now?"

"You may."

His cock sprang up, standing at full mast.

Kneeling by his side, Tessa inched closer. She smacked her lips as she wrapped her palm around the base, then lowered her head and flicked her tongue over the head. She looked up, smiled, and then did it again, circling all around in little teasing licks.

Already, this was nothing like the other time.

Yeah, Tessa was kneeling, but over him and not at his feet. This time, she was playful, enjoying tormenting him with little flicks of her wet tongue, and not trying to get him off. But even though she refrained from giving him the pleasure of taking him deep down her throat, Jackson preferred the teasing a hundred times over to that professional display of skill from before.

This was fun.

He was going to let her play for a little bit longer, then show her something new and exciting. "Are you having fun, kitten?"

"Mm-hmm." She took the head into her mouth.

"Then let me show you something that is even more fun." Reaching for her hips, he lifted her up and twisted her around to straddle his head.

She let his cock slide out of her mouth but kept her palm wrapped around the base as if afraid it would flop the moment she let go. Silly girl. His dick knew what was good for him. He wasn't going anywhere other than her hot, welcoming mouth.

Tessa looked at him over her shoulder. "What are you doing?"

In response, Jackson pulled her sweet bottom closer and licked her slit.

She moaned. "Oh. I like this."

He chuckled. "I thought you would. It's called sixty-nine."

She giggled, but her laughter died out when he flicked his tongue over her clit.

"Oh, oh, keep doing that."

Her head thrown back, rocking her sex against his tongue, Tessa was too absorbed in her own pleasure to remember that this was supposed to be simultaneous.

Not one to be petty about things like that, Jackson gave her a few moments of his undivided attention, both of them concentrating solely on her pleasure.

But he wasn't a saint.

With his heels digging into the comforter-covered floor, he thrust up, reminding Tessa that his dick was waiting for some tender, loving care.

She took him into her mouth again, just a small portion of his length, treating the rest of it to up and down pumping with her soft palm.

This was good, better than good. He loved driving her crazy with his mouth and his tongue and his fingers.

The girl who'd been so skittish at the beginning, the one whose expectations had been limited to being able to endure sex as opposed to truly enjoy it, had turned into a most wonderfully responsive woman who loved what he was doing to her and reached climax with ease.

He was lucky beyond belief.

Splaying his hands over her tight little ass, he gripped her and licked in bliss, making growling sounds while at it to let her know how much he loved eating her up.

The growling must've excited Tessa. She moaned around his shaft and took him deeper.

When he let go of one hip and pushed a finger inside her tight wetness, she groaned, the vibrations almost sending him over.

He wasn't going to last. But he'd be damned if he didn't bring her to the finish line first.

Withdrawing his finger, Jackson came back with two and flicked his tongue over her clit. Her juices running down his fingers and onto his chin, Tessa groaned again and took him all the way to the back of her throat.

This time he was all for it.

As he shouted his release and pushed deeper, her tight channel contracted around his fingers. Driven by instinct, Jackson moved his mouth to the side, flicked his tongue over a soft spot on her inner thigh, and bit down.

Tessa climaxed again.

When the fog lifted from his blood-deprived brain, Jackson felt her little tongue licking him clean. The venom wasn't affecting her as strongly as it had the first couple of times. He, on the other hand, was losing his fucking mind every time he bit her.

Damn it. He shouldn't have come inside her mouth.

Lifting her up by her hips, he turned her around and laid her over him like a blanket. Exhausted, she put her head on his chest and sighed.

He cupped her cheeks and lifted her head. "I'm sorry, kitten, can you forgive me?" He looked into her eyes.

A satisfied smile spread over her sweet face. "What am I supposed to forgive you for?"

"I didn't plan on coming in your mouth."

She braced her elbows on his chest and rested her chin in the cradle of her laced fingers. "I know you didn't plan to do it, but I'm glad you did."

From his experience, very few girls actually liked that part.

"Are you sure? Because I don't want you to do anything you don't enjoy. And I don't mean just the things you really hate, but also the stuff you think I like but you could do without. I want you to do only what brings you pleasure."

Tessa smiled and dipped her head to plant a soft kiss on his lips. "I did enjoy it because it was you. Giving you pleasure makes me feel wonderful. I'm sure you get it because I know you feel the same."

"I do."

She kissed him again. "You better marry me, Jackson, because I don't want to ever be with anyone else."

His arms came around her in what would have been a crushing hug if he hadn't reminded himself to be careful with her. "I'm yours, Tessa, forever. There will never be anyone else. For you or for me."

CHAPTER 23: CALLIE

"Goodnight, I'll see you tomorrow." Callie waved at Miri before ducking into the employee lounge—a small room with a row of lockers on one wall, hooks for hanging things on the other, and one wooden bench. Not as nice as the one at Aussie's, but then no one ever hung out in there. It was a place to store personal stuff and not much more. Franco couldn't afford a lavish lounge for his employees. Not yet. Maybe once Brundar helped him make the place more profitable he would.

Opening her locker, Callie collected her purse and her light jacket. The club was always warm, but it was getting cold outside at night. Unable to help herself, she pulled her phone out, hoping like an idiot to see a message from Brundar, or maybe even a missed call, but of course there was nothing.

Third day in a row and no Brundar. Not in person or any other way.

After the talk she'd had with her neighbor, Callie itched to confront Brundar about his deception. But after having a full day to cool off, she'd decided to wait and see if he'd confess. Maybe she would drop hints, leading him to talk about it.

The problem was that he was avoiding her again. Just when she'd thought they were making progress, he'd retreated into his shell, and was hiding from her like a coward.

That evening, he hadn't even shown up at the club.

Callie had been waiting to catch Franco and ask him if Brundar had called him. Maybe he was sick and couldn't come in, or something had happened to him...

Crap. She shouldn't give a damn, but she was worried about the jerk.

Except, Franco had been busy in the basement and hadn't surfaced at the nightclub throughout her shift. Unless he had, and she'd missed him because she'd been taking orders or delivering drinks.

Should she text Brundar?

Ask him if he was okay? A bodyguard's job was inherently dangerous.

Now that her thoughts had wandered in that direction, her worry kicked into overdrive. She had to text him. Otherwise she wouldn't be able to sleep.

Hi, just checking if you're alive. With her finger hovering over the send button, she decided to add *I'm worried.* Just in case he got mad at her for texting him.

A couple of minutes later he answered, and the tightness in her chest eased.

Working.

At least he was alive. But would it have killed him to ask if she was doing okay? Show that he cared even a little?

He was such an infuriating man. When he was near her, she felt that he cared, that he liked her as a person, and that he liked spending time with her. But when he was away, Brundar behaved like she didn't exist, like nothing had happened between them, and like he didn't give a damn about her.

How did the saying go? Absence makes the heart grow fonder? In Brundar's case, it was more like out of sight, out of mind.

She put the phone back in her purse and headed outside.

"Hi, Donnie. Ready to call it a night?"

"I was waiting for you, girl."

"Thanks. Brad was a no-show, and Franco spent the entire night in the basement. So I guess you're stuck with me."

Donnie wrapped his thick arm around her shoulders. "I love walking you home."

The truth was that he never complained and was always upbeat during their walks. He was such a nice guy. Why the hell did she have to go for the complicated and the troubled?

If Donnie were her boyfriend, he would probably call her and text her throughout the day and be happy if she called and texted back. That was what normal couples did. Wasn't it?

But Donnie had his eye on someone else. Besides, as hunky as he was, she wasn't attracted to him.

"Are you going to give Fran your comic this weekend?"

Donnie shook his head. "I'm too big of a chicken."

Callie chuckled. "An enormous chicken. The size of a bull. But seriously, why not?"

"What if she thinks it's stupid?"

Callie patted his bicep. "Then she is not worthy of you, and you should set your sights on someone who thinks your comics are fabulous."

"Would you mind taking a look at it?"

She stopped and put her hands on her hips. "Mind? I've been asking you to show me your work since the night you told me about it. I'm dying to see it."

Donnie patted his jacket. "I have one in here."

"Then you must come up and show me."

He looked unsure. "I don't know about that. Do you think Brad is going to be okay with that?"

Callie pulled out the key to the building's front door and unlocked it. "Brad has no say in who I invite to my apartment."

She held the door open, but Donnie didn't come in. "It's the middle of the night."

She reached for his jacket, grabbing it to pull him in. Not that she was under any illusions that she could've moved that mountain of muscle if he hadn't let her, but it seemed Donnie needed the pretense of being coerced. "Come on. I'll make us coffee, and you'll show me your work."

"Fine. But if Brad rearranges my face, it's on you."

"Donnie, what are you worried about? You don't even need to fight him, you can sit on him. You outweigh him by about a hundred pounds." Callie kept walking, Donnie's sneakers making squeaking sounds behind her.

"I don't know about that. He is freakishly strong."

"How so?" Callie opened the door to the staircase and waited for Donnie to catch up.

"Once, when I was sitting in my car in the club's parking lot, I saw him pick up a Suburban with one hand. He must've dropped something, and it rolled under the car. He just held the thing up and reached with his other hand for whatever was under it, then lowered the Suburban back down as if it was a cardboard box filled with toilet paper."

"Impressive. But I think you could've done it too."

"I could. With two hands and a grunt."

"Nevertheless, as I told you before, Brad has no say in whom I invite over. I can entertain whomever I want, when-ever I want."

Subconsciously, Callie suspected Brundar hadn't told her

the truth about where he was and what he was doing. Now that Donnie was going on and on about not wanting to anger her so-called boyfriend by coming up to her apartment, her own anger was pushing the subconscious suspicion to the surface.

She could accept that on occasion Brundar's cousin would need his bodyguards in the evenings, or even on an out of town trip. But while in town, this time of night the big shot was most likely asleep in his bed.

For as long as she'd known Brundar, which admittedly wasn't all that long, he worked for the cousin during the day and at Franco's during the evenings and nights, which meant that the cousin didn't need his services while at home.

Only two scenarios could support Brundar's claim of working that late at night. One was that the cousin was making a transaction at night, which implied some illegal activity she knew Brundar wouldn't have taken part in, and the other was that he was partying somewhere and needed his bodyguards with him. Which again, didn't follow the normal pattern of Brundar's employment.

Something smelled fishy.

Callie opened the door to her apartment and flicked the lights on.

Donnie took a look around. "Nice place."

"Thanks." She dropped her purse on the kitchen counter and grabbed the carafe. "Make yourself comfortable while I make coffee."

Donnie sat on the couch, opened his jacket, and pulled a rolled up comic out of an inside pocket that must've been really deep.

Watching him flip through the pages while she loaded the coffeemaker, Callie observed that his sitting pose was nowhere near relaxed. The poor guy was anxious to see her response to his work.

He shouldn't be. She was going to gush all over it even if it wasn't great. Friends didn't put friends down. Not unless she thought it was a complete disaster and he shouldn't waste his time on it. But even then she would only suggest that he take a course to improve his skills.

When the coffee was ready, she loaded a tray with two cups, some sugar cubes, creamer, and a few store-bought cookies. As talented as she was with cooking, Callie sucked at baking.

"Okay. I'm ready for the grand reveal." She lowered the tray to the coffee table.

Donnie handed her the comic, then got busy with the coffee, dropping in several sugar cubes and following with creamer.

As soon as Callie opened the comic, she had to slap her hand over her mouth to stifle a laugh. Not only because it depicted Brundar with uncanny accuracy, but also because she was relieved that Donnie was really good and she wouldn't have to pretend to be impressed.

"That's Brad." She pointed to the comic's hero. Donnie hadn't changed anything. The same long pale hair, the same austere expression, just the clothes were different. The comic hero was wearing leather pants and a muscle shirt.

Donnie nodded. "He is so perfect for the role, I couldn't change a single thing about him."

"And that's Miri." Callie pointed to the hero's sidekick. "But you said she didn't fit as his sidekick, and that you needed someone less colorful."

"I decided she does. What do you think?"

"I think you're amazing. This is so well done. But I have second thoughts about you showing this to Fran. She might tell Brad. Or Miri."

Donnie pretended to shiver. "Right. I don't know who's scarier."

"I have an idea."

He lifted a brow.

"Make a comic strip starring Fran. Nothing elaborate, just a page or two. There is no way she wouldn't go out with you after seeing how much effort you've gone to and how talented you are. Make sure she looks amazing in it. It's a rare woman who is immune to flattery. I'm sure Fran isn't."

Donnie clapped her on the back. "Callie, you're a genius."

CHAPTER 24: BRUNDAR

*B*rundar's rotation had ended when the sun came up at five in the morning. There had been one false alarm, a drunk couple necking in a parking lot, but thankfully no murders.

If he didn't have a full workday ahead of him, Brundar would've gone straight to Calypso. That one text had shattered his resolve to try and stay away from her as much as he possibly could.

She'd been worried about him.

Or perhaps he was just looking for an excuse. Blaming Calypso for his weakness was much easier than admitting he had no willpower where she was concerned.

He was so screwed.

At this stage, no matter what he did, they were both going to get hurt.

There was no elegant solution.

After a quick shower, he lay down in bed, trying to catch a couple of hours of shuteye before having to report to Onegus for his daily duties. But sleep eluded him. All he could think of was Calypso; her sexy smile, her bright green eyes, her laughter.

She'd been through so much, and yet she seemed happy. He would've expected her to be reserved, subdued, maybe even a little sad. But she'd proved to be more resilient than he'd given her credit for. Or maybe it was in her character to be upbeat and positive, and external forces had little to do with how she felt.

Did it mean that he was naturally unhappy and cold? And that what had happened to him hadn't really shaped who he was?

Those were questions better addressed to a professional, and Brundar wasn't planning on visiting Vanessa anytime soon. Or ever. Maybe he could buy a book on the subject. Get some information without visiting a bloody shrink.

Later, while waiting for Kian to be done with his lunch meeting, Brundar was bored enough to actually search the Internet for such a book, but he didn't find anything he was interested in reading. It could have had something to do with Anandur peeking over his shoulder and asking him what he was looking for. The truth was that he wasn't much of a reader. Whatever little free time he had was usually spent training, and lately with Calypso.

Damnation. He couldn't wait for his tasks for the day to be done so he could go to her. So much for willpower.

At four o'clock, after completing a short investigative assignment Onegus had sent him on, Brundar informed the chief Guardian that he was leaving early.

"Go get some sleep. You look like hell." Onegus allowed him to cut one hour off his schedule. After spending most of the night on rotation, he shouldn't even have to ask.

Nevertheless, sleeping was not what Brundar had in mind.

Fighting against Calypso's pull was like resisting an

elastic tether, but one that was made of carbon fibers. At first, there had been some give, the pull bearable, but with each passing hour the pull became stronger, and digging his heels in the ground wasn't helping.

Brundar parked his car in front of her building and pulled out the keys to its front door from the glove compartment, but then reconsidered and put them back. After neglecting her for so long, it would be inappropriate for him to come unannounced.

He walked up to the door and punched the buzzer.

A moment later, he heard the door lock release, but not a word from Calypso. She was allowing him in but refusing to acknowledge him. Obviously, she was mad. He couldn't blame her.

Taking the stairs two at a time, he was at her door a couple of moments later. It was ajar, and he pushed it in.

Sitting on the couch, Calypso was watching a show on the tube, ignoring him. Perhaps she hadn't heard him?

Brundar cleared his throat. "May I come in?"

"You're already in."

Yep, she was mad. But that wasn't the only thing that made him tense.

There were two new scents in the apartment. An old one, female, and a recent one, male.

He crossed the distance to the couch and stood in front of Calypso, blocking her view of the television. "Who was here?"

"None of your business."

Damn it. He couldn't tell her that he could smell people's residual scents long after they had left. But then she hadn't denied having someone over.

"I asked you to text me if you invite anyone in here."

"I was in no danger from either."

He crouched, forcing Calypso to look at his face and not his belt buckle. "Are you angry?"

She rolled her eyes. "Duh."

He tilted his head. "About what?"

"Don't play dumb, Brundar. You know exactly why."

"Because I didn't come over for a few days?"

If looks could kill he would've been dead already. Calypso's green eyes were shooting daggers at him. "Because you didn't call. Because you didn't text to let me know you're alive, and because your answer to my text was super jerky." She crossed her arms over her heaving chest.

Scratching his head, he tried to remember what his answer had been. "I said I was working."

"Yeah, you did. And that was it. You didn't ask how I was, or if everything was okay. Nothing. You made me feel like the clingy clueless girlfriend who should've gotten it through her head that you're not interested but didn't." She looked away. "Well, you succeeded."

"Succeeded in doing what?"

"Ugh, you're infuriating. I get it that you're not interested. You can go home." She pointed at the door.

"I don't want to go home. I came because I wanted to be with you."

Calypso shook her head. "Well, I don't want to be with you. I don't want to be with anybody. Men are all jerks and are good only for one thing that I can do without. I'm taking a vow of celibacy."

What happened next was totally unexpected.

Brundar felt laughter bubble up from deep in his belly, and, once he let it out, it just kept coming in wave after wave until there were tears in his eyes and a stitch in his side.

If Calypso had been pissed at him before, now she looked ready to do him harm. Shoving on his chest, she sent him toppling down on his ass. "It's not funny!"

Brundar laughed even harder.

The idea of Calypso taking a vow of celibacy was just ludicrous. She wouldn't last more than a week.

"I'm sorry—" he croaked between peals of laughter, "—it has been so long since I laughed, I forgot how it felt—" He tried to breathe in to stop. "It's bad... It hurts..." He pressed a hand to his middle.

Calypso's lips quivered with an effort to stifle her own laughter. "Good. I want you to suffer."

It took a few forceful inhales and exhales before Brundar regained his composure. "Please forgive me. I meant no disrespect." He pushed up and sat on the couch next to Calypso. "When I got your text, I was in the middle of a situation. But that's not an excuse. I could've texted you later that night or this morning. I'm not adept at social interactions."

Calypso's rigid posture relaxed a fraction. "This is not about social etiquette. I'm allowing for your no-nonsense military style. This is about caring and showing it. But I guess you don't. Not enough, anyway."

Damnation.

Brundar cared a lot. More than he should. Except, telling her that might appease her in the short term, but later, when he would be forced to sever the inexplicable bond between them, it would cause her more grief.

"I'm not adept at interpersonal relationships either. Whatever expectations you may have, forget them and save yourself a shitload of disappointment." He had done his best to avoid saying anything that would've sounded as rejection, going for self-deprecating and noncommittal. The less she thought of him, the better.

Calypso sighed, her shoulders slumping. "You're right. You are who you are, and I can either take it or leave it. I told myself a long time ago that I shouldn't try changing anyone because it's a waste of time and energy. The only one I can change is me."

"Smart." Especially for a woman so young. She was a quick learner.

She shrugged. "If I were smart, I would've stayed away from the complicated and the brooding and gone after the simple and upbeat. A nice guy who would treat me right and call me ten times a day to tell me he loves me."

Her words cut deep. Brundar wished he could be that guy she'd described, but even if she were an immortal female, and he loved her dearly, he would've never called her ten times a day to tell her that. Or even once. That just wasn't who he was.

With a frown, Brundar tried to imagine the guy she'd described. Was it anyone he knew? Was it the same man who had visited her last night?

Had she had sex with him?

Anger and jealousy washing over him like a tsunami, Brundar took a deep sniff. If she had, he would smell it.

Thank the merciful Fates, there was no lingering scent of sex. Not even his and Calypso's from several nights ago. Still, he had to know who it was. "Who did you invite over here?"

"I already told you. It's none of your business. Don't play the part of a possessive boyfriend when you keep telling me you're not mine." She waved a hand in the air. "You spend your nights in that dungeon, doing God knows what with God knows who, and I can't even invite anyone for coffee?" She huffed. "Please. Give me a break."

"I haven't been with anyone but you since I helped you leave your husband."

She pinned him with a hard stare. "And I'm supposed to believe that? You are the co-owner of a kink club. It's your job to play." She waved her hand again.

Brundar didn't take offense easily, but being accused of

providing sexual services was too much. "I'm not whoring myself out, Calypso. That is not part of my job."

"So what do you do down there all night?"

He itched to repay her in kind and tell her it was none of her business, but that was before he'd scented her distress. Calypso was putting on a brave face, masking her hurt with anger, but her eyes were shining with unshed tears.

"I instruct, I demonstrate, and I monitor. I don't participate in sexual acts unless I want to. And ever since I brought you here, I haven't wanted to play with anyone else."

"Really?"

At first, her doubting his veracity angered him, but on second thought he realized Calypso needed reassurance.

"I can't promise you much, but I can promise you exclusivity as long as we are together, and I demand the same from you. No more inviting men to your apartment without letting me know who and why."

Calypso nodded. "I can live with that." She smirked. "It was Donnie. He walked me home, and I invited him for a cup of coffee."

As if that was supposed to ease his mind. Donnie was a good looking human, with exactly the kind of mellow personality she'd described as desirable in a male.

"Why did you invite him up?"

"What do you mean, why?" Calypso lifted her hands in exasperation. "That's part of the social interactions you don't get. He was kind enough to walk me home, and the least I could do was to offer him a cup of coffee. Besides, you have nothing to get jealous about. Donnie is not interested in me. He has his eyes on Fran. All we talked about was him mustering the nerve to approach her."

That was good. Donnie's face was no longer in danger of getting beaten into a pulp. Except, Calypso hadn't clarified about her interest, or lack thereof, in the bouncer.

But inept as Brundar was at interacting with people, especially women, he knew it would be a mistake to ask her directly. Instead, he could keep her talking about the guy and sniff for arousal. Her body couldn't lie.

"Donnie is handsome. Why would he fear approaching Fran?"

Calypso shrugged. "She is a little snooty to him, barely acknowledging he exists. Donnie believes Fran thinks of him as all brawn and no brain. A dumb muscleman."

No arousal.

Brundar allowed himself to relax. "I can ask her for him."

Calypso shook her head. "Don't. He needs to do it himself."

"What if she says no?"

"So it's a no, and he can move on. Dealing with rejection is part of life. Getting turned down is not as bad as never trying."

"Come here." Brundar leaned and scooped Calypso into his arms, positioning her in his lap. "The lady is both smart and beautiful. A killer combination."

CHAPTER 25: CALLIE

*H*ot and cold. Cold and hot. Brundar was a man of extremes.

It was so satisfying to have seen him getting jealous over Donnie.

As much as he pretended that their relationship was nothing more than a string of exclusive hookups, Brundar wasn't fooling Callie.

He had feelings for her. The problem was his attitude toward those feelings. He regarded them as a curse or a disease and not something wonderful between two people that was rare and special and should have been cherished.

Callie couldn't change him or who he was, but she could change his mind about that—give it her best and hope it would be enough.

She wanted to touch his face, caress his clean-shaven cheeks, run her fingers through his hair. But, of course, she did none of that, keeping her hands tucked between her thighs as a reminder. "This was our second fight. I would say it's an achievement."

Brundar's left brow arched. "You consider an argument a good thing?"

"Sure, I do. Getting a rise from someone as stoic as you means that you care."

Brundar kissed the top of her head. "I think you have things turned around. Both times you got mad at me."

"True. But you took the effort to engage with me. I guess you don't do that with others. You walk away."

"That is correct." Brundar seemed to ponder her observation. "I wonder why that is?"

The guy didn't understand the most basic elements of human interaction.

"Because you don't care what others think or feel toward you. Well, maybe other than respect. I think that is important to you. But with me, you want more than my respect."

"You bet, I do. I want your moans, and your whimpers, and your screams." His thumb brushed over her puckered nipple, stoking the simmer of desire his words had started.

"So what are you saying? That I make a lot of noise?" Callie teased.

"Music to my ears." He brushed his knuckles over her other nipple.

He was teasing her back, not with his words but with his hands. To touch her over her shirt and bra instead of her naked skin was like letting her smell something delicious but not allowing her to taste it. This was so like him, expressing himself through touch and not speech, probably because he was so good with the first and so inadequate with the latter.

Days without him had created so much pent-up need that Callie felt like crawling out of her skin. Touching herself, which was the only relief she'd gotten for the past few days, had been pleasant at best, but she needed Brundar to take her higher. To make her wild and wanton the way he'd done before.

Sex with him was so intense that everything else seemed devoid of color and flavor in comparison.

It scared her.

What were the chances of her ever finding another man who could so perfectly satisfy her? Who could bring her to such heights of ecstasy?

As inexperienced as she was, Callie figured out that a precise match like theirs was rare. Given the huge spectrum of shades and variations, a perfect alignment was nearly impossible. She was just a slightly darker shade of vanilla, while Brundar was on the lighter shade of kink, and they were both flexible enough to stretch a little and meet where they were both comfortable.

Unless she was reading him wrong and he was holding back to accommodate her.

"Am I enough, Brundar? Tell me the truth. Are you holding back on what you want, what you need?"

He shook his head. "Not in the way you think."

"Please explain, because I'm having an insecure moment here."

Dipping his head, he kissed her forehead. "I told you what I need, and I didn't omit anything. You agreed to it. Why would you think I would want more?"

That was true. The only thing Brundar listed as an absolute must was bondage. The blindfold was probably part of that. But he admitted that something was lacking.

"What are you holding back?"

He chuckled. "I have incredible stamina. If I had my way, you would need a transfusion by the time I was done with you."

"Is that a challenge?"

"No, sweetling. I know when you have had enough."

"But what about you? I hate thinking that you're left unsatisfied."

"Who said anything about not being satisfied? The fact that I can go on doesn't mean I'm unsatisfied."

Callie tilted her head back to have a better look at Brundar's face, wondering how was it possible to want more but at the same time feel satisfied.

Was it like eating chocolate?

She was an unrepentant chocoholic. One or two squares were never enough, and she would keep coming back for more until there was nothing left. But there was a price to pay for the overindulgence, and not only in extra pounds. The nausea and upset stomach were an unpleasant reminder that she should've stopped at no more than one-third of a pack. Except, she usually smartened up only after the fact, not while obsessively devouring one piece after another.

Maybe for Brundar sex was the same. The fact that he could go on didn't mean he should.

"Okay."

"Okay what?"

"Okay, sir?"

Brundar chuckled. "And you were accusing me of unclear communication. Okay as in, I understand? Or okay as in, take me to bed right now?"

"Both. I accept your explanation, and I want you to take me to bed."

"I will. But first, there is the small matter of your punishment."

Callie felt herself melt into a puddle. Except, she needed a cause to make the game fun to play. "Punishment for what?"

"Let me see." Brundar looked up as if he was concentrating on recounting her misdeeds. "First, you didn't believe me when I told you that I haven't been with anyone but you since we got together. Just for that, you deserve a thorough spanking. Then you suggested I was whoring myself out to club members. That's a strapping offense, but you're too green for that."

Callie shivered, and not in a pleasant way. "You mean like with a belt?"

"Yes."

"I will never be ready for that." What could be sexy about that much pain? Not that she would know. No one had ever done that to her, and Callie was adamant about keeping it that way.

"Never say never."

She smiled, thinking he was teasing, but Brundar seemed serious. Her smile turned into a frown. She would've dismissed his remark as nonsense, but the thing was, he seldom made claims about things he wasn't an expert on.

"Why would you say that?"

"I've seen it before. Some start easy and never venture into darker places, while others get the taste and want to experience more. I always try to guess which camp a new member will end up belonging to, but I miss more often than I get it right. Each person is different."

"Which camp do you think I belong to?"

"The second one. But as I said, I'm often wrong."

Callie looked away, embarrassed even though she was sure he was mistaken. Pain wasn't her thing. She liked the feeling she got from submitting, and a little spanking was the perfect catalyst to help her get there; bondage was too, but that was as far as she was willing to go. "I'm curious to hear what makes you think that."

"Mostly because you're gutsy. You don't back away from trying new things even when you're scared."

True, but she was also a reasonable woman. Callie's willingness to stretch her comfort zone in the name of experimentation didn't mean she would abandon it for just any thrill.

If Brundar stayed around for long enough, they might find out who was right. It saddened her to think that he might not.

Callie's arousal dissipated along with her good mood.

"What's going on in your head?"

As usual, Brundar didn't miss the slightest change in her. Which was weird given how obtuse he was about almost everything else.

"I just thought that you need to stick around for a while to find out if you're right about me."

CHAPTER 26: BRUNDAR

*B*rundar felt trapped.

What could he say to her?

Even though he wanted it more than anything, he knew he wasn't going to stick around. And he wasn't about to lie to Calypso either.

Which left him with only one choice. Change the subject and make it about the present, not the future.

"Enough stalling, sweetling. Right now we have some business to attend to." Hands on her waist, he flipped her around, so she was sprawled over his lap, bottom up. He grabbed one of the decorative pillows and put it under her cheek. "Comfortable?"

"I am, but not for long." She wiggled her cute little ass.

Reaching under her, he popped her jeans button, then pulled her pants and panties down to her mid thighs.

Calypso's arousal, which had taken a nosedive during their talk, was back and climbing with each passing moment.

"Do you want to hold my hands?" she asked.

"I'm not going to restrain you. Not unless you want me

146

to. But I want you to close your eyes and not open them under any circumstances. Can you do that for me?"

"Yes, sir." She sounded so happy that he was making a concession and trusting her to follow his rules without enforcing them by tying her up and putting a blindfold over her eyes.

Brundar was well aware that he was taking a risk.

His fangs had already elongated just in response to Calypso's scent of excitement and the sight of her perfect globes. In a few moments, they would reach full length, and his eyes would start glowing. If she disobeyed him and opened her eyes, he would have no choice but to thrall her, and that would end their playtime.

He never engaged with a woman who was drunk or high, and a thrall reduced mental capacity just as much if not more. He wanted Calypso to participate while fully cognizant.

His palm resting on her beautiful ass, he reiterated, "I'm trusting you to follow the rules. If you break them, this play-time will end immediately. Do you understand?"

"I do. I promise not to look and to keep my hands right here." She tucked them under the pillow.

"Good girl." He caressed her butt cheeks. They were so small that he covered both with one hand.

His first smack was more of a love tap. Calypso felt so good draped over his knees, her trust in him tasting so sweet, that he wanted this to last. Getting into an easy rhythm, Brundar tapped her butt cheeks, caressing and kneading after every two or three taps.

It wasn't what she'd expected, but she wasn't complaining. He was stoking the embers of her desire slowly, enjoying the closeness. She seemed to be enjoying it too.

To mix things up a little, he surprised her by delving his finger between her moist folds. Unprepared for the new sensation, she sucked in a breath and arched up, seeking more. He reached with his other hand and pressed the heel against her sensitive nub, then pushed inside her, first with one finger, then with two.

Undulating her hips, Calypso rubbed against his palm, pleasuring herself on it while he slowly pumped his fingers in and out of her.

This wasn't enough to bring her to a climax, but then he was in no hurry.

For a few minutes, Calypso played along, but he knew it wouldn't last. His girl was patient in many ways, but not in this.

"Please, Brundar, I need more."

With a swift tug, he got rid of her pants; her T-shirt and bra were gone next. When she was gloriously nude, he lifted her hips and slid from under her.

"Stay here and don't move. And no peeking either. I want to see your face buried in that pillow when I come back," he commanded, laying her legs back on the couch.

"Where are you going?"

"To the bedroom, to get a condom."

"Okay."

He was back before she'd finished sighing contentedly.

"You're fast," she commented.

You have no idea.

With her face firmly pressed into the pillow, he allowed himself to move at his natural speed, shedding his clothes and sheathing himself in the hateful rubber in seconds. This was something he needed to address, the sooner the better. Bridget could produce a clean bill of health for him, and Calypso could get on the pill.

Keeping up the charade was taking pleasure away from both of them.

"Lift." He tapped her bottom while grabbing another

pillow, then tucked it under her pelvis. "You're so beautiful. I could just stand here and look at you."

She giggled, the sound muffled by the pillow. "I hope not for long."

"Impudent girl." He smacked her bottom, harder than before.

She moaned.

Fates, that throaty sound went straight to his cock.

Getting into position behind her, he covered her body with his like a blanket, enjoying a moment of skin to skin and prolonging their anticipation. His cock nestled in the crease between her butt cheeks, and he wanted to grab her chin and turn her head around so he could take her mouth before surging inside her, but he didn't dare.

As it was, he was already playing with fire. He couldn't risk her opening her eyes and seeing him in his full alien mode.

That was the disadvantage of not using a blindfold and leaving Calypso unrestrained. He didn't feel as free to do as he pleased, and the underlying stress wasn't conducive to a good experience.

Next time he would go back to business as usual.

Both of them would enjoy it more.

CHAPTER 27: RONI

"Wat's the verdict, doctor?" Roni looked hopefully at Bridget.

"The verdict is that you don't need to stay here. You're still sick, but your symptoms are milder. If Ingrid can find you an apartment, you can move to a more comfortable setting. No exercise and no other strenuous activity for at least two weeks."

Bridget glanced at the contraption William's students had built for him. She'd pushed it aside to conduct her examination, and it was now blocking the entrance to the room. "Take this thing with you. I know you'll not listen to me and rest, so the next best thing is working from bed the same as you did here."

"Thanks. What if Ingrid, whoever she is, can't find me an apartment? Can I stay here?" He'd kind of gotten used to the hospital bed, which he could adjust for maximum comfort with the remote, programming into its memory his two favorite positions, one for working and the other one for resting.

A regular one was never going to be as comfortable. One could only do so much with pillows.

Fuck, would there be pillows? And blankets? And the other things he'd always taken for granted?

And who was going to feed him?

Andrew's wife had been kind enough to send down meals, and the nurses pampered him with sandwiches and other things from nearby restaurants. He had no money, and if he did, he was pretty sure he couldn't leave the building to go shopping. Sylvia would have to buy him groceries until he figured shit out. The problem was that he'd never cooked anything in his life, and as far as he knew neither had Sylvia.

"Don't worry. She'll find you a place."

Yeah, don't worry, right. He was on the verge of panicking.

"Will the apartment come with pillows and blankets and towels and all of that shit? Because I don't have money and I don't know where and how to get things. I've never been on my own."

Bridget patted his shoulder. "Everything you need will be there, and if anything is missing, you can call Ingrid, and she will get it delivered."

Roni exhaled a relieved breath. "That's one less thing to worry about. What about the transition, though? When should I attempt it again?" Not anytime soon, that was for sure. He was so weak that a walk to the bathroom was a strain. Getting on the mat with an immortal was a no-go if he couldn't even stay upright without aid.

"You need to wait at least a month, maybe longer, and not before I give my okay. If you want it to work, you need to let your body get back into peak condition first. You might have been carrying this virus with no symptoms for weeks, and that could be the reason you didn't transition."

Having a plausible explanation for not transitioning was

comforting and made his outlook way more optimistic. But waiting so long to try again was going to be a bitch.

"I hate waiting."

"Patience, Roni." Bridget patted his arm again. "I'm going to call Ingrid."

"Thanks."

"You're welcome."

Now that he was about to get discharged, Roni needed to figure out some basic logistics before he could leave. First of all, he needed clothes. With the state he'd been in when snatched from the human hospital, Roni hadn't noticed if anyone had bothered to collect the clothes he'd arrived in. Or if Jerome or Kevin had had the presence of mind to bring his wallet to the hospital.

Fuck. He could probably say goodbye to all the money he had saved up in his bank account. He of all people should know he could never touch it again without giving the feds a way to find him. Money left a trail no matter how carefully it was hidden.

Andrew might have an idea of what was going on, but he was still avoiding contact with Roni. He wouldn't come without a hazmat suit, and Roni doubted the clan kept those on hand.

Or they could talk on the phone.

Reaching for the one next to his bed, Roni pressed zero for the operator. Bridget had told him the line went straight to the keep's security office and nowhere else, but they could connect him with Andrew.

"What can I do for you, Roni?" an unfamiliar male voice answered.

"Do I know you?"

The guy chuckled. "No. But your name is programmed as the occupant of the room you're calling from."

"Obviously." The fever must've destroyed a good number

of his brain cells for him to ask a dumb question like that. "Can you connect me to Andrew Spivak?"

"Sure. Let me check if he is home. I'm going to put you on hold."

"No problem."

A few moments later Andrew picked up. "What's up, kid? How are you feeling?"

"Better. Bridget is letting me out of here."

"Good. I'm glad to hear that."

"Yeah. How are things at work? Anyone talking about my disappearance?"

Andrew chuckled. "It is assumed that you hacked your way out of the hospital."

Sylvia had been questioned by Barty the day after Roni's escape, even though Yamanu made sure the staff remembered her leaving shortly after the agent and his wife. According to her, she'd been very convincing, crying about what a jerk Roni was for leaving her without a word.

"Did any of you get my clothes? Or my wallet?"

"Sylvia has them. But what do you need your wallet for?"

"I have a few bucks in there. The money saved up in my bank account is probably gone. I don't want to hack into it because I know they booby-trapped it to hell and back. If they release it to my parents, and providing the bastards will cooperate and not snitch on me, I can then hack into their accounts and take it out."

"How much do you have in there?"

"Close to a hundred thousand. I spent almost none of my pay."

Andrew whistled. "Yeah, that sucks. But I wouldn't touch it anytime soon even if they transferred it to your parents. They will be watching for that. Besides, you can probably make it back in no time."

"If I were free, I could. But I'm not."

"I'm sure some kind of an arrangement could be made."

"I want to talk to the head honcho, Kian. Can you arrange a meeting? I hate not knowing what to expect. And by the way, Dr. Bridget says I need to wait at least a month until I attempt transition again. She says I might have been carrying the virus for weeks without showing symptoms and that's why it didn't work."

"That would explain it. You're the best candidate for transition the clan ever had. Better than I was, that's for sure. I was racking my brain trying to figure a plausible explanation for your grandmother's picture on those driver's licenses other than her being an immortal. But I couldn't find one."

"Yeah, same here. So are you going to talk to the boss for me?"

"Not yet. I think you need to get settled first. If I were you, I would want to be healthy enough not to look like the living dead when I meet him. Well-dressed too. You want to leave a good first impression."

"Yeah, you're right. It's like a job interview."

"The most important one you'll ever have."

"Right."

CHAPTER 28: CAROL

"*H*ere you go." Carol handed Anandur the plate with the sandwich he'd ordered. "And just in case you're about to ask, I'm not going hunting with you."

Leaning against the counter, Anandur lifted the sandwich to his mouth and took an enormous bite, shoving in at least one third of it. He chewed and swallowed, then grabbed a napkin and wiped his beard. "It needs to be done, Carol. You know it's a crucial step."

Yeah, Brundar had made it very clear that he wasn't green-lighting her for the mission unless she proved she could kill an animal and remove its heart.

Crazy asshat.

Of course, he would think it was critical for the mission. The guy was the deliverer of death. What did he know about the art of seduction and manipulation?

Absolutely nothing.

"This is not the place to have this conversation." Carol handed Anandur another paper napkin. "You have mayo on your mustache."

"Thanks." He grabbed it, dabbing at the wrong spot.

"Here, give it to me." She took the napkin and wiped his mustache for him. Men with facial hair, especially as bushy as Anandur's, were walking germ farms. Tiny food particles always landed in there, providing a fertile breeding ground. "You should shave this bush off. It's not sanitary."

"But it's sexy, and the ladies like it." He waggled his red brows.

"If you say so." Carol wasn't a fan. One of the things she'd liked about Robert was that he was always clean shaven.

Had she been too hasty throwing him out?

Probably. After years of living alone, she'd expected the transition back to single life would be smooth and easy, but it hadn't been. As annoying as Robert was, she missed his presence. The apartment felt lonely without him.

Still, it would've been wrong to keep him around just because she couldn't tolerate the silence, or to have a male available for shagging at her disposal. Carol was quite proud of herself for setting him free. Contrary to what everyone else thought, she wasn't a heartless bitch, and freeing Robert to seek his someone special had been a selfless move.

"Can you take a break?" Anandur asked.

She glanced around the café. It wasn't too busy, and Onidu was there in case anyone ordered a sandwich. Everything else was handled by the vending machines.

"Do you want to come up to my place?"

"Nah. Let's take a walk outside."

Imagining herself trotting behind him, Carol grimaced. The guy was huge, especially compared to her. She would have to take two steps for each one of his. "On one condition." She pointed a finger at his chest. "You walk at my pace. I can't compete with your long legs."

"Done."

Removing her apron, she signaled Onidu that she was taking a break.

"Let's go." Carol stuffed her phone in one pocket, her wallet in another.

Anandur waited until they were out of the building. "Did you change your mind about the mission?"

Other than the two of them, there were no pedestrians on the street. Even the traffic was sparse this time of day.

"If I have to kill animals, then yeah. I can't do it. No way."

Anandur stuck his hands into his jeans pockets. "Let me ask you something. Are you a vegetarian?"

"No. I'm an omnivore with a preference for vegetarian dishes."

"If eating a piece of meat that you bought raw in the supermarket or already cooked in a restaurant doesn't bother you, but killing the animal you are going to eat does, it's not a moral issue for you. You're just squeamish."

"I can't argue with that. But knowing that doesn't make it any easier for me. Besides, I'm too busy. I'm running the café during the day and teaching self-defense beginner classes in the evening to free your time for patrolling. I have enough on my plate."

Anandur's strides were getting longer, and Carol found herself trotting behind him. "Slow down, big guy."

He stopped. "I'm sorry. I forgot." Scratching at his beard, he waited until she caught up and was standing next to him. "I'll make you a deal."

Making deals with Anandur could be tricky. The guy was a prankster. The good thing about his brother was that she'd never had to second guess Brundar's motives.

"I'm listening."

"With Brundar so busy lately with whatever he is doing in his off time, I offered to take over your training. Even if you later decide to scrap the mission, I think you should keep on pushing to improve your skills. We will train twice a week, an hour each time. That way you'll stay in shape, I'll fulfill my promise to Brundar, and if you later decide to do what's needed to get green-lighted for the mission, your skills will be where they need to be."

"Sounds very reasonable. Except for the fact that neither of us has any spare time."

Anandur shook his head. "Two hours a week is nothing. We will make the time. This is important."

CHAPTER 29: BRUNDAR

*B*rundar halted in front of Onegus's office and knocked. If the chief was going to chew his ass for taking another half a day off, he would be well justified. Everyone was stretched to the limit, working double shifts. The thing was, Brundar and Anandur's job allowed them more free time than the others.

When Kian didn't have meetings outside the keep, they could choose to help out with other tasks or not.

Lately, Brundar was mostly opting to take time off. Between his second job helping manage Franco's club and seeing Calypso, he just couldn't afford to volunteer any of his free time.

Today, he was taking her to UCLA, even though Roni had made it unnecessary by changing the records. The kid was amazing. Calypso's old name had been replaced by the new one Brundar had chosen for her in each and every one of the admissions records the university kept.

For some reason, this outing was important to him. As a guy who'd never taken a woman anywhere, it would be a first for him. He didn't want to give it up unless he absolutely had to.

"Come in," Onegus called out.

Brundar pushed the door open. "I'm taking the rest of the day off. I'll be back for my night shift."

Onegus shook his head and waved him off without a comment. The dismissal was worse than the chewing Brundar had been expecting.

Closing the door, he wondered whether he should've offered an explanation. But what could he have said? That he was choosing to escort his lady friend over helping his fellow Guardians? Promise that it was the last time?

Both options would have made him look bad. It was better to keep his mouth shut. Anyway, no one expected him to explain, because he never bothered.

Not Calypso, though. She had a way of pulling words out of him like no one before her had managed. Which reminded him that he should text her to get ready.

He pulled out his phone. *On my way. Be there in twenty.*

I'm waiting, was her reply.

As he tucked the phone into his back pocket, Brundar frowned, wondering why the text exchange bothered him. For some reason, he felt uncomfortable, as if he was wearing shoes that were rubbing his feet the wrong way or an article of clothing that didn't fit well.

He was still trying to figure it out when he knocked on Calypso's door.

She opened the way, her broad smile taking his breath away. How was it possible for her to look more beautiful every time he saw her? And it wasn't as if she was dressed to kill. The thing was, simple jeans, sneakers, and T-shirt looked better on her than an evening gown on another woman.

"Don't just stand there, come in and give me a kiss."

He could do that.

Taking a step in, Brundar kicked the door closed and wrapped his arms around her middle. Trapping her arms as he lifted her up, he kissed her until she pulled back to suck in a breath.

"You must have huge lungs," she said after catching her breath.

Brundar set her back down. "I do." His lungs could go without air much longer than a human's.

"Can I see the papers?"

He'd kept the name she was going to use a secret, wanting to surprise her.

Reaching inside his pants' back pocket, he pulled out the envelope with her new birth certificate, social, driver's license, and passport.

Calypso walked over to the kitchen counter, upended the envelope, then picked up the driver's license first.

"Heather Wilson?" She grimaced. "That's so boring."

"I agree, which is exactly the reason I chose it. You need a name that's forgettable. A unique name would stand out. You don't want people to remember it."

"Yes, you're right, of course. I need to memorize it."

"Do you want me to start calling you Heather?"

"Oh, God, no. It's weird enough that you call me Calypso when I think of myself as Callie."

She should've told him she didn't like her given name. He thought it was beautiful, like the woman herself.

"If you don't like it, I can start calling you Callie."

"No. For some reason, I like the way you say it. It sounds so regal coming out from your mouth. Calypso." She imitated his serious tone, then chuckled nervously. "Ignore me. I'm talking nonsense."

"No, you are not. I like using your given name because it sounds special. Like you."

"Thank you." Calypso opened her purse and put her new

documents inside. "Heather Wilson is ready to tackle the administration offices."

Brundar shifted his weight to his other foot. "I have another surprise for you."

"What is it?"

"My hacker took care of everything, changing your name in the university's database. There is no real need for us to go there. Only if you want to."

Calypso lifted her purse and tucked it under her arm. "First of all, I still want to verify that everything is all right. Secondly, they might keep a paper trail."

He hadn't considered the possibility. "I don't think any institution does that anymore these days. Why waste space on endless paper files?"

"Maybe you're right. But we need to check."

"Agreed."

Brundar pulled the door open for her.

"How long do you have?" she asked while locking it. "Do you need to go back to work? Or just the club?"

Brundar held the door to the stairs open for her. "I have a night shift, so no club. But other than that I have the rest of the day off." He took her hand as they descended the stairs.

"After we are done with the administration, do you want to have an early dinner with me?"

"I would love that."

"I mean out in a restaurant. Like a date. Our first." She cast him a hesitant glance.

A date. He'd never been on one. Did hookups count as dates? Not likely. Not his kind of hookups. The kind that required a signed contract.

Calypso was still waiting for his answer, her heartbeat getting faster by the second. He assumed it wasn't due to physical exertion. Going down the stairs wasn't a strenuous activity.

"Of course. I owe you for all those amazing home-cooked meals."

Her face fell and he knew he'd botched it.

"What I meant by that is that it is my turn to treat you, and since I don't know anything about cooking, I should invite you to a good restaurant."

Calypso smiled, but it was forced.

Could he have said it better? How?

The uncomfortable feeling from before was back.

Calypso was expecting too much from him, and he was feeling trapped by her expectations, trying to accommodate them because he wanted to make her happy. Or at least not sad. That was why he'd felt weird about the texting earlier. With all her talk about caring and showing that he cared, she was trying to turn him into someone he was not and would never be.

He wasn't her boyfriend, and he didn't do the things a boyfriend was expected to do. He would never fit into that mold.

Friends with benefits. That was what she'd called their arrangement. It was a good definition for what they had, and they should never cross that line.

CHAPTER 30: CALLIE

The campus was beautiful. Old trees, large grassy areas, and walkways meandering between the various buildings. Callie had been there before, but it was Brundar's first time, and she was excited to show him around.

"Where did you go to college?" she asked as they left the administration building. Just as the hacker had promised Brundar, he'd had her registered as Heather Wilson. She'd picked up a bunch of forms even though everything was available online. Tomorrow she would sort through them and fill out everything needed.

"I didn't." Brundar turned to look at one of the buildings. "Must be stifling to sit in one classroom or another all day."

"Not if you're enjoying the subject you're studying."

He shrugged.

Some people were more physical than cerebral, but for some reason, Brundar struck her as someone who was both. Perhaps circumstances had prevented him from pursuing higher education. Not everyone could afford it. Given that he and his brother had been raised by a single parent, money had probably been tight.

Damn it. What if she'd embarrassed him by asking?

"I guess not everyone likes studying," she offered.

"When I was young, my brother thought I would become a scholar. He said I didn't have the soul of a fighter. But I proved him wrong."

There was a note of pride in Brundar's tone, which was a big deal since he'd rarely expressed any emotion. Apparently, he valued fighting skills more than scholarly pursuits.

Good. It meant he hadn't been offended by her question. "How long did it take you to master swordsmanship?"

"Centuries," he deadpanned.

Callie chuckled. "It must have seemed that way."

"Yes, it did. Endless hours of grueling training. I wanted to be the best."

"Are you?"

"Yes."

No hesitation there. Was it the truth or his ego? "Did you win any tournaments?"

He chuckled. "Many. I'm still alive. My opponents are dead."

Was he joking? No one went to war with a sword anymore. Even if he served during the last one, she doubted he'd killed anyone with a blade. And competitors in fencing tournaments didn't kill each other, either. He must have been talking about mastering a different weapon.

"You must be very good with rifles and machine guns as well."

"I am."

"Which war did you serve in?"

"Not any that you're aware of."

A secret war? He was probably a member of some special commando unit that went on undercover missions.

165

Casting Brundar a sidelong glance, Callie took in his harsh profile, his straight posture, his determined strides. He was a soldier through and through—from the way he talked to the way he thought. It was like he'd never known anything else, and civilian life with all its loose social rules baffled him.

"Did you go to a military high school?"

"No."

Brundar's curt tone was a good indication that he was starting to get annoyed with her incessant questioning. She'd overdone it. The trick to getting information out of him was to limit her inquiries and spread them out over time, but once again curiosity had gotten the better of her.

On the one hand, it was frustrating to have to do all this careful maneuvering to get Brundar to lower his shields a fraction at a time. On the other hand, it was challenging. Even professional psychologists had to work months and sometimes years to get a person to open up, or deal with problems, or even acknowledge having them.

In fact, Callie was convinced that no psychologist would have been able to make the smallest crack in Brundar's shields, for the simple reason that he didn't think there was anything wrong with them. Furthermore, there was no chance in hell Brundar would have ever consulted one.

The silence that stretched between them felt uncomfortable. Callie needed to fill it with something other than addressing personal questions to Brundar. A strategic change of subject was in order. "I'm thirsty. Do you want to check out the student cafeteria? I would love a cup of coffee."

Brundar scanned the grounds again as he had continually done throughout their walk. Always on high alert, the guy never relaxed his vigilance. "I don't see one, but I can smell food."

"You do? Can you find the source, or should I ask someone for directions?"

His lips compressed, showing his displeasure. Guys were so weird about that. Suggesting that they needed assistance to find a location was like an insult to their manliness. On the other hand, they had no problem getting help finding their socks, their car keys, their wallets, and any other item they misplaced in the house. Somehow that was okay.

Brundar took her hand. "With me around, you'll never need to ask for directions."

She chuckled. "The nose that knows."

"In this case, yes."

Following a smell she couldn't detect, Brundar found the cafeteria with ease. The place was huge, the coffee was meh. But then Callie hadn't expected it to be good.

Brundar tossed his cup after taking one sip without slowing his steps, hitting the trashcan's flap with an unerring accuracy.

"That bad?" she asked.

"I've had better. My cousin's wife bought a fancy cappuccino machine, and she keeps experimenting with it. Naturally, she chooses my brother and me for the taste tests."

Another little tidbit of information. Should she chance a couple more questions?

Not as finicky as Brundar, Callie took another sip of her coffee. "I'm guessing you're talking about the wife of the cousin you work for."

Brundar nodded.

"Do you like working for him? Does he treat your brother and you well?"

"Kian is a good and fair leader. I've never had any grievances with him. My brother, however, finds great satisfaction in aggravating me any chance he gets."

This was another piece of information to add to her collection.

"And yet you choose to work with him every day, and to share an apartment with him."

A ghost of a smile flitted through Brundar's austere features. "Anandur never means to insult. He's a trickster and a joker and he thinks he is funny. As annoying as he is, I wouldn't want anyone else fighting by my side."

That was as close as Brundar got to admitting that he loved his brother.

"I would really like to meet him. Your cousin and his wife too."

Brundar didn't respond. Was he pretending he hadn't heard her? Or maybe he hadn't understood the implied suggestions that she wanted him to arrange a get-together?

Pushing the subject could backfire, but Callie felt compelled to do so despite the possibility of it blowing up in her face. "Do you think we could maybe all go out together to a restaurant? Does your brother have a girlfriend? Because a three couples outing could be fun."

"No."

God, she felt like slapping the infuriating man.

"What do you mean, no? No, as in it's not going to be fun? Or no, as in you don't think we could all go out to dinner? Be more specific."

With a sigh, Brundar pinched his forehead between his thumb and forefinger. "My brother doesn't have a girlfriend. That's the only question I can answer."

Crap.

The rest of the walk to the parking lot passed in even heavier silence. Callie searched her brain for something to say, but for once came up with nothing.

She wasn't going to apologize for wanting to meet his family. And she wasn't going to apologize for bringing it up either.

Was he still taking her out to dinner, or was that idea

scrapped together with what passed for Brundar's good mood?

When they reached his Escalade, he opened the door for her as he usually did, and she thanked him politely even though the lump in her throat was the size of a frog.

"Are you taking me home?" Callie asked as he turned on the engine.

He lifted a brow. "Do you want to go home? I thought we were going out to dinner."

Well, at least there was that. "I thought you changed your mind."

"Why would I do that?"

The guy seemed genuinely puzzled, but she was not in the mood to spell it out for him. It was getting tiresome. Callie felt like she was the only one putting in the effort for their so-called relationship to work.

Except, even as peeved as she was, she knew it wasn't true.

Brundar was taking days off work to be with her, and he was doing so much to help her out, like taking her to the campus because she didn't have a car and was afraid of going by herself, in case Shawn was stalking the place.

They were both making an effort, each in her or his own way. It was vitally important to remember that, especially when annoying things popped up, making her doubt her resolve.

People had different things going for them, different skills, different comfort zones, and judging everyone by the same standards, usually her own, was wrong. She was verbally competent where Brundar was not. She was outgoing while he was not. On the other hand, where he would bravely meet an enemy head on, she would cower in the darkest hidey-hole she could find.

The most important thing they had in common was

loyalty. Callie would do anything for the people she cared for, and she believed Brundar would do so as well.

What about honesty, though?

She had laid herself bare for him, keeping nothing back, while he was still more secretive than an undercover agent in enemy territory.

Maybe that's what he was.

What if that story about being a bodyguard for his businessman cousin was a lie? What if he was a Russian spy?

Callie shook her head. With way too much time on her hands, she was reading too many suspense novels lately. Still, if Brundar were a spy, he would be Russian. With his pale complexion and hair color, he could hardly be spying for anyone else.

As far as she knew, the USA had no conflict with Scotland or any of the Scandinavian countries, and she'd already dismissed the Mafia scenario. A Google search had revealed nothing. No mention of anyone named Brundar or Brad who matched Brundar's description.

What the heck was his last name?

After today's fiasco, Callie wasn't about to ask. She could either search his wallet and check his driver's license, or invent a good reason for needing to know it.

"What are you thinking so hard about?" Brundar asked.

Callie plastered a smile on her face. "I'm trying to guess where you're taking me."

"Do you like Italian?"

"I love it."

"Then I'm taking you to Gino's. Best Italian cuisine in L.A."

CHAPTER 31: RONI

"*J* brought you clothes." Sylvia lifted a hefty shopping bag. "I hope they fit. I went by the sizes of what you had on when they brought you to the hospital."

Fuck. Did he have enough money in his wallet to cover it?

Roni pushed up on the pillows. "Thank you. How much do I owe you?"

"Not a thing. It's a present from me. A welcome to your new home present." She hopped onto his bed and leaned to kiss him. "Do you want to see what I got?"

"Sure."

Upending the huge plastic bag on the bed, she started grouping the items. "Five pairs of jeans, size twenty-nine; ten T-shirts, size medium; three hoodies, size medium as well."

She put the aforementioned items back in the bag and continued with the inventory. "Two nice button-downs, a sweater, two packs of boxer-shorts, five in each pack, and ten pairs of socks." She added those to the bag. "I didn't know if you wear pajamas, but I can get them when I go back to get you training clothes. I forgot about those."

Sylvia had forgotten some other necessities as well, but he was too embarrassed to remind her. As it was, she must've spent a lot of money. She'd bought him an entire new wardrobe.

"Thank you. You have no idea how much I appreciate this. I feel even more helpless here than I felt there. All I had to do to get something was to put in a request. I don't know how things work here. Besides, I can't access my money, which means that all I have are the few dollars in my wallet."

Dr. Bridget had a stash of new toothbrushes and disposable razors. He could ask her to give him some until he settled in. Or maybe he could ask Andrew if he had any he could spare.

Sylvia reached for her purse. "I have your wallet here. Not that you have much use for it. You need a new name and a new driver's license."

"I know." He took the wallet and put it on the table by his bed. It was all he had. Never mind that he hadn't had much use for a driver's license before, and he wouldn't have in the foreseeable future. He was still a prisoner. The dream of touring the country with Sylvia in a convertible was just that. A dream.

"What about shoes? I don't think I was wearing any."

"Right." Sylvia pulled out her phone. "You weren't. Another thing I forgot. What's your shoe size?"

"Ten and a half. And I'm going to pay you back for all of this once I get paid myself. I don't know when that will be, though. Andrew thinks I should get better before talking to Kian."

"He is right. Kian is a cool guy, and I don't think he would mind that you look sickly, but you'll feel more confident, and that's what's important. You just need to remember not to be rude to him. He is not known as a forgiving kind of guy. In fact, he is pretty intense."

Roni had met his share of type A personality assholes. Almost every fucking agent thought he could push the scrawny hacker around. Wrong. The only way to deal with them was the opposite of polite. The ruder he'd been to them, the more respectful they had been. Showing weakness was the worst thing to do with these types.

Except, the agents had had no power over him. If they'd wanted Roni's help, they'd had to grovel, not the other way around. Here, he was at the mercy of that Kian guy, and Roni didn't like that at all.

True, Kian needed him, but Roni needed Kian just as much if not more. Damn it, for a smart guy he'd been incredibly stupid not to consider the precarious position he was putting himself in.

He'd been blinded by fantasies of living with Sylvia. Going to sleep with her each night and waking up with her each morning. The other promises Andrew had made had been just a bonus.

Even the immortality.

Roni had been lonely and friendless for most of his life. Even before the prank he'd pulled that had gotten him in trouble and had taken his freedom away, he'd been the geeky kid who'd spent all of his time alone in his room with only his computer for company. Other kids his age had been dumb and boring. The guys had behaved like adolescent chimps, and the girls had ignored him.

Sylvia was his salvation. Much more than a lover, she was his only friend.

"Knock, knock." A woman sauntered into the room. "I'm Ingrid, the housing fairy." She offered her hand to Roni.

He shook it, painfully aware of how pitifully weak his grip was, while the foxy lady in charge of housing arrangements could smash the bones in his hand if she so wished. "Nice to meet you in person."

They'd spoken on the phone earlier. Ingrid had promised to check the available inventory and then come talk to him.

"I assume you know Sylvia."

Ingrid put her hand on Sylvia's shoulder. "Of course I do. Roni tells me that the two of you are going to share the apartment."

Fuck. He hadn't asked Sylvia about it. But Ingrid had made it clear that there weren't enough vacant apartments and that he would have to share. Roni didn't want to room with some strange guy. He wanted to be with Sylvia and only Sylvia.

"I can't. I wish I could. I'm going to spend as much time with you as I can, but I can't move in with you. I'm sorry."

"Why not?"

Sylvia sighed. "My mother. She is clingy. She'd be devastated if I left. I have to get her used to the idea over a long period of time. Maybe in the new place, she'll have more company and won't feel as lonely."

Ingrid shook her head. "I got you your own apartment under the assumption that Sylvia would be moving in with you. So until I run out of options and have to stick you with a roommate, you can enjoy your solitude."

"Thank you."

"Here are the keys." She handed him two plastic cards like the ones used in hotels. "The apartment number is on the sticker attached to each key. First two numbers indicate the floor it's on. Welcome to the keep, Roni."

When Ingrid left, Sylvia leaned and kissed him again. "I'm sorry, baby. I told you about my mom. I thought you figured out that I'm stuck with her."

"Being with you was the most compelling reason for me to leave my old life behind. I can't help feeling disappointed."

"It will happen. Just not right away." She hopped off the bed. "Come on. Get dressed and let's get out of here."

"What about my equipment?" Roni pointed at the monitor stand.

"I'll ask someone to bring it up."

A few minutes later, dressed in his new clothes and with socks on his feet, Roni came out of the bathroom holding a new toothbrush and a disposable razor.

Sylvia noticed the items and pulled out her phone. "I forgot those too. I'll get them when I go for the other things." She typed on the small screen, adding to her shopping list.

Roni threw them in the plastic bag and lifted it off the bed, pretending it wasn't a huge effort to hold the thing up.

"Give me that." Sylvia snatched the bag away from him.

He was too weak to fight her for it. "Way to make me feel like a man, baby."

Holding the bag in one hand as if it weighed nothing, Sylvia wrapped her arm around his waist and propped him up. "You're a man who is weakened by pneumonia. Once you're back on your feet, I'll let you carry all the heavy things. Deal?"

"Deal. And also let me pay you back."

"Nope. I don't want to hear another word about it."

The arguing continued all the way up to the apartment.

"I'll tell you what." Sylvia inserted the keycard into the lock and pushed the door open. "When you get your first paycheck, I'll order a bunch of stuff for myself, and you'll pay for it. A present from you to me for being an awesome girlfriend."

That sounded reasonable, and it gave him an idea. He didn't need to wait for a paycheck to buy his girlfriend things, or for himself. As one of the best hackers in the States, he could get her anything without paying for it, and no one would ever find out. There were two problems with that. One was the delivery; he didn't know if he was allowed to have things delivered to him in the keep. The other problem would be keeping it a secret from Sylvia. She wouldn't accept stolen gifts.

"Okay?" She put her hands on her hips.

"It's a deal."

Sylvia's face lit up. "Wonderful. Now let's take a look around."

She took his hand and tugged, urging him to follow her to the bank of windows. "Look at this view!"

Roni glanced at the high-rises across the street. It was a better view than the one he'd had before, but nothing spectacular. What interested him more was the big television screen hanging over the low fake fireplace and the comfortable couch facing it.

"The sofa looks comfortable." He tugged on Sylvia's hand. "Let's check it out."

They plopped down at the same time, bouncing up from the springy cushions. Roni leaned back. "Now, that's what I call a sofa. Every couch potato's dream come true."

Sylvia cast him a smirk. "How about we check out the bed for bounciness?"

"Most important system check. Lead on, captain." Roni imitated *Star Trek* Scotty's accent.

Sylvia tugged her T-shirt down and straightened her back. "So I'm the captain?"

"Who do you want to be?"

"Commander Deanna Troi, of course."

"Not the same *Star Trek*. Troi is from the Next Generation. Scotty is from the old one."

"Then you can be Geordi."

"I don't want to be Geordi. How about Worf? I always wanted to be a Klingon."

Sylvia chuckled. "Works for me. Deanna and Worf had a fling."

"In a hallucination. It wasn't real."

Sadly, in his current state, all Roni could do was hallucinate.

CHAPTER 32: SHAWN

"*S*ee you tomorrow, Jerry." Shawn passed his fellow salesman on the lot.

Jerry glanced at his watch. "You're leaving early today. What gives?"

"I have a thing, and I'm late for it." Shawn hurried up his steps.

He wasn't late; in fact, he was leaving an hour earlier than needed, but it was none of Jerry's fucking business where he was going.

If word got out about Shawn joining a support group for jilted men, he would become the laughing stock of the dealership. It would be like admitting that he'd gotten his dick cut off and had grown a pussy.

Deciding to check it out had surprised him too. Something in that Facebook ad had resonated with him, touched a sore spot, and the only way he could think of getting rid of that soreness was to go there and make a mockery out of all the sad saps who showed up.

In the end, the joke was on him. A few of the guys were obvious losers, but the majority were other angry men like him. Shawn had felt right at home. He wasn't the only one who felt like a ticking bomb. There were others like him.

The coolest part was the shrink. That dude not only understood Shawn and the other guys, but he also approved of their anger and their right to vengeance.

There was none of the hippie-dippie nonsense about forgiving and forgetting and moving on. The guy got it that it was not going to happen until revenge had been exacted.

Today was the second meeting, and Shawn couldn't wait for another session. He only hoped that none of the pussies came back.

His trip to Aussie was the first step in tracking his wife. He didn't give a shit about the divorce papers. Callie belonged to him. He owned her and her whoring cunt. She would learn that the hard way.

Her phone was still at the restaurant. The battery was long dead, but he knew where she'd left it. One of the waitresses called asking if she was coming back to work and if not if it was okay to clear her locker. Which meant she hadn't told her coworkers about her plans.

He'd told Kati, or whatever the cunt's name was, that Callie had had an emergency back home, something about her father, and that she'd had to leave unexpectedly, but that he would come to collect her things.

A perfect excuse to question the other cunts working there.

As he entered the restaurant, he stopped by the hostess.

"How many in your party?" She flipped her hair back as she smiled at him.

The cunt was fuckable, and he would've gladly done her if not for the charade he needed to keep up. Callie's devoted husband wouldn't fuck her coworker.

"I'm here for my wife's things. Callie. Is there anyone who can help me with that?"

Her smile turned into concern. "What happened to her? Nothing bad, I hope?"

Not yet, but something bad was going to happen to her soon.

"Callie is fine. It's her father. She had to go home, and she has no idea when she'll be able to come back."

The hostess shook her head. "It must be really bad if she didn't even call to let us know she wasn't coming in for her shift."

Shawn plastered on an apologetic expression. "You know how it is when a family crisis hits and they need you. Everything else gets forgotten."

"Yes, of course. I understand. Let me get Kati for you. She can help you."

"Thank you. Your help is much appreciated."

"Of course." The chick hurried to get the other one.

A few moments later, she came back with another hot piece of ass. He should've come here when Callie had asked him to. She'd failed to mention how hot some of her coworkers were. Apparently, she'd failed to mention a lot of things. Like the guys she'd been screwing on the side.

"I'm Kati. You're Callie's husband?" The hottie offered her hand.

"Shawn."

"Nice to meet you. Follow me." She kept talking while leading him to wherever Callie's things were. "So weird the way she took off and forgot her phone. Who forgets her phone?"

"It was probably out of charge. Callie never remembers to charge it." Shawn wondered if his affectionate tone was fooling the waitress. She looked smart, smarter than his fucking wife.

At the employee room, she pointed at an open cardboard box sitting on top of one of the tables. "It's only her phone and a couple of Aussie T-shirts. We all keep spares just in case. People are so clumsy. Someone can bump into you while you're carrying a tray, and boom, you're covered in BBQ sauce."

Shawn shook his head in fake commiseration. "Tell me about it. I also work with customers. What a nightmare."

"What do you do?"

He was glad that Callie hadn't told them anything about him. The question was why? Had she been ashamed of him?

Nah. He was handsome and made good money. Any other woman would've been bragging about what a catch she'd landed.

"I sell luxury vehicles."

Kati put her hand on her hip. "Rich people are the worst, treating everyone as if they are beneath them, and they don't tip well. Unless they are celebrities. Those are the best tippers because they still remember being poor, just like us."

The waitress was talkative, which was good, but Shawn didn't know how to steer the conversation to Callie and whoever she'd been meeting at Aussie.

After mulling over it for days, he decided there was no other place she could've managed a secret affair. He'd known where she was every minute of the day, and she'd never spent long at the supermarket or even clothes shopping. She hadn't gone to nail salons or gotten facials either, and she'd had her haircuts at Supercuts. She must've been meeting her lovers at Aussie.

"Who was your best tipper? Anyone famous?"

"I'm not sure he was a celebrity, but he left a huge tip. In cash. He looked like a rock star, with long blond hair and a body to die for. You should know him. Callie said he was her cousin from Scotland."

"Right. That cousin. I think he plays in a band." Shawn was putting on the best performance of his life. He deserved a fucking Oscar for keeping his murderous rage bottled up and smiling like an idiot. "I keep forgetting his name. Do you remember it?"

Kati scratched her scalp. "Nope. Nothing comes up. It's like a black hole in there. Let me ask Susan. Maybe she remembers."

"Much appreciated. It's so embarrassing. Callie must've told me his name at least ten times and I still keep forgetting it."

As Kati walked out, Shawn paced the small room, counting numbers to keep himself from exploding. His face felt hot.

A few minutes later Kati came back. "Sorry, Shawn, Susan doesn't remember his name either. She doesn't even remember what he looks like, which is really strange because a guy looking like that sticks in a woman's memory." She winked. "But she remembered something about him that I forgot. Susan says he sounds like a robot or a computer. Flat."

Something about a guy who sounded like that tugged at Shawn's memory. But when he tried to focus, it felt as if needles were being shoved into his brain. Shaking his head, he tried again, but again lost the thread and the headache got worse.

"Anything else I can help you with?" Kati asked.

"Thank you. You were most helpful. I'll just take the box."

"Tell Callie we miss her and to come say hi when she's back. Also, that I pray for her father's health."

"I will. You're a good friend."

CHAPTER 33: CALLIE

hank God it was the middle of the week, and the club was closing at two in the morning. Callie was counting the minutes until Franco turned on the lights and called it a night.

After their dinner at Gino's, Brundar had brought her home just in time for her to change into her uniform, then dropped her at the club and headed for his night rotation. Which meant that tonight he was free and could walk her home. Or drive her. But she preferred the walk even though her feet were killing her after seven hours of running around taking orders and delivering drinks.

Breathing the fresh air and enjoying the quiet was calming. It helped her sleep better, but not always. Some nights she was plagued by nightmares about Shawn finding her; others, she kept tossing and turning because of wet dreams about Brundar doing all kinds of wicked things to her.

"What are you still doing here?" Miri asked on her way out.

"Waiting for Brad."

"What's the matter, Donnie can't take you?"

The barmaid still wasn't convinced nothing was going on between Callie and the bouncer, and Callie didn't have the heart to tell her that Donnie had his eyes on someone else.

"I'm sure he can, but I want Brad to take me tonight." In more ways than one. At the end of their walk, Callie intended to invite Brundar up to her apartment and have her way with him.

Miri shook her head as if Callie was deluding herself. "Goodnight. I'll see you tomorrow."

"Goodnight to you too."

To pass the time and not look like she was waiting to catch him, which she was, Callie got busy helping the busboys clear the tables.

A few minutes later, Donnie walked in. "What's up, Callie?"

Crap. She should have told him he didn't need to wait for her and could go home. "Sorry. I forgot to tell you that I'm waiting for Brad tonight."

Donnie lifted a brow. "Does he know that you're waiting for him?"

"Nope. But he is going to find out."

"What if he can't take you?"

"He will have to if you're gone. Don't worry. I'll tell him I sent you home."

Donnie plopped down on a bar stool and crossed his arms over his chest. "I'll wait."

Stubborn man. "Why?"

"First of all because I don't want to lose my job. No offense, but Brad is my boss, not you. And secondly, Miri is outside, lying in wait for me. I told her I need to take you home. I hope she gets tired of waiting and drives off."

Poor Miri. Callie knew all about pining for a guy who wasn't interested. But at least Brundar was attracted to her.

He just didn't want a relationship. Donnie didn't find Miri attractive.

"Just tell her you're not interested."

Donnie grimaced. "I can't say it straight out like that. I don't want to hurt her feelings. Besides, she is scary. I don't want to go on her shit list."

Callie chuckled. "I know what you mean. That's one more reason why you should go after Fran. When Miri sees you with someone else, she'll give up."

"It's happening this weekend."

"Good for you." Callie patted his shoulder.

"What's happening at the weekend?" Brundar asked, startling both her and Donnie.

Hand on her racing heart, she turned around. "Could you please make more noise when you walk? You scared the bejesus out of me."

There was no amusement in his tone as he stared daggers at the bouncer. "Donnie?"

The guy looked so extremely uncomfortable that Callie decided to come to his rescue.

"Donnie is going to ask someone out."

"Is it someone who works here?" Brundar was still staring at Donnie who seemed to be shrinking under that intense scrutiny.

"Yeah. It's Fran," he finally admitted.

Brundar relaxed. "Good luck with that. Just remember to keep your hands and other body parts to yourself on club grounds. Anywhere else it's none of my business."

"Yes, boss."

Callie rolled her eyes. First of all, considering what went on down in the basement, telling Donnie to keep his hands to himself was hypocritical. And secondly, Fran hadn't said yes yet. She might prove to be a snooty little bitch and turn sweet Donnie down.

"Are you taking me home?" She turned to Brundar. "Donnie waited to make sure I have an escort."

"Yes."

"Good." She turned to Donnie. "Thank you for waiting. I hope the coast is clear."

The bouncer pushed to his feet. "Me too."

"What was that about?" Brundar asked after Donnie left.

Forgetting his aversion to touch, Callie threaded her arm through his, but surprisingly he didn't pull away.

"It's a soap opera. Miri is waiting for Donnie outside because she likes him, but he likes Fran. He was hiding inside under the pretense of waiting for you to make sure I had an escort, hoping she'd give up and go home."

They stepped out into the cool night. Callie huddled closer to Brundar. It was a little windy, and her light jacket didn't offer enough protection.

He wrapped his arm around her and held her tight against his side. "You're cold. We should take my car."

"I like to walk home. It's soothing after the hustle and bustle of the nightclub. Helps me sleep better."

He frowned as he looked down at her. "You have trouble sleeping?"

"Sometimes. I have nightmares about Shawn finding me and threatening to kill me." She couldn't tell him about the other types of dreams that had been keeping her awake.

"Would you feel better if I slept by your side?"

Wow. That was such an unexpected and wonderful offer. "Of course. But what about your night rotation?"

"It's every other day. I can come in the morning after my shift ends."

She stopped and turned her face up to him. "That would be amazing. I hate sleeping alone."

He grimaced, and she immediately regretted her words. The only other person she had slept with had been her husband and the number one threat to her life. Sleeping with him hadn't felt safe in a long time.

"Perhaps you should get a dog. A big one."

"That's not a bad idea. But what about the times when I'm at work? Who is going to take care of it?"

"True. I hadn't thought of that." He wrapped his arm around her waist as they kept walking.

"I can get a cat. They don't need as much company."

"A cat is no protection."

"I don't even know if pets are allowed in the building." Brundar should know. She was certain that he'd rented the place and not his imaginary friend, and it still bothered her that he'd lied. But she didn't want to confront him about it. Their relationship was too tenuous to withstand a big blowup over a lie that was rooted in good intentions.

The problem was that it sat like a nasty sediment at the pit of her stomach. If she could somehow get Brundar to confess and explain why he'd done it, she could get rid of that bad feeling.

"Did your friend have a pet?"

"What friend?"

"The professor. The one who's teaching abroad. By the way, you never told me which university he's teaching at. Or even in what country."

Brundar shrugged. "I don't know. I can ask the manager if pets are allowed. Did you see any of your neighbors walking a dog?"

"No. The only neighbor I've talked to was the lady in the apartment right next to me."

Brundar frowned. "I thought she was always traveling."

"She is. But she came back, and we had lunch together."

Callie was watching Brundar's expression closely. The changes were so minute, it was easy to miss them. Except, she'd learned to pay attention. Brundar might be a closed book to everyone else, but not to her.

There was the slight tightness of his jaw, the crease on his forehead, and sometimes she caught his eyes glowing. Or at least they seemed to when he got angry or sexed up.

"Did you like her?"

"I did. She knows your friend. The professor. But she is convinced he moved out and is teaching somewhere else in the States. Not abroad."

Brundar stopped walking and put both hands on Callie's waist. "She must be mistaken."

Pulling her against his body, he kissed her, his lips smashing over hers, his tongue slipping inside her mouth without preamble, taking, possessing as he backed her against a block wall fence.

She knew what he was doing, but his distraction tactic was working. His aggression turned her on, making her feel boneless, needy, hungry.

When his palm closed over her breast and kneaded, the neighbor and the lie suddenly seemed unimportant.

"Brundar," she breathed.

Pressing his hard length against her, he pushed his hand under her club T-shirt and tweaked her nipple through her bra. Hard. "Let's go back to the club and play. Everyone has left already." His words came out sounding like a hiss—as if he was in pain.

Brundar was in a dangerous mood tonight, and Callie knew that whatever he was planning to do to her, he wasn't going to be gentle, and it turned her on even more.

"Okay," Callie whispered.

She was more than ready to play.

CHAPTER 34: BRUNDAR

*C*alypso's heartbeat had been drumming a rapid beat throughout their short walk back to the club. It accelerated as Brundar opened the door to his favorite playroom, the one he'd taken her to their first time together.

"Do you think they've had time to clean it up already?" Her voice shook a little.

Some of it was nervousness; most of it was excitement. His girl was in the mood for something darker. She was eager to play.

Good, because so was he. Typically, he didn't care one way or another. As long as his basic requirements were met, he was game for most kinds of play, but it was more like willing to eat a treat than craving it.

Tonight he was craving it.

Because it was Calypso, and because she'd pushed him to his limit and he needed to assert his dominance over this feisty female who was trying to turn him into someone he was not.

In here he was the teacher, and she was the pupil. He instructed, and she obeyed. The beauty of it was that he wasn't going to hear any arguments from her. On this subject, they were in agreement.

In here she accepted his authority without question.

In her bedroom he had let the boundaries slip.

It wasn't working for him. He had caved, wanting to satisfy her need for intimacy, but he could provide it after the scene was over and the sexual energy released, when he was no longer sporting two-inch-long fangs and glowing eyes and could let her see him.

"The room was cleaned. It's on the chart outside the room."

"That's smart," she mumbled, eyeing the equipment. Now that she knew what it was for, it must've looked more ominous to her.

"Strip," Brundar commanded, watching Calypso's eyes widen.

He hadn't used that tone on her before because she'd been a newbie, and he'd thought she was fragile and vulnerable. He'd learned since that Calypso was neither. She was a fighter, she didn't cower, she plotted and schemed, and she got her way one way or another.

Not tonight. Not in this room.

The only say she had about what was going to happen was either submit or abort by safe-wording out of the play.

Leaning against the door, Brundar crossed his arms over his chest and waited.

Unmoving, Calypso stared right back at him.

He wasn't going to repeat his command. He wasn't going to do anything until she obeyed. He had the patience of a sequoia tree.

The standoff didn't last long. With a slight nod, Calypso walked over to one of the nightstands and put her purse down, then gripped the bottom of her T-shirt and yanked it over her head.

Watching her strip, the smile tugging on his lips made keeping up the stern expression difficult.

Calypso was obeying him, but in the most defiant, non-submissive way possible, while at the same time careful not to cross the line into giving him an excuse to punish her.

Although baring her body to him was arousing no matter how it was done, she wasn't making the slightest effort to make it a sexy striptease. Undressing unceremoniously as if she was about to step into the shower, she didn't let her eyes leave his for a moment.

The woman was a force to be reckoned with.

When she was bare, she mimicked his stance, crossing her arms over her breasts in a futile effort to hide them from his eyes.

"Arms by your sides, Calypso."

She closed her eyes for a couple of seconds, then did as he commanded.

"Get in position on the bench."

A hurt look flitted through her beautiful green eyes, tempting him to drop the charade and take her into his arms. But a moment later, it was gone and she tilted her chin, straightened her back, and walked over to the bench.

When she got in position, he walked over to her, pulled her hair to one side and kissed her exposed neck. "Good girl," he said in a soothing tone as his palm traveled down her back, caressing her incredibly smooth skin, then kneading her taut buttocks.

With a sigh, she relaxed the tension in her shoulders.

"How come your palms are not calloused?" Calypso blurted out of the blue.

His hand stilled on her body. No woman had asked him that even though he'd listed fencing as his main hobby on the questionnaire. No one had ever wondered how come his hands were smooth despite supposedly playing a sport that was known to produce callouses. No one had paid enough attention, or cared.

Damnation.

Two things were obvious. One—the woman was dangerous if she was so observant. Two—he was doing something wrong if this was what she was thinking of during play.

"I use gloves." A lie, but the alternative was some bullshit about a hand moisturizer. Not very manly. Especially given where they were, and what they were doing.

He delivered a hard smack to her butt. "No more talking."

"Not even please more, or this is so good?"

Impudent girl.

He delivered another smack, then leaned against her back. "That's allowed. But no more questions. Is that clear?"

"Yes, sir."

To her credit, Calypso stayed in position, not looking back or reaching to rub her stinging ass even though he hadn't restrained her yet. Something he was about to remedy right away.

It took him less than a minute to have her secured to the bench, the blindfold going on last. He didn't ask if she was okay. By now he knew Calypso wouldn't hesitate to tell him if anything felt uncomfortable.

That was the advantage of playing with a woman who wasn't a true submissive. Calypso wouldn't endure excessive discomfort or pain just to please him. A relief. He didn't have to keep checking and reassessing to make sure she wasn't suffering. Or rather not suffering more than she wanted to.

In that regard, she was the perfect playmate for him. Hell, in every regard.

She took to bondage like a pro. As soon as he'd fastened the last restraint, she relaxed into the bonds holding her body, and as soon as he'd finished tying the silk scarf around her eyes, she uttered a contented sigh.

Beautiful.

Brundar caressed her back, kissing one side of her neck down to her shoulder then moving to the other side.

Calypso purred like a kitten, and when he cupped her butt cheeks and kneaded the warmed up flesh, she laid her head back on his shoulder and purred even louder.

A little mewl of protest left her throat when he stopped touching her to pull his T-shirt over his head and toss it behind him. But when he leaned over her back, covering it with his bare chest, she once again let her head drop back on his shoulder and sighed.

The contraption she was strapped to supported her front only up to her breasts. There was an extension he could've pulled up, a narrow beam that went between the breasts and terminated in a padded chin support, but he didn't think Calypso would have liked it even though it would've made her more comfortable. The strap that went around the neck would've prevented her from leaning her head back on his shoulder.

Besides, it required a level of submission he didn't think she had in her.

Palming her breasts, he rubbed his erection against her soft bottom, regretting that he hadn't shucked his pants along with the T-shirt.

For a few moments, he was gentle, kneading and stroking, thumbing her nipples, stoking her need and her hunger for something spicier.

CHAPTER 35: CALLIE

*C*allie was on fire.

His rhythm unpredictable, Brundar moved from drawing lazy circles around her areolas to plucking at her nipples, then pinching, then gently stroking again. She never knew what would come next, a zing of pain or a soft caress.

Everything about tonight felt different.

Brundar was different, and yet the same. Not as careful or gentle as before, his touch rougher and more demanding, he was nevertheless in full control of his emotions. It was still about her pleasure, Callie didn't doubt that for a moment, but he was upping the ante and testing her limits.

Apparently, he'd been right. Painting the experience a shade darker was pushing all of her buttons.

Bound and blindfolded with Brundar's hard length rubbing against her bottom, her whole body singing to the tune of his torment, she was on the brink of orgasm before he even touched between her legs.

"Please," she groaned.

As his grip on her stiff nipples tightened, she pushed

forward to escape the rough treatment, but the restraints allowed her no more than an inch of wiggle room.

The realization that she was at Brundar's mercy finally hit home.

Until tonight, he'd been holding back, his treatment of her more gentle than what she would've liked. Even the spanking had been more playful than painful. This was different. He was pushing her boundaries, testing her willingness to submit.

It should have scared her, but it didn't.

With a throaty moan, she relaxed into the pain, trusting that Brundar's cruel touch was a means to an end. It wasn't about inflicting pain for pain's sake, it was about helping her unlock a place inside herself for which this was the only key.

Pulling a shocked gasp out of her throat, his grip tightened.

The buildup was more of a leap than a gradual climb. Before she was done processing the confusing messages her body and her mind were sending, Callie snapped, lights exploding behind her closed eyes and her mouth opening on a scream.

If not for Brundar's body pressing against her back and the bonds that were holding her up, the force of the climax would've brought her down to her knees.

As bliss slowly receded, she registered Brundar's warm palms cupping her breasts, soothing, and his muscular chest glued to her sweaty back. He was unbuckling the restraint on her left wrist, then moved to the right.

Disappointed, Callie whispered, "Are we done?"

A few moments to recuperate were desperately needed, but she didn't want their play to be over yet. As tired as she was, Callie had another climax or two in her.

"Not by a long shot." His warm chest abandoned her back as he bent to tackle the restraints holding her thighs spread wide. When he was done with those, he moved to the ones strapping her calves to the lower supports.

"That's good to know." Despite the incredible release, she was still craving a spanking, and the tiny sting from the two smacks he'd delivered before was long gone.

The blindfold remained as Brundar lifted her into his arms, cradling her to his chest and carrying her to the bed. It felt amazing to be held like that. Like she was precious, and he didn't want to let go.

She refused to dwell on the fact that Brundar didn't have feelings like that. He was holding her tight only because her body was so limp that he was afraid she would fall. The rest was the product of wishful thinking and her imagination.

Laying her on the bed, Brundar's palm tenderly cradled the entire back of her head. His lips were soft and warm as he kissed her, his tongue parting hers and gaining access without waiting for her permission.

It seemed that he was done asking.

Callie had thought it was his style, but apparently, he'd only been testing her and learning her responses until he had her figured out.

She liked that he was letting the dominant in him take over. It added a level of excitement to their play. As long as he dropped the autocratic attitude outside the bedroom, she was perfectly fine with being his willing subject in here.

Guiding her arms over her head, he once again restrained her hands with the soft Velcro ties. This time, though, he didn't tie each one individually to an opposite corner of the headboard. He bound her hands together and tethered them to a central post.

Her legs were left unbound.

Was he going to flip her around on her tummy? Maybe she would still get the spanking she'd been craving?

Just imagining that wrested a moan from her throat, and new moisture seeped from her still untouched core.

"Brundar?"

She heard him kick off his boots and unbuckle his jeans.

"What is it, sweetling?"

"I need you."

"I'm right here." He climbed on the bed. Lying on his side, his hand slowly caressed her from collarbone to hip as if there was no urgency, but his ragged breathing told a different story. It was amazing how much could be discerned from sound, smell, and touch when sight was not available.

Even if the evidence of his arousal weren't pulsing against her thigh, Brundar's labored breathing told her everything she needed to know. The guy was in such incredible shape that he could run a marathon and his breaths would come out as calm and as even as if he were taking a casual stroll.

He was turned on. Big time.

Callie smiled. Brundar could huff, and he could puff, but the real big bad wolf in this bed was her. Well, not really, but they could take turns.

"What's that smile about, beautiful?"

With his palm circling from her hip to her stomach and traveling south, so close to where she needed him, it was hard to formulate words.

"Touch me," she commanded.

His hand halted. "Who is in charge in here, sweetling?"

His stern tone had woken a flurry of butterflies in her stomach.

Damn it. She didn't like these kinds of games.

Or did she?

Hadn't he told her that this was all about her? And that ultimately she was the one in charge?

One word from her could stop everything. She could use a safe word, while Brundar couldn't.

She needed to remember, though, that her pleasure depended on keeping her head in the game and not in the real world. Out there, Callie would have never tolerated him talking to her like that. But this was not the real world. It was a fantasy. The rules were whatever they wanted them to be for this particular game. Other games would have different ones.

"You are." Should she have added 'sir'?

Maybe next time she would. After all, there was no sense in playing the game if she wasn't going to use all its pieces.

"That's right, sweetling." Mercifully, his hand returned to her stomach. "In here, I decide when to touch you and how."

Callie held her breath as his palm finally made it to her aching center, but he only cupped her, holding her there as if her feminine center belonged to him.

She almost issued another command before catching her lower lip between her teeth to keep herself quiet.

Brundar leaned and licked at the lip she was chewing until she released it, then sucked it into his mouth, at the same time parting her folds with his finger and pushing it in.

Her hips arching off the bed, Callie groaned.

"Please..." He'd said it was okay to plead, just not to command.

His finger left her sheath, and she was about to cry out her protest and complain when he seized her by her hips and flipped her around onto her stomach. A moment later he tucked a pillow under her belly, then another one, until he was satisfied with the angle.

Oh, God, was he going to spank her?

Could she at least hint that she wanted him to?

Would he stop their play if she did?"

Brundar had discovered that the most effective punishment for her disobedience wasn't his hand on her ass, but the lack of it, there and everywhere else.

Experimentally, she wiggled her butt a little and arched further up.

Crap, she must've looked like a cat in heat. How embarrassing. Her behind was high enough propped up as it had been. Immediately, she lowered herself back down until her pelvis rested on the pillows.

When she heard a drawer open, Callie wondered what Brundar was looking for—a condom or an implement of punishment?

A condom was fine. But a paddle or a strap was not. She specifically marked those as hard limits. Listening intently for a clue, she heard him remove the wrapping from something that sounded a lot bigger than a condom.

Her butt cheeks clenched a moment before something that felt like soft strips of suede touched her back.

"It's a flogger," he said, dragging the strips down her to her bottom. "It's very soft, and is meant for pleasure, not pain." He waited for her to okay it or not.

Apparently, when introducing something new, Brundar was still going to ask.

She was willing to try an implement of pleasure. And if it proved unpleasant, she could always tell him to stop. But what if she didn't want their play to stop, just the use of the flogger?

"I want to add another color to red, yellow, and green."

Brundar chuckled and kept caressing her with the flogger, not an unpleasant sensation. "That should be interesting. Why would you need another color?"

"In case I don't like the flogger or some other implement you want to try on me, and I want you to go back to using only your hands, which you know is my preference, I will say purple."

"Does that mean you're giving me the green light to try other things?"

"Yes." Even if Brundar decided to use one of those horrid paddles, or a strap, or even his belt, one smack wasn't going to kill her or her mood, but it could satisfy her curiosity.

He chuckled again. "Purple is officially added to the list of safe words."

The tails dragged in a slithery caress up across her shoulders, then down again to wrap around her inner thighs. Brundar's palm followed, with two fingers seeking her moist entrance from behind and pushing in, retreating and then pushing back.

She clenched around his fingers, trying to hold them in, but he withdrew. A moment later she tensed at the sound of the tails swinging, but the flogger struck gently, slapping her bottom with barely any force.

It didn't even sting.

Callie relaxed, relieved, but also a little disappointed. The flogger retreated again. Its caress was gentle as it landed on her left shoulder blade, then the other, then going back to her bottom, a little more forceful this time, but still just a little more than a caress.

She knew where it was going and welcomed it.

Finding his rhythm, Brundar landed soft strokes on her shoulders and thighs, heavier ones on her bottom, playing her like a musical instrument.

Her soft moans sang the perfect tune to accompany the steady beat.

She was writhing now, her lower body moving to the rhythm of the flogger, her skin tingling, her bottom stinging but not hurting. Awash in sensation, Callie decided she liked the flogger and the man who wielded it so expertly.

Through the haze of arousal, Callie was dimly aware of a drawer opening. A moment later, she heard the unmistakable sound of a condom wrapper tearing.

Brundar's rhythm never faltered. The flogger landed

several times in quick succession on her upturned behind before delivering one last hard sting, then getting tossed to the floor. A split second later, Brundar surged inside her, filling her in one powerful thrust and detonating the orgasm that he'd been steadily building.

She cried out, the exquisite pleasure like an electrical current pulsing through every part of her body.

Without pause, Brundar pounded into her, his groin smacking against her warmed up behind, each thrust into her soaking sex making a lewd wet sound and bringing her closer to another climax while his own rushed to the front.

Hanging on for dear life, Callie was barely aware of Brundar's mouth latching onto her neck. A split second later, his teeth pierced her skin. There was a distant sensation of burning pain, and then she climaxed again.

CHAPTER 36: BRUNDAR

*B*rundar discarded the condom, grabbed a few washcloths and came back to bed. Releasing Calypso's wrists from the restraints, he wondered whether he should thrall her while she was still out of it, or wait to see if she remembered his bite.

He removed her blindfold and examined her neck. The bite marks were already gone, so there would be no evidence of it, and even if she remembered, he might be able to talk his way out of it.

Damnation. He hated all the lying necessary to keep his people safe.

Except, it was for a very good cause, and he would do so as long as he had to in order to preserve Calypso's sharp mind. Even every other day or every third day could cause irreversible damage to a human's brain. He had developed a good system that allowed him to refrain from using the thrall too often, and it worked well in the club, but Calypso wasn't as easy to fool.

She didn't miss much.

After a quick wipe down with a washcloth, he tucked her

into his chest and held on. So soft and so perfect. Nothing had ever felt as good and as right.

She opened her eyes and looked up at him with a smile. "Did I pass out again?"

"Just for a few minutes." Her body was getting accustomed to his venom. Soon, she wouldn't black out at all.

"You must be so proud of yourself," she teased. "It takes skill to have a woman pass out each time you make love to her."

The phrase making love grated on his mental synapses. Why did humans have to use euphemisms when talking about sex?

He didn't like the word fucking either; there was a demeaning connotation to it that he wanted nowhere near Calypso. Plain old sex worked best. Not making love, not sleeping together unless they were actually sleeping, and not fucking or screwing either.

He and Calypso had sex.

But he wasn't going to correct her. Calling the act of sex making love obviously meant something to her, and if he commented on it, she would get offended, maybe even start crying. The petty peeve he had with the euphemism wasn't worth ruining her orgasm afterglow over.

"Did you enjoy the flogger, sweetling?"

"A lot. I'm so glad we added purple as a safe word. Now I feel like I could get adventurous and try new things. Nothing is so bad that I can't endure a few seconds of it."

"You can always say red and everything stops. Isn't that enough?"

Calypso eyed his chest, then leaned forward and kissed it. "Is this okay? Or is it the same as touching?"

He cradled the back of her head and kissed her forehead. "It's okay. You can kiss me anywhere you want."

"Anywhere?" She waggled her brows.

He slapped her behind. "Answer the question I asked you."

She made a pouty face. "Meanie. What was the question?"

Perhaps she was still loopy and unfocused from the venom. "Why do you need purple when red stops everything?"

"Because I don't want everything to stop. It's a downer. Purple is about implements only. There are so many of them that they deserve a color of their own."

There was some logic to it, though he doubted it would make sense to anyone but the two of them. But then the two of them was what mattered. Until he could no longer stay around, Brundar wasn't going to play with anyone else, and neither was Calypso. Which meant the condoms could and should go.

"I want you to go on the pill. I don't want any barriers between us. I'll get checked up and bring you a letter from the doctor as proof that I'm clean."

"How do you know you are? Were you always safe?"

"I was. But I don't want you to take my word for it. Never do that with any guy no matter how much they swear on it. Always ask for documents."

Her smile vanished, her chin quivering a little. "How can you talk about me with other men?"

He couldn't. The words had left his mouth before he had time to let the implications sink in. "It's hypothetical. I want to make sure that no matter what the future holds, you're always careful and protected."

Calypso nodded. "You're right. But by the same token, you should also ask me for a certificate. What if I'm infected?"

Brundar chuckled. "You married the first guy you had sex with, was with said guy for two years, and I'm the second one. I don't think there is a chance you caught something."

Calypso chewed on her lower lip. "What if Shawn cheated on me?"

"You think he did?"

"Why else would he be so suspicious of me cheating on him all of the time? Everyone judges others by their own standards or lack thereof."

He nodded. "Yeah. That's why it never crossed my mind that the lowlife could've brought diseases back home to you."

She kissed his chin. "You're a good man, Brundar."

Was he?

Not really. But he was honorable. He would've never cheated on a life mate even if their match wasn't a true love one.

"I can arrange an appointment for you with my other cousin who is a doctor." Bridget would do it for free, saving Calypso unnecessary expense.

Calypso chuckled. "Not another cousin, Brundar. I want to do this one on my own."

"Why? My cousin would do it for free."

She shook her head. "Not this time. I'm going to find a nice doctor and make an appointment like everyone else."

"I'll drive you to the appointment."

She rolled her eyes. "We will talk about it later."

Which in Calypso speak meant forget it.

He didn't understand why she'd refused getting checked up by a relative of his, or why she wanted to do this without him.

Was she trying to hide something?

Nah. Calypso was like an open book. Whatever bothered her about his involvement must have been something else. Probably one of those strange female-specific issues no male would ever understand.

CHAPTER 37: RONI

"*How* do I look?" Roni pulled down on the skin under his eye, stretching out the dark circle that had formed there.

Sylvia straightened his shirt collar. "Sickly, but at least presentable."

"Tell me more about that Kian dude, so I can mentally prepare."

She shrugged. "I don't know him that well. From what I hear he is cranky and short-tempered but not a pompous ass. The Guardians all admire him."

"Anandur is a Guardian, right?"

"Yes, and Onegus is the chief Guardian."

"How many Guardians do you have?"

She hesitated. "I'm pretty sure it's classified information."

"But you know."

"I do, but I'm not supposed to talk about it."

Sylvia seemed distraught by the situation he'd put her in. As his girlfriend, she should have no secrets from him, but some secrets were not hers to share. He didn't want to make her uncomfortable.

"It's okay, baby." He pulled her into a hug. "I love you."

She kissed him lightly on the lips. "I love you too."

He took her hand. "Let's go. I don't want to be late."

"You don't want to be early either. He gave us fifteen minutes, not because he is a megalomaniac, but because he really doesn't have time."

That remained to be seen. People in positions of power usually didn't get there by playing nice.

Roni was surprised to see Sylvia press the button for one of the underground levels. "Where is his office?"

"Down in the basement. Most of our facilities are there. There is a gym, a swimming pool, a movie theater, classrooms, a grand hall, a commercial kitchen. The list goes on. Oh, and the catacombs. And a dungeon."

Roni wiped a hand over his mouth. "I'll be damned. A dungeon? Can I see it? Is it like a medieval torture chamber or a place to have kinky sex?"

Sylvia slapped his arm. "You're so juvenile. The dungeon is a level with several holding cells that are supposedly pretty nice. Nothing medieval about them. You can ask Anandur to show you. I don't think there is anyone there at the moment."

They exited the elevators and continued down a wide corridor, identical to the one leading to the clinic. Anandur was waiting for them outside a set of glass doors.

"Hey, Roni, my man." The big guy's hand landed on Roni's shoulder with a surprisingly light touch. "How are you feeling? I hear you got a place all to yourself."

"It's temporary. Ingrid told me she would have to pair me with someone."

Anandur scratched his beard. "Yeah, we are a little short on lodging here. But pretty soon we will have room to spare in a village-like atmosphere with lots of green stuff to look at." He leaned to whisper in Roni's ear. "Personally, I'm tired of the concrete jungle."

Sylvia sighed. "That's why my mom refuses to move into the keep. She says it's depressing."

Anandur glanced at his watch, then knocked on the door. "It's time, kids." He pushed the door open.

"Are you coming in?" Roni asked. No one had asked Anandur to come talk on behalf of Roni, but it seemed the guy had volunteered. Andrew, who was the ideal candidate for the job, was still playing chicken and refusing to get anywhere near Roni until Bridget reassured him that the virus was no longer contagious.

"Yes, I am. But I'm going to be quiet. With that big mouth of yours, I'm sure you can manage on your own."

Sylvia groaned. "That's what I'm afraid of."

"That's what I'm here for." Anandur winked. "To kick him under the table if he forgets his manners."

"Are you guys going to be standing out in the corridor much longer? Because I have shit to do," came a gruff voice from inside the room.

Roni liked the guy already.

He strode inside, ready to offer his hand for a handshake, when the guy pushed up to his feet and rounded his desk.

Holly shit, the dude was good-looking. Like in movie-star, girls throwing their panties at him good-looking.

Roni swallowed. Jerks with attitude didn't intimidate him, but guys like Kian did. Too attractive, and too full of themselves because every female in their vicinity drooled like an idiot.

"I'm Kian." The guy offered his hand, and Sylvia nudged Roni to reciprocate.

Falling back on years of experience dealing with people who thought he was easily intimidated because he wasn't big and buff, Roni shook Kian's hand. "It's good to meet you, Kian. I heard a lot about you." He was proud that his voice came out sounding steady and professional.

Kian regarded him with a pair of eyes that were the most intense Roni had ever seen.

"Let's all sit at the conference table." He pointed to the oblong thing that was taking most of the floor space of his office.

The boss sat at the head of the table, Anandur to his left, and Roni took the seat to his right. Sylvia sat next to him. Evidently, Kian intimidated her as well, though not sexually.

Roni felt ridiculously grateful that sexual relationships between clan members were prohibited. According to Sylvia, it was something about all of them sharing the same blood-line. Because there was no way any woman who wasn't a blood relative wouldn't be attracted to that dude.

"What can I help you with, Roni?"

"I need to know what my status here is. If I transition, that's obvious, I join the clan. But at the moment it seems doubtful."

Kian nodded. "I understand that you prefer to stay on, even if it means you're a prisoner here."

"You understand correctly. I want to be with Sylvia. We love each other."

A pitying look flitted through Kian's eyes. "A relationship between an immortal and a human is doomed from the start. But you're young. You still have many years ahead of you even as a human. On the other hand, you can have a full life outside of here. I can arrange for a new identity, a new place to settle in, and we can even use your services without you knowing who and what we are. The problem is that erasing your memories would be next to impossible. You've accumulated a shitload of those with Sylvia."

Kian cast her a reprimanding glare. "You shouldn't have done it. Not for so long. I understand we are talking months, right?"

Sylvia nodded without looking Kian in the eyes.

"We face several challenges here. Completely wiping Sylvia from your memory is impossible. I can give it a shot and erase just the part about her being immortal, but I doubt it would work on you. Your brain is too powerful. Which brings me to the next complication. I would hate to damage it even slightly. It's like ruining a one of a kind work of art. Unforgivable."

"Thank you. I appreciate the compliment. But that leaves only one option, and that's of me staying on. I'm fine with that. I was a prisoner where I was before, so that's not a big change. Hopefully, I'll be treated better here. It was so fucking lonely there. I'm not going to miss that."

Sylvia gasped in horror, but Kian grinned.

"I think you're going to miss those days when you realize what a bunch of fucking busybodies your new friends are. Privacy? Forget about it. Keeping secrets? Only if you don't tell a soul."

Roni felt a heavy weight lift off his chest, and it had nothing to do with the pneumonia. "Does it mean I can stay?"

Kian shook his head, scaring the crap out of Roni, but then he nodded. "There is a precedent. Andrew was allowed in because of Syssi, his sister and my wife. Syssi transitioned, so we knew Andrew was a Dormant as well, but he was older, and there was a fear he wouldn't make it. It all ended well, and he transitioned, but the point of the story is that we welcomed him regardless. You don't have a blood relative who we know has transitioned, but you have Sylvia. Not as strong of a case as Andrew's, but I can work with that."

Roni slumped in his chair. "Thank God."

Kian lifted a finger. "But, I have to take precautions to ensure the safety of my people. You will be fitted with an unremovable cuff that will track your location at all times and sound the alarm if you try to leave."

Unable to stop himself, Roni snorted. "With all due respect, Kian, do you think I can't disarm a thing like that?"

Kian's smile was part conceited, part evil. "You might be smart, even brilliant, but our William is just as smart and has the advantage of advanced technology you've never even heard about. Try to mess with that cuff and it will explode, taking your arm with it."

Roni gulped and instinctively cradled his forearm.

His expression menacing, Kian leaned toward him. "Just think about it, Roni. How are you going to do all that hacking of yours with only one hand?"

CHAPTER 38: JACKSON

a box of pastries under his arm, Jackson walked into the keep's café and scanned the small crowd. It was late morning, after the breakfast rush was over and before the lunch one began, and yet four out of the café's twelve tables were occupied, most by more than one immortal.

Mid-morning coffee break for those working in the keep.

He put the box down on one of the barstools. "Hi, Carol, how are things going?"

She shrugged. "Business as usual. What about you?"

"Same, though not for long. Everything is going to change after the move to the new place."

She nodded. "I'm still stuck with running the café unless someone volunteers to take it off my hands. I don't think Nathalie is ever coming back. Not until little Phoenix is old enough to go to preschool." Carol shook her head. "The little darling will have a long commute. I don't know how far it is to the nearest school, but my guess is about an hour's drive. The place is so isolated that it will make socializing with people outside the clan difficult."

"Do you prefer it here?"

"No. I prefer my own little home, which I'm renting out."

So did Jackson's mother. As a therapist, she worked mostly with humans and shared a clinic with several other therapists in an office building that wasn't anywhere near the keep but was ten minutes' drive from their home.

Her home, he corrected himself.

Jackson no longer lived there, and he had no intention of going back. The next place he was moving into was the house he and Tessa were going to share in the village. Which would make his commute a nightmare too.

"I've been thinking. What if I take over the new café?"

Carol's eyes widened. "What about Nathalie's old café? I hear it's doing very well."

"It is. But I'm thinking about the commute too. Besides, Vlad and Gordon are starting college. Vlad is staying in town so he can work part-time, but Gordon is going out of state."

"You can hire humans."

Jackson swiped his long bangs back. "I will, if I have to. But what do you think about my idea?"

Carol tilted her head, taking a few moments to think. "If Nathalie doesn't mind about the other place, then I'm all for it. I can work part-time too, help you out until you get settled." She sighed. "I would love to reclaim my old life and chill a little. I miss the clubs and the partying and inviting friends over for dinner."

Fates, he knew the feeling. Ever since he'd taken over the café and then started dating Tessa, everything else had become less of a priority, which meant nonexistent. When was the last time he'd chilled with his friends? Except for performing and practicing their music?

With the guys leaving for college, even that would be over.

It hit him then that he and Tessa were like an old married couple. Tessa didn't know any better, since she'd missed the entire high school experience and started working for Eva at sixteen or seventeen, but he did. They should get together with other couples. Go out dancing or something. For Tessa's sake more than his.

There was a whole chunk of life she'd missed out on, and it was up to him to help make up for that.

Jackson opened the large box and pulled out a smaller one. "Here are your pastries." He closed the bigger box and tucked it under his arm. "I'm going to restock the vending machine."

"We are all out of muffins."

He patted the box. "I have plenty of them here."

The vending machine needed to smarten up and send messages when it was running low on something. The technology was available. He should check it out. Someone must've thought of that and already built smart vending machines.

Perhaps he should suggest it to Kian. Unless they were available for lease, Jackson couldn't afford to buy even one. But the good thing about Kian was that he was generous with money if he deemed the expense justified. Given that automation was the only alternative to employing humans, which Kian was refusing to consider, Jackson had a feeling the boss would be all for getting the new and improved vending machines.

Not that he could blame the guy. Jackson didn't like working with humans either. It was a constant strain to watch himself and not let on that he could hear conversations from across the room, or lift things that took the strength of two human males.

Opening the machine, he started filling up the slots with wrapped pastries, when a pair of legs stopped next to him.

"Is it going to take long?"

Jackson lifted his eyes. "Sylvia? What are you doing here?"

"Same as everyone else. I want to grab something to eat."

"I meant in the keep."

"I came to be with Roni."

"Who?" He didn't know any Roni.

"Didn't you hear about him?" Sylvia rolled her eyes. "Where have you been, on the moon? I thought everyone knew."

Jackson went back to filling the machine. "Apparently not everyone."

"I thought you were tight with Andrew. Roni is, or rather was, a hacker for the government who worked with Andrew. He found Eva's trail. That's how Bhathian knew to look for her in Brazil."

"Now I know who you're talking about."

"Long story short, Roni's maternal grandmother, who had supposedly drowned when Roni's mom was a young girl, applied for a driver's license not once but twice since, looking the same way she did at twenty-something. So naturally, we assumed she was an immortal and that Roni was a Dormant, right?"

"Right." Jackson closed the vending machine.

"So we staged this elaborate setup, a dojo where he was supposed to train, and Anandur pretended to be the instructor. He got bitten several times, and after the last time, he developed a fever and we thought he was transitioning, but it turned out to be pneumonia. So now he is here, and Kian agreed for him to stay even though he is a human."

Jackson rubbed his jaw. "I'm obviously missing some important parts of the story. Why the elaborate setup? And since when are you working for Kian?"

For some reason his questions caused Sylvia to blush. "I don't work at the keep. I'm Roni's girlfriend. And the reason we needed the dojo excuse was that Roni wasn't free to go as he pleased. When he was a kid, he hacked into some classified information, got caught, and instead of going to prison, or a juvenile correction facility, he was offered a job. He couldn't go anywhere without his handler. Andrew convinced the bosses that Roni needed physical activity to keep his mind sharp, which was obviously important to them as he was their top hacker, so they agreed, and we staged the dojo."

That was one hell of a story, and there was probably much more to it. But Jackson couldn't spend all day chatting with Sylvia. The guys needed him back at the café. Still, there was one quick question that could satisfy his curiosity for now.

"How old is your Roni?"

"About your age."

"You don't say." Jackson smiled, an idea forming in his head. "And he now lives here in the keep?"

"Yes."

"Did you move in with him?"

"Not yet. But I'm here a lot."

"How about we all get together? My girlfriend and me, you and Roni."

"Roni is not allowed to leave the keep."

"We can hang out at his place. Who is he rooming with?"

"For now, no one. And that's a wonderful idea. Roni could use some friends his age. He spent the last few years surrounded by agents who were way older than him."

This was just perfect. Both Roni and Tessa had missed a big chunk of normal growing up. They should get along splendidly.

Jackson pulled out his phone. "Let's exchange numbers. Check with Roni when is a good time and let me know. We'll come over, and I'll bring the pastries."

Sylvia frowned. "Who's your girlfriend? I'm not aware of any girl who has recently transitioned."

"She didn't. Tessa is a Dormant just like your Roni, and Kian gave me permission to tell her who we are."

Sylvia put her hands on her hips. "How come your girl-friend knows about us and is free to come and go, while my boyfriend is a prisoner?"

Damn. Telling her about Tessa's special situation was the last thing he wanted to do. Having a good time with people their age didn't involve sharing her horrific past with them.

"How about we talk about it when we get together? I have to go back to work."

"Fine." She pointed a finger at him. "But you owe me an explanation."

Not really, but he didn't want to argue the point with her. Before the four of them got together, he would think of a good excuse that didn't involve revealing Tessa's past.

CHAPTER 39: TESSA

"$\mathcal{H}$ ow do I look?" Tessa asked.

"Amazing." Jackson grabbed her by her waist and lifted her up for a kiss.

Usually, she loved when he did that, but they were right outside Eva's house. "Stop it. Put me down."

"No one is looking. And if they are, they are jealous." Instead of letting go of her, Jackson carried her to the other side of his car, letting her slide to the ground only because he needed his hand to open the passenger door for her.

"Your car always smells of pastries." Tessa buckled up and turned her head to glance at the back seat. A big pink box was the source of the smell.

"I told Sylvia I'd bring some." Jackson turned the ignition on and eased into the street.

"How many people are going to be there?" She was mentally prepared to meet two new people. Not a big bunch of them.

"Just us, Sylvia and Roni."

It would be fun to spend an evening with another couple. Especially since one was an immortal and the other still a human. The human boy was Jackson's age, and the girl was a few years older than Tessa. The reverse age difference was another thing they had in common.

She wondered if Roni was as mature as Jackson. He had to be for a twenty-five-year-old woman to find him interesting. But then the guy was some kind of a genius hacker, so naturally he must be fascinating.

Except, Nick was a great hacker too, and he wasn't mature at all. All he cared about was scoring with girls and watching sports or reality shows on TV. Tessa loved him like a brother, but that didn't mean they had anything to talk about other than job-related stuff.

"I think you overdid it with the pastries. Unless that box is mostly empty."

"It's full. My motto is that it is always better to bring too much than too little. They can put some in the freezer for later."

At the keep, the security guy waved them in with no questions asked. She could understand Jackson getting in without showing identification. After all, he or one of the other guys were delivering pastries to the café on a daily basis, but it was strange that they had let her through without asking her to show her identification or frisking her for weapons or having her pass through a metal detector. The keep's security was supposed to be top notch.

"How come no one asked me who I am? Did you call ahead of time?"

Jackson shook his head. "You were entered into the system the first time you came here, and apparently given a security clearance to come and go as you please. Kian must've been really impressed with you."

Or had felt really sorry for her. Jackson claimed he'd never told Kian any details about her ordeal, but Kian seemed like a guy who didn't shy away from the ugliness of this world. He must've known what her captivity had entailed.

When Jackson knocked on the door, the young woman who opened the door smiled wide and pulled Tessa into a hug. "You have no idea how happy I am to meet you, Tessa."

"And what am I? Chopped liver?" Jackson squeezed by them with the big box. "You forget who is holding the pastries, woman."

Sylvia let go of Tessa. "I happen to love chopped liver." She sauntered over to Jackson and kissed his cheek.

A sick-looking guy waved at them from the couch. "Excuse me for not getting up. This fucking pneumonia is killing me."

"Roni!" Sylvia gasped.

"What? If we are all supposed to get friendly, I'd rather be myself."

Jackson walked over to Roni and offered his hand. "I have no problem with cussing, and neither does Tessa. She only looks fragile, but she can kick butt."

It was Tessa's turn to gasp. "Jackson!"

Jackson plopped on the couch next to Roni and wrapped his arm around the guy's narrow shoulders. "Let's make a deal. There will be no pretending to be anything other than who we really are. Deal?"

Tessa and Sylvia exchanged glances in female solidarity.

Sylvia shrugged. "You guys want an excuse to cuss, then be our guests. But Tessa and I are ladies."

For a moment, Tessa was afraid Jackson would snort a *yeah right*. But apparently he was smarter than that and so was Roni. Both guys nodded in agreement.

"Who wants tea and who wants coffee?" Sylvia asked.

"Coffee," Roni said.

"I'll have whatever soft drink you have." After a day at the café, the last thing Jackson wanted was another cup of coffee.

"I would love some tea. Do you have herbal?" Tessa followed Sylvia to the kitchen.

Sylvia pulled out a box from one of the cabinets. "I'm afraid we don't have much. Roni moved in just a couple of days ago, and I'm still working on stocking this place with food."

"How is he feeling? Jackson told me he has pneumonia."

"He's better, but as you can see, he is still sick."

They walked back into the living room with Sylvia carrying two cups of coffee and Tessa her tea and a can of ginger ale for Jackson.

He took the can from her. "Ginger ale?"

"Roni gets nauseous. The ginger ale helps."

Sylvia went back to the kitchen and came back with a plate loaded with pastries.

Jackson popped the lid and took a sip. "Not bad."

There was an uncomfortable moment of silence, with each of them pretending to be busy with their beverages.

Tessa put her tea on the coffee table. "So I know that Roni is a hacker. What do you do, Sylvia?" Talking about work was always a safe subject. Even she knew that.

"I'm a student."

Jackson lifted a brow. "In what field?"

Sylvia smirked. "Several. I figured there is no rush, so why not study whatever I'm interested in, like literature, psychology, criminology, philosophy, ancient languages, archeology, etc."

Must be wonderful to have no financial worries and be an eternal student. Except, Jackson had told her that clan members didn't start getting a share in clan profits until they were twenty-five.

"What did you do for money before you turned twenty-five?"

"I see Jackson told you about that silly rule. But there is a loophole. Those who finish a bachelor's degree get their share when they graduate. Annani is big on education, and that's her incentive for clan members to get it. I finished my first bachelor's degree at twenty."

"My woman is smart." Roni patted the spot on his other side. "Come sit with your man."

Tessa stifled a smile. Roni was so thin and young looking. Calling himself a man was a stretch.

But apparently to Sylvia, he was. She got up and went to sit with him, lifting her legs and tucking them under her as she snuggled up to him.

Cute.

It was apparent the two were in love.

"What about you, Tessa? What do you do?"

"I work in a detective agency."

Roni looked impressed. "Must be exciting."

"Not really. I'm just the personal assistant and bookkeeper."

"You never get any field work?" Sylvia asked.

"When Eva, my boss, needs someone who can pull off looking like a twelve-year-old, she calls on me."

The look-over Roni gave her made it clear he thought she was all woman. It used to make Tessa uncomfortable, sometimes even scared, when men gave her appreciative looks, but Roni seemed so harmless that all she felt was flattered.

"You look all grown up to me," he concluded his assessment.

To say that Jackson was not too happy about Roni's appraisal was a huge understatement. The glare he directed at the guy was murderous.

She patted her hair. "It's the haircut and makeup. Take those away, and I can play the role of a kid easy."

Jackson shifted in his seat. "What do you do for fun, Roni?"

"Hacking."

"Other than work."

"I love hacking. I listen to music while I'm hacking. When I can't hack, I read and listen to music."

Roni's love of music softened Jackson's attitude. "What do you like listening to?"

By the time Roni was done reciting all the groups he liked, Jackson was regarding him like he was his best friend. "You have good taste in music, bro. Do you play any?"

Oh, so now Roni was a bro. Men were so weird. Even the good ones.

"When I was a kid, I used to play the drums. But that was years ago."

Jackson perked up. "Were you any good?"

Roni puffed up his chest. "I'm good at everything I do."

"I'm asking because I have a band and our drummer is leaving for college. I can use you."

Sylvia cleared her throat. "You're forgetting the small detail about Roni not being allowed to leave the keep."

Both guys' moods plummeted from their temporary high.

"You can perform here," Tessa offered. "And later in the village square. It looks like the perfect place for a rock concert."

Roni and Jackson exchanged looks.

"I like it," Jackson said. "We will have to get Kian's approval, but I'm sure he will be okay with that."

Roni groaned. "I don't have a drum set to practice on, and until I get paid, I can't buy one."

Sylvia caught his chin with her fingers and turned his head to face her. "I can loan you the money."

Roni shook his head. "No. You already bought me clothes and filled up the fridge and the pantry. The drums can wait."

For a moment, Sylvia looked like she was going to argue, but then she seemed to have decided against it. For now.

Tessa had a feeling she would raise the issue as soon as she was alone with Roni.

"Fuck," Roni exclaimed. "I forgot to talk money with Kian." He turned to Sylvia. "You think he would agree to see me again?"

"How about you send him an email? He is so busy he might get annoyed by another request for a meeting."

Roni banged his head against the back of the sofa. "I'm such a fucking moron."

Sylvia patted his hand. "No, baby. You're brilliant. You are just not well."

Roni turned a pair of smitten eyes on his girlfriend. "You're so good to me. I love you so much." He leaned and kissed her as if Tessa and Jackson weren't there.

"I love you too," Sylvia mumbled into his mouth.

Tessa cast Jackson an amused glance. "I think that's our cue."

CHAPTER 40: ANANDUR

*S*itting in the old truck he'd borrowed, the same one he'd used when pretending to be a lowly deck boy to get close to Lana, Anandur waited for Brundar's Escalade to leave the underground garage and hit the street.

It was an underhanded, dishonest, and all around crappy thing to do, but Anandur was sick and tired of his brother's secrecy. Today, he was going to check out the mystery woman who had his brother wrapped around her little finger.

The guy was so inexperienced with women that a smart one could've taken advantage of him. Having plenty of sex, even the kinky kind, didn't make Brundar an expert on female manipulation or immune to the magic some women wielded.

On the contrary. All those silly contracts and agreements they insisted on in those places defined the rules of the game and left little to chance.

Real life didn't work like that.

And if all Brundar was familiar with were hookers who did what they were asked to, and/or kink partners who did what was written in their contract, he was in for a very rude awakening.

Out in the real world, where emotion ruled supreme, Brundar was like a helpless little lamb. It took acumen and experience to decipher women's intentions. They were so much more careful and subtle in their scheming than men. Anandur wasn't going to let some shrewd manipulator take advantage of his brother.

He didn't have to wait long.

The good thing about Brundar's rigidity was that he tended to follow an exact timetable, and his routine made it easy to anticipate his moves. That was how Anandur had discovered his brother was a regular visitor to a nightclub, which had seemed odd until Anandur had learned about the basement level, which housed a secret kink club.

Naturally, Anandur kept pretending that he didn't know. It wasn't a big deal. Brundar was entitled to his privacy, and his sex life was none of Anandur's business. He just wanted to make sure his brother was safe.

One slip was enough for a lifetime. It had cost Brundar his soul, and laid a burden of guilt on Anandur that he was still carrying around every day of his goddamn life. Even though Brundar was more than capable of taking care of himself, Anandur couldn't let go of the constant worry.

Thank fuck Brundar's car was a monster. It made following him from a good distance easy. Not that it would be a big deal if Brundar caught him spying on him. Anandur could always claim it was a lark.

Heading in the direction of the club, Brundar stopped a couple of blocks away from it and parked his car next to an apartment building. A few moments later he came down with a girl who was wearing the nightclub's T-shirt.

Was he picking up a waitress? Or was this the mystery woman?

She was a looker, that was for sure, but a bit too skinny and delicate for Anandur's taste. He liked his women sturdier, but then his size demanded it. Brundar, on the other hand, wasn't as big or as bulky, which made the girl perfect for him.

Just like her body, her face was small and delicate. Her honey-colored hair was pulled in a ponytail, but he could tell it was long. It wasn't straight either. The ends curled up.

He'd parked a considerable distance away, so other details like her eye color and the exact shape of her lips remained a mystery.

Not a problem. Once Brundar left for his rotation tonight, Anandur would go in and have a talk with the little missy.

Heck, he didn't even have to follow them to the club. He would come later after Brundar left.

AT NINE O'CLOCK, Anandur parked in the guest parking lot of the club and headed for the entry. He nodded at the bouncer, who nodded back, a professional courtesy from one guardian to another. Different positions, and yet similar. They were both keeping the good guys safe.

The receptionist was cute, and Anandur flirted with her because he always did. When she took his money, she gave him a coupon for one free drink, and he felt bad about leading her on.

"Enjoy," she said.

"I will."

She looked disappointed that he didn't take his flirting further than that. It was too bad. If he weren't on a mission, and this wasn't his brother's playground, he would've asked when she was getting off and arranged for a hookup.

It was mid-week, so the club wasn't packed, or maybe it

was still too early. Whatever the reason for the sparse clientele, it made it easier locating the two waitresses and figuring which area Brundar's girl was in charge of.

He took a seat and waited.

A few minutes later she arrived. The tag attached to her T-shirt identified her as Calypso. An unusual name, but he liked it.

"What can I get for you?" she asked with the pleasant smile of a professional waitress.

He took a good look at the girl as she placed a napkin on his table. Beautiful, in a fragile small-boned way. Except, he had a feeling she was anything but. There was strength in those small bones that had nothing to do with their physical composition.

Nice. Brundar had good taste.

"Chivas, please."

For some reason, his choice of drink made her narrow her pretty green eyes at him as if she was trying to figure out where she'd seen him before. He was about to crack a joke when she waved a finger at him.

"I know who you are."

"And who might that be?" He leaned his elbows on the table and cast her a flirtatious glance from under his long lashes. Not that he had any intentions of hooking up with Brundar's woman, but he wanted to see what she would do.

Calypso bent a little and lowered her voice. "You're Brundar's brother. Right?"

That took him by surprise. "How did you know?"

She smirked. "He described you as really big with lots of crinkly red hair all over your face and body. I doubt many guys fit that description."

"Busted. I'm Anandur."

He offered his hand, and she shook it, pointing to her name tag. "Calypso."

"Nice to meet you, Calypso. May I ask why are you whispering?"

She leaned closer. "He uses the name Brad around here. Besides, I don't want anyone to notice us talking. He would get mad if he knew you came spying on him."

"I'm not spying on him. I just happened to stop by for a drink."

She shook her head. "Right. And I'm Sleeping Beauty."

Anandur couldn't help himself. "A beauty you are, just not a sleeping one."

She waved her finger at him again. "Flirting with your brother's girlfriend is against the bro code."

Anandur grinned. He liked the girl, but he wasn't done poking at her. "Are you his girlfriend?"

That must've hit a nerve because she grimaced. "Sort of. We are exclusive, but he told me not to get my hopes up because he is married to his job."

The girl had just done a clever role reversal, milking him for information.

Anandur nodded. "He is, and so am I. Did he tell you what we do?" He was curious how much his tight-lipped brother had revealed to the girl.

"He said you both work as bodyguards for your cousin who is an important businessman. But I know it's more than that. Your brother has contacts everywhere." Her eyes holding his with an unwavering gaze, she waited for him to spill some more information.

Gutsy girl. Clever too.

What Anandur wanted to know, however, was who Brundar had mentioned to her and why.

"We've been in this business for many years, so naturally we got to know a lot of people. Anyone specific you're referring to?"

Calypso narrowed her eyes again. "I don't know if it's

okay for me to talk about it. I know you're his brother, and you work together, but I'm not going to drop names without asking him if it's okay first."

Gutsy, smart, and loyal. Anandur approved.

He clasped her delicate hand. "I prefer he didn't know I came here. Brundar is a secretive bastard. I just wanted to make sure he was okay."

She shook her head. "You guys and your appalling choice of words. You're not bastards. You're love children."

Anandur laughed. "Did you tell him that?"

"You bet I did."

She was just too cute. "Good for you. Our mother is sending her thanks."

Pulling her hand out of his grasp, she glanced around. "Let me get you your drink and see what those guys want." She tilted her head toward the next table over. "I've been standing here for too long. We'll talk some more when I come back.

"I'll be here."

When she returned with his Chivas, it was just the way he liked it. Straight, no ice. Brundar had taught her well.

"Can you take a break so we can talk outside?"

"I can, but it's not a good idea. Donnie, the bouncer outside, is keeping an eye on me for Brundar. He would tell him I talked with a big red-haired guy and you'd get busted."

"We are talking now."

"Not the same. Lots of guys like to talk." She winked. "And we are not supposed to be rude to customers unless they get handsy."

He nodded. "I wish we could talk some more."

"Me too. I wanted to invite you to dinner, but Brundar said no. He is a tough nut to crack."

Anandur pulled out a pen and wrote his phone number on a napkin. "For emergencies." He handed it to her. "Or if you just need someone to talk to. I know my brother is not easy to be with. He has his issues, but he is a good man."

"What issues?" Calypso took the napkin and stuffed it in the back pocket of her black jeans.

"Oh, you know." Anandur waved a dismissive hand, regretting his slip of the tongue. Brundar's secret was safe with him. No one knew what had happened all those years ago, not even their mother. He'd sworn to take it to his grave. "He is brooding and rigid and has no sense of humor. It takes a special girl to stick around a *charmer* like him."

Calypso put a hand on her hip. "He is also honorable, loyal, and brave."

Anandur liked her even better for defending Brundar. She was a keeper. For a little while, at least. What a shame the girl was a human.

"That he is."

CHAPTER 41: CALLIE

Callie filled a pot with water and put it on the stove to boil.

After their lunch at Gino's, she'd promised Brundar an Italian dinner to outshine anything he'd ever had at that restaurant. Not that it hadn't been good, but her lasagna was better.

It was a complicated recipe that took about an hour and a half to make, and she planned to have everything done at least half an hour before Brundar arrived. It should be enough time for a quick shower and the rest of her minimalistic beauty routine. A little mascara, a clear lip gloss, and that was it.

The dress would have to be the same strapless one she'd worn before because she didn't have anything else nice.

Clothes shopping was in order, but the thing was, Callie felt odd about using an Uber to get to the mall and back. Seemed frivolous.

She really needed a car.

Tomorrow, she would have no choice but to take a taxi or

an Uber to get to her doctor's appointment. On second thought, she couldn't use Uber.

Brundar had provided her with new identification but no new credit cards. The ones she had were joint with Shawn. She couldn't use them. In fact, she should cut them up and get rid of them, together with everything else that was left over from her marriage. The fewer reminders, the better.

Hopefully, the taxi driver would have no problem with her paying cash.

Another solution was to buy one of those prepaid credit cards. Yeah, that was better. Tomorrow morning she would stop by the supermarket and get one.

There were so many details to remember when hiding and on the run. She'd almost made the mistake of booking the doctor's appointment under her real name.

The best thing would be to switch identities entirely and get used to the new name. Heather Wilson. The problem was that everyone at the club knew her by her real name. Perhaps she should find another job.

Crap. She liked working for Franco, especially since Brundar was there. The best part was access to the basement when no club members were there.

God, the basement.

Remembering their time there, Callie felt shivers rock her body—the good kind. So intense. So amazing. She wanted more of that.

Except, she didn't need to work at the nightclub for Brundar to sneak her into one of the playrooms down below when no one else was there.

Did Anandur know about his brother's involvement in the club?

Did he know about the kinky sex?

She should've asked him. No, she should not have. That would have been one heck of an awkward conversation.

Especially since she was willing to bet Anandur was pure vanilla.

The brothers were each other's opposites. Brundar was shrouded in darkness while Anandur basked in the light. Brundar's perfect features were hard—like a statue's. Anandur was all smiles and flirtation.

The one who snagged Anandur would be a lucky woman.

And yet, Callie would never trade her brooding, dark angel for his sunny counterpart. Or anyone else for that matter.

Brundar was the one for her. The one she was destined to be with. Callie felt it with every fiber of her body and soul. That being said, she would have loved having Anandur as a brother.

Brother-in-law.

Feeling silly, Callie shook her head. Next thing she would be doodling her name with Brundar's inside a heart and drawing flowers around it.

It was way too soon to be thinking about anything permanent. Especially since Brundar had made it clear that it wasn't going to happen.

CHAPTER 42: BRUNDAR

a good bottle of wine in hand, Brundar knocked on Calypso's door.

The smells coming from her apartment were mouth-watering, as was the woman who opened the way.

That strapless black dress would be the death of him.

As hunger seized him by the throat, not the kind that could be satisfied by the appetizing smells, he reached for her with his free hand and pulled her into his arms. She melted into him, parting her lips and sucking his tongue in as if her hunger was just as potent as his.

There was an easy solution to that. Lifting her up, he stepped in and kicked the door closed, then marched in the direction of her bedroom.

Calypso laughed. "Put me down. I didn't spend all this time cooking for it to go to waste. Save that enthusiasm for after dinner."

Brundar growled, but the sound that would've terrified a grown man had no effect on this woman.

She pushed on his chest. "Save that growling for later too. I prepared a feast for you, and I'm going to feed you first."

Reluctantly, he put her down. "I would rather feast on something else."

"Hold that thought." She reached for the wine. "Let's add this to the table. You didn't even look at it."

Fuck. Who could think about the table setting with her looking like that?

Women.

Sulking, he followed her back to the living room. It looked like Calypso had set the table for a romantic dinner for two, complete with candles and flowers and cloth napkins.

"It looks nice," he said, thinking Calypso expected him to say something about it. Brundar couldn't care less. He would've enjoyed this dinner just as much or even more if they were eating it at the kitchen counter.

She pulled out a chair. "Sit down. I'm going to serve you the best Italian food you ever had."

He shook his head. "I should be the one pulling it out for you, not the other way around."

She patted the back of the chair. "I'll make you a deal. Whenever you take me out to a restaurant, I'll wait patiently for you to do the gentlemanly thing."

"Can't I help in the kitchen or something?"

She chuckled. "Nope. You stay here and uncork the wine. That's the only thing I'm allowing you to do other than eating and praising the cook. A few moans of pleasure are acceptable as well."

"Mine or yours?" Relenting, he took the seat.

"Mine will come later." She winked.

Brundar moaned. A lot. First when Calypso served the minestrone soup, which was the best he'd ever had, then his eyes rolled back in his head when he took the first bite of her lasagna. Even the salad was terrific, and he wasn't big on salads or any other kinds of greens.

When she served the tiramisu, he was so full he felt his stomach had doubled in size.

Calypso smiled with satisfaction. "Well? Is my Italian better than Gino's?"

"The food definitely. The language, I'm not sure. I've never heard you speak Italian."

She poured him coffee from the carafe. "I'm afraid Gino wins in this department. I don't speak anything other than English and a tiny bit of Spanish. Do you?"

"I know a few languages. Not well enough to speak, but I understand." For some reason, absorbing new languages was easy for immortals. Naturally, some were better at it than others, but most were better than the average human.

"How about your brother, is he good with languages too?"

"Yes." The last thing he wanted was to talk about Anandur.

"How about other family members?"

"I guess so."

"I would really like to invite your brother to dinner. He doesn't have to bring a date when it's here."

"No."

"Why not?"

"Because I don't want him here."

"Why?"

Stubborn woman. What did he have to do to make it clear that meeting his family wasn't on the table?

He couldn't tell her she was a forbidden pleasure he shouldn't have let himself indulge in, and that his family wouldn't be happy about that indulgence. As long as him having a woman was just a rumor or a guess, no one could demand that he forsake her. As it was, he was living on borrowed time with her, and he had no wish to shorten it.

"It's complicated. I'm not supposed to have a relationship.

It's one of the conditions of my job. If anyone found out, I would be ordered to stop seeing you."

Calypso's lips tightened into a thin line as she glared at him.

"You're lying."

Her words felt like a punch to his gut. He might have omitted things and had twisted the truth when he had no choice, but he'd never outright lied to her.

"Are you really accusing me of being a liar?"

She crossed her arms over her chest. "That's exactly what I'm doing. You're lying straight to my face and not for the first time. Though I'll be damned if I know why."

"What in damnation are you talking about?"

"Your friend the professor. He is not your friend. You never even met him. The landlady told you about him when you rented the apartment for me. You could've told me the truth. You should've told me the truth. Why make up the story? So I will feel less guilty about accepting your generosity? I don't understand."

Fuck. He should've known Calypso would eventually find out. Except, when he'd come up with the story, he'd had no intention of having a relationship with her. All he'd wanted was for her to accept the apartment without argument, and if she later discovered the truth, it wouldn't have been a big deal.

"I didn't have any friends who needed a house sitter. But you needed a place to stay, and I knew you would refuse the apartment if you knew I was paying for it."

"So you decided to lie about it."

His palm landed on the table with a thud. "I did what I thought was right at the time. I wanted you safe, and frankly, I didn't care if you learned about it later. I had no intention of having a relationship with you. I still don't."

"Why?" There were tears in her eyes.

Brundar was too angry to care.

She should be grateful and thank him for his kindness and generosity, not attack him as if he'd done something despicable. Other than the fucking apartment, which was a non-issue as far as he was concerned, he had been upfront with her as much as he could've been under the circumstances.

"Because I can't, and I told you that time and again. I'm breaking the rules by being with you."

"Why?" The tears were running freely down her cheeks. "Why are you breaking the rules for me?"

The woman was driving him mad, using her tears and her incessant questions like weapons and spurring his aggression.

An enemy holding a sword to Brundar's throat would have been less of a provocation.

He did the only thing he could to regain control. Brundar retreated into the zone—the cold and unfeeling place that was his safe haven, where nothing could touch him. Including Calypso's tears.

"It was a mistake." He pushed his chair back and stood up. "Thank you for dinner." He walked out.

Her sobs followed him all the way to his car. Intellectually, he acknowledged them and regretted causing her sorrow. Emotionally, he felt nothing.

CHAPTER 43: CALLIE

A full bladder forced Callie out of bed. She didn't want to wake up, she didn't want to feel the pain, she wanted to stay asleep and pretend her heart hadn't been broken into a million shards.

After Brundar had left, she'd cried for hours, had called in sick and cried some more, until finally falling into an exhausted sleep.

Trudging to the bathroom, she relieved herself, then went back to bed. But sleep wouldn't come back. How could it when her mind was racing, and her heart was aching, and her soul was crushed?

How could he have turned so cold?

It had happened in front of her eyes. Brundar had shut down, his shields slamming down with an almost audible thud, his eyes becoming flat. No emotion, nothing. Like he wasn't even there.

And the worst part was that she couldn't help blaming herself. What had possessed her to push him like that? Accuse him of lying?

But it hadn't been a false accusation. Brundar had lied to her face.

If his employment terms prohibited him from having a relationship, Anandur would have said so.

That was the second lie she'd caught him in, and he'd admitted the first one. How many were there?

Was he married with a bunch of kids, and had all his talk about being married to his job been a smokescreen? Did he want to keep her as a mistress? Would Anandur have told her if that was the case?

God, she felt like a loser playing the 'what if' game.

Her mouth felt disgusting, she needed to brush her teeth, and she desperately needed to get some caffeine in her. Everything would look better once she had her morning coffee.

As Callie waited for the coffeemaker to provide her salvation, her thoughts kept jumping around like a bunch of helium balloons in a cage, bouncing from the walls to the ceiling and the floor, chaotic.

Coffee helped her put some order into the mess.

It didn't make sense to think Brundar was married. Anandur would've been much less accepting of her, or would have at least looked uncomfortable on behalf of his brother. Unless he was a cheater himself.

But that was a far-fetched scenario, and she pushed it aside.

His explanation about wanting to ensure her safety sounded true. She hadn't known him then, and accepting his offer of a place to live was much easier the way he'd presented it. She would've refused to let him pay for the apartment, and according to the neighbor, Callie could not have afforded the rent.

The question was why. He'd been attracted to her from the start but had resisted her not too subtle advances. Which was consistent with the story about his job and not being allowed ongoing relationships.

But what kind of a job demanded such a thing? Even commandos and other Special Forces soldiers could have girlfriends and wives. Many probably chose not to, given the constant danger they were in, but it certainly wasn't prohibited.

Brundar and Anandur's situation was most likely the same. Getting involved in a long-term relationship wasn't recommended, but it was not forbidden.

Which left her with the conclusion that Brundar just didn't want that. It was about time she accepted that the man was emotionally handicapped and incapable of sharing his life with anyone.

Even before his brother had hinted at it, she'd known that Brundar had issues. It was quite obvious.

Her mistake was a classic female pitfall.

Callie had deluded herself that she could fix him. The worst part was that she'd convinced herself that it wasn't what she'd been doing. She'd called it pushing, helping him out of his shell, teaching him to communicate better.

All of that boiled down to her trying to fix him.

Except, the man didn't want her to fix him. Furthermore, she knew that trying to change someone was futile. But she'd listened to her heart, and that little liar had made her believe that love conquered all.

It was time to face the facts.

She was in love with the idiot. But she wasn't going to waste her life trying to fix the unfixable. Callie had made that mistake before, and it had landed her in her current predicament. She should've learned her lesson.

Only an idiot kept making the same mistakes and hoping for different results.

If Brundar wanted her, if he was willing to make an

effort, he knew where to find her. At least until she found a new apartment. And a new job. Because she wasn't going to hang around and live off his charity.

Today was as good a day as any to start.

It was a little after nine o'clock in the morning, and her doctor's appointment was at eleven, which meant she would probably be done by twelve. Plenty of time to go apartment and job hunting.

If only she had a car.

Change of plans. After her doctor's appointment, she was going to get herself a car—a used one she could buy for cash. Heather Wilson had no credit history, and no employment record, so leasing one was out of the question even though she would've preferred to keep her money for emergencies instead of buying a car with a good chunk of it.

But it was okay. She was young and healthy and hard working. She had plenty of time to save up for future emergencies.

Flipping her laptop open, Callie Googled Craigslist and started going over the used cars section.

A few phone calls later she had a couple of good options she was going to check out.

CHAPTER 44: LOSHAM

"Which one is the human you wanted me to take a look at?" Losham asked.

Rami pointed at a tall, handsome man. "His name is Shawn Davidson. He is a car salesman, a good one. Whenever he talks, the others listen. He has a commanding presence."

Taking a seat at the back of the group, Losham spent the next hour observing the guy closely. The quack psychologist was doing a decent job of spurring the men on without going as far as inciting them to commit violence against their exes. Shawn kept throwing around crude jokes and making comments that had the other men laughing and nodding in agreement.

As the meeting drew to a close, Losham leaned toward Rami's ear. "He has potential."

What the other men saw was a confident, charming, and easy-to-smile young man who entertained them. But underneath was a seething rage. Losham didn't like the guy. Shawn was emotionally unstable, and therefore dangerous and unpredictable. The opposite of what Losham valued in a man. But the human fit perfectly into Rami's plan.

Provided they could harness all that rage and control it.

They didn't need a loose cannon, they needed a charismatic leader. One who could turn a bunch of suburban rejects into Satan-worshipping fanatics who dressed up in robes and performed idiotic rituals, believing wholeheartedly that they were the evil one's chosen.

The question was whether the human was not only charismatic but also capable of managing the cult and growing its numbers. Losham was willing to finance the operation, but he wanted to hand the management over to a competent human.

His and Rami's time was too valuable to waste on this smokescreen operation.

As it grew, the cult could start collecting membership fees, and Losham would no longer need to finance it. Maybe he could even make a profit. After all, that was what cults were for—to make their leaders rich by convincing the brainwashed members to surrender their money, and sometimes even their women.

They could keep the females. Losham wasn't interested in their subpar stock, only in the profits.

"Bring him to me," he told Rami.

"Yes, sir."

The human smiled confidently, even though he was clearly suspicious, and offered his hand. "Shawn Davidson at your service."

Losham shook the guy's hand. "Logan Foresight. Could I have a few minutes of your time, Shawn? I want to make you an offer, but I'd rather not do it here."

Shawn chuckled. "Me neither. If you want to talk, let's do it over beers."

"Excellent idea. Do you have a place in mind?"

I. T. LUCAS

When Losham and Rami arrived at the bar Shawn Davidson had chosen, the human was already there, clasping hands with the bartender as if they were old friends. They probably were. Mr. Davidson smelled like a guy who liked to drink. Since he hadn't started his drinking yet, his body odor was too faint for a human to detect, but not to an immortal. It was the ever-present scent of a heavy drinker.

Shawn showed them to a booth at the end. "I ordered beers. Domestic okay?"

Losham wouldn't touch the thing if he could help it, but he smiled and nodded as if it was fine.

"How are you enjoying our support group?" Losham started.

Shawn shrugged. "The shrink is good. No bullshit from that guy. He knows we all have been wronged and doesn't try to sugarcoat it."

Losham nodded. "That's right. We have been wronged, and we need an outlet to express our anger."

The waitress arrived with their beers and a bowl of mixed nuts. Shawn didn't even pretend to pull out his wallet, waiting for Losham to pay. Good. The guy was cheap and greedy. He would do anything for money.

"So what's your story, Logan? Your wife left you? Cheated on you?"

"Something like that. That is why I founded the support group. I like helping other men get their lives back in order. The right order." He glanced at Shawn meaningfully. "Where I come from, women are not free to do whatever they want like they are here. They are owned. The way it's supposed to be."

Shawn lifted his beer bottle. "Amen to that."

Encouraged by Shawn's response, Losham pushed forward with Mortdh's age-old propaganda that had worked its magic on countless generations of humans. "Life is so

246

much simpler that way. There can be only one leader in the family, and naturally, it's the male. Women should obey and serve their husbands."

Shawn lifted his bottle again. "You're my kind of guy, Logan." He emptied the bottle and signaled the bartender to bring him another one.

"You are probably wondering about the offer I mentioned."

Shawn nodded while stealing glances at the bartender, impatient for his next drink.

"I'm a busy man, and I don't have time to manage this little pet project of mine. I need someone to lead the group and grow it into a club. I recognize leadership ability when I see it, and you have it in spades. To start with, I'm going to compensate you for your time, generously. When membership grows and becomes more substantial, we will start charging fees and you'll get a cut of the profits. Basically, I'm handing you a business and financing it. I'm sure a man as smart as yourself recognizes that this is a once in a lifetime opportunity."

The wheels in Shawn's head were turning, calculating, appraising. The guy's expression was guarded, but his eyes betrayed his thoughts—starting with greed and ending in doubt. A few moments later, he admitted he had no idea how to go about it. "What exactly do you want me to do?"

Losham leaned back in his chair. "Men need an ideology to serve as the glue that binds them together. If we want to grow this thing into a profitable business, it needs to become a cult. People like rituals, they like feeling special, better than others. We need to sell them on a belief system."

Shawn rubbed his jaw. "I'm a salesman. I can sell anything. But I'm not good at making up that kind of crap."

The waitress arrived with Shawn's beer. "Can I get you guys anything?"

"No, thank you." Losham lifted his untouched beer as if he was going to take a sip.

"Don't worry about that part. I can supply you with the script and the agenda. Do you want to have a say in what it would be?"

Losham was leading up to this. It was where Shawn was supposed to spill his own set of beliefs if he had any.

"I like your attitude toward females. That's something I stand a hundred percent behind and have no problem promoting. Other than that, as long as you don't ask me to preach turning the other cheek, I don't care what it is. If you want me to convince a bunch of guys to chant prayers to Satan or some other crap like that, I'll do it. I don't have a problem with inciting them to violence either. What I want is to grow this shit into a profit making machine and get revenge on the whoring cunt who left me and stole my money."

Losham patted Rami on the back and offered Shawn a wide grin. "Then we have a deal, Mr. Davidson. How does ten thousand a month starting salary sound?"

Shawn's eyes popped wide open. "Sounds good, what about profit sharing?"

"Once the cult starts making money, I only want to keep twenty percent. The rest will go to you, but naturally, your salary will get deducted from your share."

Shawn whistled. "One hell of an offer, Logan. When do I start?"

"You need to give notice at your current place of employment. Are two weeks good?" Losham needed time to formulate the new religion that Shawn would be preaching. Otherwise, he would've demanded an earlier start.

Shawn offered his hand. "Let's shake on it, but I would like to get this in writing too. No offense, Logan, but I don't want to leave my job for empty promises. I make good money selling luxury cars."

"Naturally."

Losham lifted his palm and Rami put a checkbook on it together with a pen.

"Would the first month's pay put you at ease?"

The guy's eyes were on the checkbook when he nodded. "Sure."

Handing the human a check for ten thousand dollars, Losham held on to it for a moment longer. "One more thing, my friend. The time for your revenge will come, but not yet, and not without my permission. I don't want my new manager getting in trouble with the law."

The guy didn't like it, but the allure of a ten thousand dollar check was apparently stronger than his need for immediate revenge.

"I will not do anything illegal."

"Good enough."

CHAPTER 45: CALLIE

The waiting room at the clinic was depressing. Out of the six women waiting to be called in, Callie was the only one not pregnant. The woman next to her was with her husband, and the two were holding hands, whispering in each other's ears, and smiling like a couple of teenagers in love.

She felt like crap.

You're only twenty-one, she kept repeating in her head like a mantra. She had plenty of time to start a family. Her heart, though, had other ideas. It wanted her to be the woman sitting next to her with her loving husband and a baby on the way.

Grabbing a magazine, Callie searched for something interesting to read, but every other story was about nursing or baby development and how to stay healthy while expecting. She dropped it on the table and grabbed another one.

"Heather Wilson?" the nurse repeated.

It took a moment for the name to register as hers.

"That's me." She jumped to her feet. "I'm so sorry for keeping you waiting. How are you doing?"

The nurse smiled. "I'm great. How about you? A lot on your mind?"

You have no idea. "I'm good. I was just reading an interesting article."

The nurse guided Callie to her station. "Please take a seat."

"Thank you." Cradling her purse in her lap, Callie sat down. She had five thousand dollars in there for the car she was going to buy later, and she needed to keep it close.

"I see you are here about contraceptives."

Callie nodded.

"Do you remember the date of your last period?"

Five minutes later, she was in the doctor's room after having been weighed, her height measured, and her blood pressure recorded. There had been an uncomfortable moment when the nurse asked about Callie's previous doctor and her medical record. Callie had mumbled something about it being in Alabama, and the nurse had dropped the subject. Perhaps she needed to write a fake history for Heather Wilson and memorize it. It would make it easier to come up with answers on the spot.

The energetic knock on the door made her jump and hastily tuck the thin sheet around her naked lower half.

"Can I come in?" A woman's voice.

That was a relief. On the phone, Callie had gotten only the doctor's last name. It didn't matter, a doctor was a doctor, but Callie preferred a female gynecologist.

"Yes."

Dr. Stone was a tall, middle-aged woman with cropped silver hair and a no-nonsense attitude.

"Have you ever taken oral contraceptives before?"

"No."

"You opted for the shot?"

"No. I never used any contraceptives other than condoms."

The doctor nodded, looking over the chart the nurse had prepared.

Callie wondered what the doctor was thinking. Until she read the part about the marriage and the miscarriage in Callie's file, she was probably assuming Callie was entering her first exclusive relationship and was ready to discard the rubber.

In a way, it had been true at the time Callie had made the appointment, but that was no longer the case. God knew when she was going to have sex again. She should wait to start the pills. It didn't make sense to stuff her body with unnecessary hormones until she had a partner again. Which was not going to happen anytime soon.

For the foreseeable future, Callie was done with men.

"You have several options. One is a pill that you need to remember to take every day. There are two kinds of pills, and I'll explain the differences later. The second is the shot which you need to remember to come for every eleven to twelve weeks. The third is an IUD which is an implant good for about ten years. Other than that there are patches and—"

By the time the doctor was done, Callie felt more confused than informed. There were too many options and possible side effects. Everything from weight gain to tender breasts to bleeding between periods and a long infertility period after the shot, which scared her the most.

"I'm starting to think I should stick with the condoms."

The doctor smiled indulgently. "I don't blame you. But you need to realize that those are only possible side effects. You may not get any, or only a mild case of a few. My job is to make sure you are aware of them and the risks involved with each method. Condoms have their problems too."

Callie knew it better than most.

"What do you recommend?"

"If you trust yourself to remember to take the pill every day, I would start with that. Out of all the options, it has the fewest side effects."

"The pill it is, then."

"Good choice. Keep using the condoms for the first seven days. But if you have reason to suspect your partner isn't clean, don't stop using them."

Callie looked down at her hands, gathering the nerve for her next question. "How do I know that I'm clean?"

The doctor turned around from the keyboard where she'd been typing in her notes. "When was the last time you had unprotected sex?"

"Over a month ago. With my ex-husband," she added, not wanting the doctor to think she was irresponsible. "At the time, he was the only one I ever had sex with, but I'm not certain of his fidelity."

The doctor looked unfazed. Probably not the first time she'd heard that particular concern.

"I can perform two tests. One will give you a rapid result, the other takes longer but is more accurate."

"Can I do both?"

"Sure."

Callie was afraid to ask how much all of that was going to cost. Several hundred for sure. But whatever it was, her peace of mind was worth it.

Thank God, the rapid test came out negative.

The doctor gave her a free pack of pills and a prescription. "Call me if you have any concerns, or if you experience bothersome side effects. There are many other brands you can try."

"I will. Thank you."

The free sample saved Callie a trip to the pharmacy,

which meant she could go straight to see the first car on her list.

She pulled out her phone and called the owner. "Hi, it's Heather. I can be there in half an hour. Is that okay?"

"Yeah, no problem."

Callie called a taxi, which took fifteen minutes to pick her up, causing her to arrive a little late at her destination.

The owner was waiting outside when she got there, and after a short negotiation, she was the proud owner of a 2009 Chevy Aveo. The guy agreed to shave off two hundred dollars of his asking price because Callie was paying cash, which brought the cost down to thirty-five hundred dollars. Not a bad deal for a car that was in good condition and had low mileage given that it was eight years old.

Now it remained to be seen if her fake documentation would pass the test of registering the vehicle in her new name. She also needed insurance.

One thing at a time.

The important thing was that she'd taken the first step toward her independence. A new job and a new apartment were next.

CHAPTER 46: ANANDUR

inally. Anandur smiled as his phone chimed with the ringtone he'd assigned to Carol. He'd known she was going to cave in. The mission, although dangerous in the extreme, was too tempting for her to give up just because she was squeamish about killing an animal.

"Carol, what's up?" He was already thinking about where he should take her hunting.

"You need to come down to the gym."

He frowned, switching the phone to his other ear. "Why? What's going on? Is anyone giving you trouble?"

Taking over the self-defense classes when Carol herself was still a trainee must have been difficult. There were always assholes who liked to mouth off to the instructor, especially when she was a small, soft woman like Carol.

"It's Brundar. He's been training for hours, and he looks like he is going to drop any moment but pushes himself to keep going. No one dares to approach him, but maybe you can talk sense into him. Do you know what's eating him?"

Anandur had an inkling that it had something to do with a certain green-eyed girl.

"I'm coming down. In the meantime, clear the gym."

"Already did."

Anandur had seen his brother in that state before. Not lately, though. It hadn't happened in decades, but he knew the signs.

When Brundar couldn't handle his emotions, he retreated deep into himself. His pale blue eyes, which looked cold and unfeeling on any given day, turned so flat and deadened that he looked soulless.

But he wasn't. Brundar was hurting, and the only way he knew how to deal with emotional upheaval was to beat it into submission either by storming into battle or keep training until he dropped.

The thing was, there was not much Anandur could do about it besides watch over the guy and make sure he didn't attack any innocent bystanders. When he got like that, Brundar turned into a machine, oblivious to the fact that his body was made of flesh and bone and not titanium, and that not everyone around him was the enemy.

When he got there, Carol was waiting for him outside the gym, her big eyes showing her worry. "Do you know what's wrong with him?"

He patted her shoulder. "When other guys drown their sorrows in booze or go brawling, Brundar trains, or fights if there is an enemy who needs killing. He is too dangerous to indulge in what other dudes do to relieve stress."

Carol nodded. "Is it safe for you to go in there?"

"Don't worry, I'm not going to fight him. Not unless he is so far gone that he attacks me."

"That's what I'm worried about."

"It hasn't happened yet, and I've seen him in this state before."

"I'll stay here in case you need me." She patted the handgun strapped to her thigh. "As a last resort."

"Good idea. Aim for the knees. But only if it looks like he is about to take off my head." Carol was an excellent shot. She wouldn't miss.

Entering the gym, Anandur stayed near the entrance. He leaned against the wall, crossed his arms over his chest, and watched his brother.

Bare-chested and barefoot, his pale skin covered in a sheen of sweat, Brundar wielded his sword with the fluid grace of a dancer, executing each series of moves flawlessly even though his arms must've been killing him. Anandur was well familiar with the burn that came from swinging a heavy sword for hours.

Being ambidextrous, Brundar could go on wielding it for much longer. He kept switching, letting one hand rest while using the other. His brother hadn't been born with the ability. He'd trained until he achieved mastery with either hand.

Oblivious to Anandur's presence, Brundar kept going until his movements began slowing, imperceptibly at first, then gradually getting more and more laborious. When he couldn't lift his arms anymore, Brundar braced the tip of his sword on the floor, cutting a deep indent into the matting as he leaned on it.

Anandur had been waiting for that moment patiently. "Do you want to talk about it?" he asked.

Brundar shook his head.

"You should've realized by now that it's impossible to kill invisible demons with a sword, no matter how many times you imagine taking off their ugly heads."

Brundar nodded. "Do you have anything to say that is actually helpful, or do you just like to hear yourself talk?"

"I can't help you if you don't talk to me."

For a couple of minutes, it seemed Brundar wasn't going to respond.

But then, looking down at where his sword cut into the matting, he said quietly, "It's getting harder."

"What is?"

"Living in the zone. It used to be easy."

Brundar's accursed zone. The place inside his head he hid in to avoid living. "Was it ever fun? That desolate emptiness you call the zone?"

For the first time since Anandur had arrived, Brundar turned and looked him in the eyes. "It's peaceful. I need the quiet to function at my best."

Anandur shook his head. "People, even top athletes, don't live in the zone, Brundar. They slip into it when they need to. What you're doing is hiding from life."

Brundar shrugged. "It works for me."

"Does it? Because it doesn't look like it from where I stand. You're a high-functioning walking dead."

Yanking the sword out of the floor, Brundar walked over to where he'd left its scabbard, and sheathed it. "If that's all, I'm going to hit the shower."

Not today, buddy. Today you are going to talk whether you want to or not. If necessary, Anandur was going to follow the guy under the spray.

"Life is messy, and it stinks, and it hurts, but it's also beautiful and exciting. Hiding from it to avoid the pain, you're missing out on all its fucked-up glory. It's worth enduring tons of crap for a few moments of wonderful."

Brundar picked up his stuff and started walking. "Not for me."

Anandur followed. "That's what you've convinced yourself of, but it's a lie."

Stopping, Brundar turned around, his eyes blazing with fury. "Are you calling me a liar?"

With a smirk, Anandur crossed his arms over his chest. "What if I am?"

In the blink of an eye, the sword was out of its scabbard, with the rest of Brundar's stuff hitting the floor. "Do you want to repeat that?"

Anandur lifted a brow. "First, drop the sword and lift your fists." With a weapon in hand, Brundar was undefeated, but he wasn't as good in hand to hand, for the simple reason he never trained for it.

The sword clanked to the floor.

With a big grin, Anandur leaned forward and enunciated, "Liar."

CHAPTER 47: SHAWN

*T*he first thing Shawn had done after talking to Logan was to deposit the check. It hadn't bounced, the money went into Shawn's account, and he immediately withdrew it. Just in case.

Good to his word, Logan had brought the papers to the next group meeting.

Shawn hadn't been surprised that it said nothing about the group's agenda and Logan's plans for it. It wasn't something that should ever go in writing. The agreement only referred to the financial side of things and appointed Shawn as the manager.

The following day, Shawn quit his job at the dealership. There was no point in giving notice, it wasn't like he needed to train a replacement. The other salespeople would snatch up his shifts like a bunch of vultures, happy to be rid of the best closer on the lot. More money for them.

No more sweating in his suit and tie on hot California days. No more smiling at old farts with limp dicks who thought a luxury car would compensate for their impotence. No more sucking up to his manager to get the best hours on the best days of the week. The only thing he would miss were the hot cunts who had often accompanied the limp dicks. Some had been more than happy to ride his stiff, thick cock behind their sugar daddies' backs.

Whores, all in it for the money.

Now that he had time on his hands, Shawn was going to resume the search for his lying, cheating whore of an ex-wife.

The cunt hadn't even called her father or her best friend to tell them she was leaving. He knew that for a fact since he'd had their home lines and her cell phone bugged. She'd told no one. She'd gone underground and had yet to surface.

Except, there was one place he knew he would eventually find her.

The university.

There was no way she'd given up on that stupid dream of hers. Getting accepted wasn't easy, and Callie would never throw away the chance she'd been given.

In the back of his mind, Shawn suspected that one of the reasons she'd run out on him was because he'd refused to let her pursue her silly dream. But apparently, it hadn't been the only one. It had been the last push she needed to run away with her lover. The soon to be dead lover.

That morning, he'd tried calling the university's administrative offices, but he couldn't get anyone to talk to him.

There was no way around it. He needed to drive over there, which wasn't a big deal since he had nothing better to do until Logan supplied him with the agenda for their new business venture.

In person, Shawn had a better chance of getting the information he needed. Bitches responded to his charm, willing to do all kinds of favors for him to get into his pants.

Swaggering into the admissions office, he plastered his best smile on his face. "Good afternoon, pretty lady." He leaned on the desk belonging to the flustered thirty-something soccer mom type. Those were the easiest to manipulate, their dried-up pussies yearning for a young dick to make them wet. "My sister misplaced her papers and asked me to stop by and get her another copy. Calypso Davidson is the name."

The woman shook her head. "I'm sorry. She would have to come in person."

He leaned closer. "Come on. All the way from Alabama? She can't."

"Then she could call and provide her social security number to verify it's really her."

If that was all the bitchy receptionist needed, then he was good. "I have her social. Please, the girl is going crazy. She is so worried she'll miss her chance. Studying here is her dream."

The woman relented, giving him a post-it and a pencil. "Write down her name and social security number."

He scribbled it down and handed it back.

A few keyboard clicks later, the woman shook her head. "I'm sorry. I don't have anyone under the name Calypso Davidson or under that social." She handed him the post-it back. "Maybe she spelled her name differently, or you wrote the wrong number."

Shawn double checked his notes, but the number was correct. Maybe she applied under her maiden name?

"Try Calypso Meyers."

The woman typed it in and shook her head again. "Sorry, no Calypso Meyers either."

"Try Callie. She goes by Callie." It was a long shot. She would've used her legal name on the application.

"Nope, sorry. No Callie Davidson or Meyers either."

What the hell was going on? Had she made up the whole

story about getting accepted to UCLA? Had she even applied? And why would she lie about that?

Shawn ran his fingers through his hair. "Thank you. My sister is such a scatterbrain. She probably applied to a different university and sent me here for nothing."

As he walked out and headed for his car, Shawn felt like he was in an episode of *The Twilight Zone*. Nothing made sense. Was he losing his fucking mind?

Back at home, he upended every drawer and searched every cabinet for any scrap of paper Callie might have left behind. There was no trace of any paperwork. Not the acceptance letter, and not the multiple scholarship forms she'd filled out right before his eyes.

She had either taken everything with her or destroyed them before leaving.

Either that or he'd imagined the whole thing. Could too much booze and drugs induce hallucinations?

Had he even been married? Or had it all been in his head?

Except, of that he had proof. The fucking divorce papers were exactly where Shawn had left them. On the coffee table.

A constant reminder of how the cunt had screwed him over.

CHAPTER 48: CALLIE

*G*oing home with her new car had felt liberating.

Callie felt like she'd turned a new page, and even though she was still mad as hell at Brundar, she no longer felt like crying.

Keeping busy as heck had helped.

Between the doctor's appointment and the car buying, yesterday had been a full day. She had barely had enough time to grab a bite to eat and put on her club T-shirt before driving to work.

Brundar, the coward, hadn't shown up at all.

He hadn't called or texted either.

Whatever.

She was moving on.

Today, she was going to find a new job.

A list of steakhouses in hand, Callie stopped next to the first one. It wasn't that she had an overwhelming love of steaks, but the tips were better the higher the tickets, which they were in most steakhouses. The other requirement was a full bar. Besides the quality of meat, it was the most crucial factor in a steakhouse's success.

"Hi, can I speak to the manager? I'm looking for a waitressing job." She smiled sweetly at the host. The guy was about her age, but he was still a kid while she was not. Hadn't been for a long time.

The guy smiled back, his expression all about trying to look cool and flirt with her. "I'll get him for you. I don't think we need anyone, but I hope he hires you anyway." He winked.

God, it was good to feel young and free again. A cute guy was flirting with her, and it felt great even though she wasn't interested.

A few moments later, he came back with a man who she presumed was the owner and not just a manager. The guy was in his late fifties, balding, and with the belly of someone who loved to eat. Managers were usually much younger.

He offered his hand. "Damian Gonzales."

"Heather Wilson." She shook what he offered.

He motioned for her to follow him into his tiny office. "Do you have any experience as a waitress, Heather?"

"Plenty. I worked at a steakhouse for over a year."

"Which one?"

Damn it. She couldn't use Aussie as a reference. She would have to lie.

"It was in Alabama."

He eyed her suspiciously, probably noting the blush that had crept up her cheeks. She was a terrible liar.

"Would they give you references?"

Crap.

Callie locked stares with the owner, then decided to go for the truth. "I really worked in a steakhouse, and I'm a damn good waitress. But if you called and asked for references they wouldn't know who you're talking about. I just got divorced, and my ex is a dangerous man. For my protection, I've been given a new identity."

Damian still looked skeptical. "Why should I believe you?"

"Because it's the truth. Give me one shift, and I'll prove it to you. I'm good under pressure; I don't panic when I have to cover two stations at once because someone didn't show up for their shift, and I can charm even the shittiest of customers. You will never hear any complaints about me."

Damian chuckled. "Of that, I have no doubt. A pretty girl like you can get away with murder. You're lucky to show up when you did. One of the girls just called in sick. I'll give you her shift, and we will take it from there."

"What, like now?"

The owner lifted a brow. "Do you have a problem with that?"

"No, not at all. But I need to be at my other job by seven."

He nodded. "Do you intend to work two jobs?"

"Not for long. I'll quit the nightclub when I have another full-time job."

"What do you do there?" He gave her a once-over as if suspecting she was a pole dancer or something.

"I serve drinks. The tips are good, but the noise is not. I want to quit before my hearing gets damaged." It was partially true. The other part about a jerky boyfriend who wasn't a boyfriend was none of Damian's business.

"I'll tell you what. I'll test you. And if by six you prove you're as good as you claim to be, I'll hire you. How long of a notice do you need to give the other place?"

"A week or two should do it."

Franco didn't really need her, and the other servers would be happy to pick up more hours.

The owner rose to his feet and turned to the shelving unit behind him. Pulling out a T-shirt and an apron from a neatly folded stack, he handed them to her. "You can change in the ladies room. Tyler, that's the host, will show you Brenda's tables—the waitress you are covering for. Grab a menu and learn it by heart. It should be a breeze for you after working in a steakhouse for a year. We serve every cocktail imaginable and carry all the major brands. The drinks menu is three times the size of the food menu, but if a customer asks for something, we most likely have it. Just write it down, and the bartender will take care of it."

Callie tucked the garments the owner had handed her under her arm and offered him her hand. "Thank you for giving me a chance. You're not going to regret it."

He took her hand, covering it with his other one, but it wasn't a come-on gesture, more like fatherly. "I hope everything works out for you, Heather. It's a shame a young woman like you has to run and hide from some abusive asshole. If you're half as good as you say you are, you got the job."

CHAPTER 49: BRUNDAR

*A*s he got dressed in the morning, Brundar checked his reflection in the mirror, relieved to see that his eyes were back to normal with only a slight purplish hue serving as a reminder of the beating he'd taken.

Having the shit pounded out of him by his brother had been oddly therapeutic. Brundar hadn't practiced hand to hand in ages, which was a mistake, as Anandur had proven.

Several good things came out of having his face busted, not the least of which was him and Anandur getting closer than they had been in years. After his brute of a brother had proven that Brundar wasn't as invincible as he'd thought he was, the two of them had actually embraced, then had gone back to their apartment and proceeded to demolish a bottle of whiskey each, while reminiscing about the old glory days of the Guardian force.

Anandur had managed to do something extraordinary. Not only had Brundar been nowhere near the zone while fighting his brother, but he had felt great about it. In the zone, he felt nothing, good or bad.

Yesterday, even the pain had been good because it had made him feel alive.

But that was the physical pain. The other kind didn't feel good at all.

The echo of Calypso's sobs had haunted him throughout the night. He'd hurt her for no good reason. She'd had every right to call him a liar because he was. She hadn't done it to spite him or to hurt him; she'd done it to force the truth out of him.

Regardless of the fact that he couldn't have given it to her, he could've been much more understanding and forgiving about her accusation.

Bottom line, he needed to go to her and beg for forgiveness. Even if she refused to take him back, which would be the best for both of them, he needed to atone for the way he'd behaved. Brundar wanted the memory of their time together to be something they could both cherish, untainted by how badly it had ended.

He should've called, but talking, especially on the phone, wasn't his forte. He sucked at it. Besides, an apology needed to be done face to face.

Pulling out his phone he did the cowardly thing and texted her.

Can I come over this afternoon?

There was no response.

She was probably still sleeping. Or what was more likely, she was mad at him, and rightfully so.

He hadn't gone to the club after leaving her apartment. The following day he'd spent working, then training, then having the crap beaten out of him, and later, after he and Anandur had spent some quality time with their friends Jack Daniels and Chivas, he'd gone on rotation.

Two days of radio silence.

What did he expect? That she would text him back with hearts and kisses?

He fired off another one. *I want to apologize.*

No response.

Fuck, that was bad.

As little as Brundar knew about females, it was a known fact that they were more forgiving than males, especially when said males were offering to grovel at their feet.

His duties calling, he had no choice but to stuff the phone in his pocket and head to Kian's office. He kept checking for messages all throughout Kian's three-hour morning meeting with Turner, and then during lunch with two dudes who needed funds for their startup and were trying to convince Kian to invest, then back at the keep.

A little before three in the afternoon she finally answered. *I was busy running around all morning. You can come anytime before my shift starts.*

Busy all morning? Doing what?

Never mind. It was none of his business.

I'll be there in an hour.

Fine. If you want to eat, bring food.

In Calypso speak, it was like telling him to go screw himself. She was making a point, informing him he didn't deserve her making an effort for him and feeding him.

Damnation. Did he have time to stop by Gerard's and beg the guy to make him a to-go dinner?

The restaurant wasn't open this early, and Brundar didn't have a membership, but he was Brundar, and very few dared to refuse him anything. Except for one green-eyed spitfire who he could lift with one finger but wouldn't dare.

A few phone calls later, and a string of profanities in French—Gerard's—Brundar headed for Calypso's apartment with a fancy dinner for two packed in an insulated food carrier and a bottle of wine.

She opened the door wearing pajama pants and an old T-shirt, her hair pulled up in a messy ponytail and no shoes—her way of telling him that she didn't give a damn.

The thing was, she looked even sexier in her homebody attire than when all decked out.

"What's all that?" She eyed the big square carrier.

"You said to bring dinner, so I did."

"I meant burgers or Chinese." She moved back to let him and his bulky cargo pass through.

Brundar put the carrier and the bottle of wine on top of one of the dining room's chairs, then pulled out another for Calypso. "My lady?"

She quirked a brow but took the seat he offered.

Gerard's crew had packed everything needed for a fancy dinner, including a tablecloth, plates, utensils, napkins, and goblets. All he had to do was to set it up.

Calypso watched as he pulled things out one after the other, doing his best to make the table look as nice as she usually did. Gerard had numbered the containers so Brundar wouldn't mess up the serving order, but there was nothing about what was in them. Supposedly, everything the guy made was as excellent as what he'd prepared for Syssi and Kian's wedding.

As he opened the first container, marked number one, and lifted the appetizer plate, Brundar understood why each individual serving came with its own plate and was packed separately. The artistic presentation wasn't something Brundar could've ever managed.

Calypso's eyes widened as he placed the small plate in front of her. "Where did you get this?"

He smirked. "I told you I have a cousin who's a renowned chef."

"Right. Another cousin."

Brundar pulled out the second appetizer plate and sat

next to Calypso. "Don't ask me what this is because I have no clue."

She lifted one of the three forks that came with the place settings and held it above the small stack of unidentifiable ingredients. "I'm dying to taste it, but I feel bad about ruining this work of art."

Brundar waited until she finally poked it with her fork and took a tiny bite. "Oh, wow. That's amazing." She narrowed her eyes at him. "How long have you been planning this?"

"Since you told me to bring food."

"Impossible. That was an hour ago. No one can prepare a gourmet meal like that on such short notice."

Brundar cast her one of his stern looks. "Are you calling me a liar again?"

Calypso let her head drop, sighed, then looked up again. "I'm sorry. Calling you a liar was rude."

She wasn't retracting her accusation, just apologizing for calling him out on it. Still, he appreciated it. It must've been difficult for her to do.

"I lied about the apartment, so I deserved it. But I didn't lie about the other things."

"What about this?" She waved a hand over the table.

Brundar smirked. "I bullied my cousin into it. He was preparing dinner for a private party tonight, and I twisted his arm to part with some of it."

"What is he going to do?"

Brundar couldn't care less. Some of those French profanities Gerard had hurled at him were quite colorful. "He has enough time to fill the shortage."

Calypso took another small forkful but didn't bring it up to her mouth. "Why did you leave the way you did? And more importantly, why did you come back?"

He admired her directness. No beating around the bush

for this gutsy girl. The thing was, he didn't know how to answer that. But he was going to try. She wouldn't let him get away without at least making an effort.

"I was doing my best under the circumstances, but it wasn't enough for you. You kept pushing for more until I snapped. I've never been in a relationship. I don't know how to play this game. It's hard to explain, but in a situation like that, when I need to calm down, the best thing for me to do is to slip into the unfeeling, cold place I call the zone. That is where I function the best. I don't need anyone when I'm there."

Calypso put her fork down. "So if I understand correctly what you're trying to say, you felt threatened, retreated into your safe place, and stayed there. That's why you didn't call or text?"

"Right."

"What has changed?"

"Anandur beat the shit out of me."

Calypso gasped. "What? Why? How? Aren't you the best?"

"I am the weapons master. Anandur is the champion of hand to hand. He challenged me, and I accepted, thinking I could best him at that too, but he proved me wrong."

"I still don't understand what sparring with your brother has to do with you coming back to me."

"A wake-up call. While he was beating me up, he talked some sense into me. He made me realize that living in the zone wasn't living. To avoid pain, I was giving up on life."

Calypso's eyes softened. "He is a smart man." She chuckled in an obvious attempt to lighten the mood. "From your description of him, I thought he was a silly clown. But apparently, he has depth."

"He is a good man."

A crease in her forehead warned him that another question was coming. "I thought you never let anyone close enough to touch you. That's why you always fight with weapons. Is it different with your brother? Is it okay for him to touch you?"

"No. That's why we never sparred like that before. I thought I wouldn't be able to tolerate it, but I did. We even embraced when he helped me up, and it was tolerable. I guess enough time has passed."

"Enough time from what?"

Damnation. Brundar pinched his forehead between his thumb and forefinger. He hadn't told anyone about what had happened all those years ago. He'd never even talked about it with Anandur, who was the only one who knew.

The last thing he wanted was to reopen those old wounds and let anyone in on the humiliation and guilt that had been eating at him for years. But for some reason, he felt compelled to tell Calypso. Not the entire story, he could never do that, but maybe a highly modified and censored version.

She was the first person he'd let get close to him since the event that had changed him irrevocably.

"Something bad happened to me when I was twelve. Someone who I thought of as a friend, whom I loved as a brother, betrayed me in the worst possible way. I got hurt, but I wasn't the only one. My entire family suffered as a result. That's all I can tell you. Please don't ask for more. Not now, and not ever."

CHAPTER 50: CALLIE

*C*allie's heart broke for Brundar, and that was without knowing what exactly had happened to him.

Her best guess was that he'd gotten beaten up severely.

That explained why he'd become such an incredible fighter, but it didn't explain his aversion to being touched. Had it been a sexual assault? Had his so-called friend been a much older boy?

It was hard to imagine a twelve-year-old committing such an atrocity.

But then some people were just born evil.

Callie would've liked to believe differently. It was much more palatable to theorize that all babies were born pure and good and that the only reason some of them became monsters was because of external factors like neglect and abuse. But it wasn't true. Genetics played a much larger role in a person's makeup than previously believed. In recent years, the old nature versus nurture argument was leaning more and more in favor of nature.

Besides, any mother could tell that each of her children

was born different. Starting from day one, kids' unique personalities were quite obvious.

Callie wasn't sure she believed in souls, leaning more toward the scientific explanation that consciousness and sense of self emerged from biological functions and not some mystical reservoir of souls. It left genetics to account for the marked differences between one child and the next.

"I won't ask, I promise. But you need to talk to someone about it. It's not healthy to carry it all bottled up inside."

Brundar shook his head. "You can't help yourself, can you? You always have to push. Let me rephrase. I don't want to talk about it, period. Understood?"

Crap. He'd opened up to her and she repaid him by offering unsolicited advice. When was she going to learn to shut up and just listen?

Was he ever going to tell her anything after that?

"I'm sorry. It will not happen again. Scout's honor."

He lifted a brow.

"I swear. Do you want me to write it a hundred times? I will. I will write a hundred times: Callie will mind her own business and not stick her nose where it doesn't belong."

Brundar chuckled. "I'll believe it when I see it."

Mission accomplished. He looked amused, which meant he wasn't angry anymore.

"Let's eat this amazing dinner before it gets cold."

When they finished the appetizer, Brundar refused to let her help serve the next dish. "It's my treat today, from beginning to end."

She leaned back in her chair. "I can get used to that."

He kissed her forehead as he put the main course in front of her. "Then do. Because I plan on pampering you as much as I can."

The change in Brundar was so drastic that Callie was almost glad about their spat. He was even talking about a future. She'd learned her lesson, though, and kept her mouth closed, not daring to make a comment that would start a new argument.

After the main course, Brundar made coffee and served it with the dessert.

Cup in hand, he leaned back in his chair. "What have you been doing this morning that has kept you so busy?"

It was on the tip of her tongue to tell him that she was entitled to her secrets the same way he was, but that would have been petty. Besides, it wasn't like she could hide it for long.

"I went apartment hunting."

He frowned. "Why?"

"Because I don't want to keep living off charity. I want to stand on my own two feet. You helped me a lot, but I'm ready to take my life into my own hands."

"Did you find anything you liked?"

"I did. It's a studio apartment, not nearly as nice as this one, but I can afford it on my salary, which is my main objective."

"I don't want you living somewhere unsafe. And how are you going to get to work? Is it nearby?"

She was about to ruin the newfound peace, but there was no way around it. Better to yank the Band-Aid in one go.

"I also bought a car and found a new job."

"You were really busy."

Brundar didn't seem angry, but he didn't look happy either. Maybe the next item would make him happier.

"I also went to the doctor and got birth control. I'm on the pill, which means we can say goodbye to condoms in about a week. I also got tested for sexually transmitted diseases. Some of the results were immediate, all clear, but some will take up to two weeks. So I guess we will have to wait until everything is in. Did you get yours?"

"Not yet. But I will."

The frown remained.

"What's wrong? Aren't you happy about finally doing away with condoms?"

"I am. But I'm not happy about you moving out of here or working somewhere else. I want you safe, and I want to keep an eye on you."

That was rich. As if he'd been doing such a great job of it for the last couple of days.

Take a deep breath, Callie, and keep your cool. He is reacting better than expected to the news.

"I went looking for a new job because of safety concerns, not because I didn't like working in the club or bumping into you on occasion. Everyone there knows me by my real name, and that's not safe. I used the fake name to apply for the new job—a steakhouse, like Aussie. I should be earning about the same as I did there. I also bought the car under the fake name, and I made the doctor's appointment as Heather, not Callie or Calypso. The fewer people who know me by my real name, the better."

"I agree."

"So you're not mad?"

"Mad? No. Why would I be mad? You did the right thing. Except for the apartment. It's rented under my name. There is no reason for you to leave."

"I can't afford the rent, Brundar. I checked. It's twice as much as what I'll be paying for the studio."

"I'll share the rent with you."

"You already have an apartment you're paying for."

"With my brother, and it's paid for by our boss. If I'm going to be spending a lot of time with you, it's only fair that I share in the expenses. And that goes for groceries and everything else as well."

He was making a convincing argument. But what would

happen the next time they fought? Would she get stuck with an apartment she couldn't afford?

On the other hand, life didn't come with guarantees. Shit would no doubt happen, and she would have to deal with it. Besides, she hadn't heard back from the leasing agent yet. Without references, she might have not gotten it.

"I'll agree to stay here on the condition that you'll really let me pay half of the rent."

"Starting next month."

"Fine." There was no point in sweating the details. Especially since pushing Brundar beyond what he considered as reasonable seemed to always backfire.

As it was, he'd been much more accommodating than she'd expected.

Heck, he'd implied that he intended spending more time with her, had made arrangements for sharing rent and grocery bills with her. This wasn't how a guy who planned to bail talked.

It was too good to be true.

What happened to the prohibition on relationships?

Had he gotten approval from his boss?

Or was he rebelling?

Callie burned with the need to ask these questions but knew better than to succumb to it. Too much had been achieved today to jeopardize because of impatience. Eventually, she would have the answers, but not today.

CHAPTER 51: BRUNDAR

*B*rundar felt as if he was digging a hole for himself he would never be able to climb out of. What had possessed him to make all those promises to Calypso?

He'd made it sound as if he was staying.

The thing was, he wanted to, and for once in his life, he was going to do the unthinkable.

Fuck the rules.

Calypso was everything that was good. Hell, she was the only good thing that had happened to him throughout his adult life.

She made him feel.

He wasn't going to give her up for anything. Fuck the rules, and fuck his goddamned honor. None of it mattered to him anymore. He was going to keep her and fight to the death anyone who would threaten to take her away.

She was his, as he was hers.

What were they going to do to him? Fire him from his Guardian job? Sentence him to entombment?

He snorted. Who and what army was going to accomplish that?

If need be, he would grab Calypso and run. It would be hard to part with Anandur, but there was a time in a man's life when he needed to make a choice between his past and his future.

Calypso was his future.

"What are you thinking so hard about?" she asked. "You're frowning as if you're trying to solve an unsolvable problem."

Very perceptive of her.

But as far as Brundar was concerned, he no longer had a problem. He'd made up his mind. Others might disagree, but then it was their problem, not his.

"I'm thinking of the best and quickest way to get you naked and under me. I wonder if this table is sturdy enough."

"You should have said so." Calypso pushed to her feet, gripped the bottom of her T-shirt, and pulled it over her head. "I would have offered solutions." She hooked her thumbs in the elastic of her pajama pants and pushed them down. "Race you to bed." She stepped out of the loose pants, which had pooled at her feet, and sprinted for the bedroom.

Didn't she know not to run from a predator?

In a split second, Brundar was out of his chair and leaping after her. Calypso managed two steps away from the dining table when he grabbed her by her waist, twisted her around, and draped her over his shoulder—fireman style.

Or was it caveman style?

Calypso laughed and pushed back.

He smacked her upturned behind. "Stay. Don't wiggle."

The more she struggled, the more turned on he became. Brundar's imagination produced images of the kinds of games they could play if she were an immortal. He would take her somewhere wild and give her a head start, then hunt her for hours as she hid and tried to evade him.

The things he would do to her once he caught her...

Yeah, if Calypso were an immortal, a lot of things would be different.

But she wasn't.

She was perfect the way she was. Human, fragile, beautiful, feisty, independent, assertive, yet willing to yield to him and offer her complete surrender.

On top of all that, to wish she was also an immortal was greedy and ungrateful. It was good Brundar didn't believe in the Fates. Otherwise, he would have feared their retribution for regarding their gifts with such ungratefulness.

Laying Calypso gently on the bed, he quickly divested her of the last two scraps of fabric still covering her body.

With a smile, she stretched her arms over her head, arching her back and pushing her perfect breasts up. "Are you going to tie me up?"

He shook his head. "Just grab onto the headboard and don't let go."

Unfortunately, he could not forgo the blindfold. Already, his fangs were making his speech slur, and the only reason Calypso didn't notice the glow coming from his eyes was that it was still daytime and her bedroom was drenched in sunlight.

He pulled out one of the five silk scarves she kept in her drawer next to the stash of condoms. The nylon stockings he'd used the first time were there as well. He loved it that she was prepared for him, that she not only accommodated his quirks but planned for them by keeping the things he needed close by.

Scarf pulled between his hands, Brundar sat on the bed next to Calypso. "Lift your head, sweetling."

She obeyed, the smile never leaving her lush lips. Did she love the game as much as he did?

"Do you like it when I blindfold you?" he asked as he tied

the ends behind her head, careful not to snag any of her beautiful hair in the knot.

"I love all the games we play, and I'm looking forward to learning more."

Gutsy girl.

"Should I buy you your own personal flogger?"

She caught her lower lip between her teeth and nodded.

"The same kind I used on you in the club?"

"Yes," she said on a moan, the scent of her arousal permeating the air and turning his erection into a steel rod.

"Soft suede?"

She nodded.

Damnation. What a shame he didn't have one with him. It seemed Calypso was craving it. Or maybe she just enjoyed talking about it?

He caressed her side, lightly brushing his knuckles against her left breast. "Perhaps I should buy a lot of different toys and bring them here for you to experiment with?" He put his hand on her stomach, feeling the small tremors his version of dirty talk was sending through her body.

"Yes. I want to have my own, brand new toys to play with."

Brundar stifled a chuckle. His girl was rushing forward faster than he'd ever imagined she could or would want to.

Feisty, brave, adventurous.

"There are online catalogs." He cupped her hot center, then leaned to nibble on her ear. "Imagine how wet you'll get just from browsing and imagining what I could do to you with each toy."

"Oh, God." She arched her back. "Keep talking like that, and I'm going to come all over your hand."

This time he couldn't suppress the chuckle. "That would be a first for me. I've never had a woman climax just from the sound of my voice."

A sly smirk twisting her plump lips, she rubbed her center on his palm. "No wonder. It would've required you to actually talk."

CHAPTER 52: CALLIE

*C*allie waited for a comeback that never came. Instead, Brundar leaned forward and clamped his hand on the back of her head, lifting it and crushing his lips over hers.

As his tongue pushed in, she parted for him, moaning into his mouth, desperate to lift her arms and hold him close to her.

What would he do? Tell her to put her hands back up? It wasn't enough of a deterrent. She could steal a moment, pretending she'd acted on instinct.

Her fingers were in the process of loosening their grip on the metal scrollwork when Brundar reminded her of the rules of the game. Still kissing her like he was drowning in her, he brought his other hand to her throat, caging it, two fingers pressed against her pulse points as if he wanted to feel the effect his kiss and possessive grip had on her heartbeat.

It sped up, not in fear, but out of pure lust. Everything felt too tight; her jaw, her nipples, her stomach muscles, her quivering sheath.

Brundar's kiss was telling her all the things he wouldn't or couldn't say. By hungrily sucking on her tongue, he was telling her that he could never get enough of her, and by gently caging her neck with his fingers, he was telling her that she was his, and he would always keep her safe, even from his own darkness.

"Brundar," she whispered as he let go of her mouth to let her suck in a breath. "Make love to me."

Callie was all in for Brundar's rough and wild eroticism, but today she craved his tender loving touch. Today she needed reassurances. Today she wanted him to show her with his body what he couldn't say with words.

CHAPTER 53: SHAWN

"Motherfucker!" Shawn woke up, a string of vile curses spilling out of his mouth.

The divorce papers lay scattered on the floor next to the couch where they had slipped from his hands when he'd fallen into a booze-induced stupor. He'd been watching *The Lord of the Rings* on Netflix, dozing on and off and sipping out of a bottle of vodka, until his eyes had closed, opening with a start when he'd woken up from a very vivid dream.

It was him—the elf lookalike fucker.

The guy who over a year ago had thrown Callie and Shawn out of the kink club. The same one who'd delivered the divorce papers, and the same one who had roughed Shawn up.

The weirdo with the long blond hair must've been some sort of a hypnotist. He must've fucked with Shawn's head. That was the only explanation for why he hadn't remembered him. Not the first time, or the second, or the third.

Shawn had collided with the motherfucker three times, and he hadn't remembered any of them until everything came back to him in the dream.

Not old enough, Shawn seethed.

The fucker had thrown them out of the club with the excuse that Callie had been too young. But apparently, she was old enough for the guy to slip her his phone number and pork her behind her husband's back.

The cunt must've been fucking the asswipe for over a year, and then he'd convinced her to leave Shawn and run away with him.

Fuck, maybe he had hypnotized her the same way he'd done to Shawn. Maybe it wasn't her fault that she'd let him bang her. Because come on, why would she leave a man like Shawn for a girly-looking pretty boy like that?

That first time in the club, Shawn had been convinced that the guy was a homo. What man let his hair grow down to his ass? Only one who wanted that ass fucked, that's who.

The fucker sure was pretty enough for even some straight guys to give it to him. Not Shawn, his dick would never touch some guy's hairy ass, not even for revenge.

Well, maybe in vengeance. But that would be the only reason.

Still, if the asswipe was banging Callie, he was either straight or went both ways.

Shawn glanced at the clock on the wall, one of the cheap junky knickknacks Callie used to buy at the discount store to hang over the holes he'd made in the walls. He should get a trash bag and get rid of all that junk, then hire someone to patch up the walls. Why live as if he were poor when he was making so much money?

It was ten after eight at night, a perfect time to visit a certain club, find the girly motherfucker, and get him to confess.

The thing was, together with the other recollections, Shawn also remembered how fucking strong the bastard was. He'd lifted Shawn's two hundred and twenty pounds as if it was nothing.

What a freak.

But even the strongest freak would sing with a bullet in his gut, or even better, his knees, but those were harder to hit. The gut was a bigger target, one Shawn couldn't miss.

Fuck, his head was pounding with the mother of all hangovers, and he needed to piss. Otherwise, he would have been in his car already. But acting without a plan and with a sluggish brain was stupid.

A long cold shower and five Advils later, he was good to go.

Shawn still wasn't clear on what exactly he was going to do once he got there, except scare the crap out of the motherfucker and get him to spill where Callie was hiding.

Armed with his two Colt Cobras, Shawn got into the car and programmed the nightclub's address into its GPS.

Shawn had been practicing with the twin beauties for years, even before his father had gifted them to him to start his own vintage gun collection. He had kept them in perfect working condition just as his father had taught him.

Most often he'd practiced in a shooting range, but sometimes he'd ventured out into the mountains. Hunting wasn't allowed just anyplace, so he'd bought silencers to avoid getting caught. He never took his kills home, leaving the carcasses to be eaten by other predators.

As he stashed the guns in the glove compartment, Shawn envisioned two possible scenarios for their use.

One was to threaten the scumbag screwing his wife, watch him as he pissed himself in fear, and get him to confess Callie's whereabouts. The other was to drive him out to the mountains, kill him, and leave his carcass for the wild animals to dispose of, the same way Shawn had done with the critters he'd killed.

Or both.

CHAPTER 54: CALLIE

"What's up, Callie?" Donnie asked as she joined him outside on her break. "I miss our walks."

She leaned into him, putting her head on his bicep. "Me too. But I like having a car and driving myself places. You can't live in Los Angeles without a car."

"That's true." Donnie pulled out a cigarette and offered her one, even though she always declined.

Callie eyed the pack. "You know what? I'll give it another try. I feel adventurous lately." She took the Marlboro Light, waiting for Donnie to light it up for her.

"Be careful. Don't inhale too much."

She chuckled. "I won't. I learned my lesson."

It still tasted awful, but she decided to give it a chance. Some things took getting used to before they felt good. Even amazing.

Callie blushed. Like the flogger. It had been such a surprise that a scary-looking instrument like that with even a scarier name could be used for pleasure. A lot of pleasure. It wasn't harmless. If Brundar had applied more force, she would have no doubt felt the sting despite how soft those suede strips were.

Maybe someday she'd be brave enough to try. A little pain enhanced the pleasure. But as she was discovering, it sometimes worked for her and sometimes didn't. She needed to be in the right frame of mind to enjoy it.

"You're getting the hang of it," Donnie commented.

Lost in thought, she'd smoked one-third of the cigarette. "I'm getting lightheaded. I think that's enough for my virgin voyage."

Stifling a chuckle, Donnie shook his head as he took the cigarette from her. "You say the damnedest things, Callie. I have to bite my cheek every time."

She waved a hand. "Feel free to say whatever is on your mind. I'm not a delicate flower."

"Maybe not, but your boyfriend may not approve."

"He is not here." It didn't escape Callie's notice that it was the first time she hadn't denied Brundar was her boyfriend. Maybe because yesterday had been the first time he'd acted like one. He'd even texted her today, twice. Once to tell her he had a busy day and wouldn't be able to come over, which was a shame since he also had a rotation tonight. The second time he'd texted her just to ask how she was doing and promised to sneak into her bed when he was done with his rotation in the morning.

Callie was soaring on a happy cloud.

"That is true. But you never know what he can hear. I swear the dude has bat hearing."

She'd noticed that. Sometimes she would mumble something in the kitchen, and he would answer her from the living room as if she was right next to him. Just one more oddity to add to the mystery that was Brundar.

But who was counting?

Donnie pulled out several folded pages from the inner

pocket of his jacket. "I finally came up with an idea for a comic strip starring Fran. She is an investigative reporter, looking for vampires. I only have a few pages done. What do you think?" Moving closer to the light, he held up the first page.

"It's Fran all right. Just better looking. It's obvious that you're smitten with her. But that's good. What girl doesn't like to be drawn as a gorgeous bombshell?"

"I was following your advice. But I didn't need to enhance much. She is already beautiful." Donnie's smile was wistful.

Leaning closer, Callie tried to read the tight writing enclosed in the bubbles, when a shadow darted behind Donnie.

Was someone trying to sneak into the club behind the bouncer's back?

She put her hand on his arm to alert him when she heard a heavy thud.

As Donnie groaned and started crumbling down to the sidewalk, her ponytail got yanked from behind, and she stumbled.

It was all happening so fast.

The moment Callie opened her mouth to scream, a meaty fist connected with her jaw, then something rigid hit the back of her head, and it was lights out.

CHAPTER 55: BRUNDAR

"*C*an you do me a favor?" The words tasted like sawdust in Brundar's mouth. He hated asking for anything, favors in particular.

Anandur fought to stifle a smirk and lost. "What type of favor?"

To his credit, his brother refrained from making his typical comments, which must've cost him real effort. The guy lived for opportunities like that.

"Can you switch rotations with me?"

"Just tonight, or in general?"

"Tonight." He would've loved to fob off all of his rotations on someone else, but the other Guardians were in no position to take on any additional load.

"Any special reason?"

Evidently, it was too much to hope for Anandur to just do it without asking questions and commenting.

"My reasons are my own. Can you do it, or not?"

"I'll do it. And if you tell me what it's about, I'll take over all of your rotations for the next month. Hopefully, by then the murders will stop, and there will be no more need for us to do it."

It was tempting.

It was extremely fucking tempting.

"I've stuff I need to do in the evenings and nights. Stuff I've been doing for a long time. This thing with the rotations is putting a real strain on my time."

Anandur crossed his arms over his chest. "Not good enough, bro. I need details."

Damnation. What to do? Confide in his brother, or keep going on the fucking rotations?

Contrary to what everyone thought of him, Anandur was good with secrets. He wouldn't rat Brundar out.

"This stays between us."

Anandur nodded. "Naturally."

"And I don't want to hear any comments or remarks from you. I don't find them funny."

Anandur tapped his chest over his heart. "You wound me, but then you have no sense of humor, and my jokes are wasted on you."

"Are you done?"

"Yes."

"I bought half of a club I'm a member of. The owner is a shitty businessman, and it was about to go under. I liked the place, so I decided to save it, thinking of it as an investment. But my money is not going to keep it afloat unless things change and it starts turning up a decent profit."

Anandur eyed him curiously as if he was seeing him in a whole new light. "My little bro is a businessman, who would've guessed?"

"Are you going to take over my rotations, or not?"

Anandur lifted a finger. "One last question."

Brundar tensed. There was no doubt in his mind what his nosy brother's question would be about. He'd been trying to get information on Brundar's mystery woman since the first day he'd guessed her existence.

"Is it working? Did you make the place profitable?"

Hell and damnation. This wasn't the question Brundar had been expecting. He was more than happy to answer this one.

"At this point, I'm glad it's no longer bleeding money. There is a small profit, but I'm working on making it bigger."

"I'm proud of you." Anandur clapped him on the back. "It's good that you're showing interest in things other than your sword, and that you're good at it too. I always knew you were smart."

As Anandur geared up and left their apartment, Brundar changed into his club attire, which consisted of black jeans and a black T-shirt. Thinking about his conversation with Anandur, it occurred to him that his brother had never asked what type of club it was.

Brundar frowned. It was not like Anandur to leave a detail like that unanswered. His brother was too shrewd for that. Which made Brundar suspect that Anandur had known about it all along. Maybe not the part about him owning half of the place, but about his membership.

Sneaky bastard had probably planted a tracker on Brundar's Escalade. The first thing he was going to do when he got down to the garage was to check every inch of that car until he found it.

Damnation. What if Anandur made a habit of spying on him and knew all about Calypso?

CHAPTER 56: CALLIE

*G*roggy and confused, Callie opened her eyes and saw a familiar room. In front of her, next to the front door, was the clock she'd bought two months ago to cover yet another hole in the wall; to her right was the couch and to her left the kitchen.

Callie's head hurt something awful, and so did her jaw. She tried to move it a little, but it hurt like hell.

The sharp pain cleared the fog in her head enough for her to realize she was tied to a chair. Duct tape secured each wrist to an armrest, her torso to the back of the chair, her calves to its legs, and her thighs to its seat. It was one of the stacking chairs they kept in the garage for when Shawn invited his buddies from work to watch a football game. The frame was aluminum. Unbreakable.

She was going to die in that chair. Shawn was going to kill her.

How had he found her? She and Brundar had been so careful.

"You're awake. Good. I want you to watch me kill your boyfriend."

Shawn entered the living room with another chair and put it down right next to her. He then walked over to the coffee table and picked up two handguns. Taking a seat, he had one gun loosely gripped in his hand, the other on his lap.

"Are you comfortable?" He wasn't expecting a response. "You should thank me for arranging a front row seat for you. You're not going to miss a thing. I hope his blood sprays your tits, same way you've let his cum do."

He looked crazed, but his tone was calm as if he was talking about the weather, which was much more worrisome than if he was shouting and raging. She'd never seen him like that before. The hatred, the cruelty, had turned his handsome face into a monstrous mask. Or had the face he'd shown her before been the mask, and this was his real one?

She'd married a monster.

Cold sweat trickled down Callie's back. Her life was forfeit, but she wouldn't let Brundar sacrifice his on her behalf. She was going to lie and plead like her life depended on it, even though she had a feeling nothing was going to save her.

"What boyfriend? What are you talking about?"

Calmly, as if he was swatting a fly, Shawn backhanded her. Pain exploded in her cheek, stars blinking behind her tears.

"Don't lie to me, bitch. Your fucking elf lover is going to come for you, and I'm going to shoot first and ask questions later. I'm not going to give him a chance to hypnotize me again."

She had no idea what he was talking about but was afraid to say so. He was obviously delusional. There was something in the elf reference, but not the one about Brundar hypnotizing him.

"You're such a stupid cunt, Callie. You could've lived like a queen. I was saving up for us to move to a nicer place. You think what I put in our joint account was all the money I made? Just shows how stupid you are. I would have never put all my money where you could put your grubby little hands on it. I have hundreds of thousands stashed in different bank accounts. Accounts no fucking divorce lawyer could've found, so don't you get any ideas."

Did it mean he wasn't planning on killing her? A dead woman couldn't contact a divorce lawyer.

"If you were just a little more agreeable as a wife, you could have had everything a woman could want. But no, you had to argue about every goddamned thing instead of listening to your husband. Your older and much smarter husband."

Delusional indeed.

As if she'd argued about anything. Throughout their marriage, Shawn had treated her as his personal maid, expecting her to do all the cooking and the cleaning and the picking up after him even though she worked too and put all of her money into their joint account, not just a small portion of it like he had done.

But there was no sense in arguing the point with a madman. He would just hit her again, and she was already in so much pain that she was fighting to stay awake and not to black out.

He turned to her. "What did you lack? Were you embarrassed about being married to a car salesman? Just so you know, I got a new job." He smiled evilly. "A very well-paying managerial job. I'm the top guy and what I say goes. They chose me because I'm a natural born leader. But only my whoring cunt of a wife couldn't see it!"

He lifted his hand again, and Callie flinched, expecting a blow, but it didn't come. His hand was gentle as he cupped her bruised cheek. "You were so young. Maybe if I slapped you around from the start, taught you to obey, none of this would have happened." He waved the gun between them.

He slapped her then, lightly, but it was over the big bruise he'd left before, and the pain was too much for Callie to keep the tears from leaking.

Shawn wiped her tears with his thumb. "I like this look on you. Beaten and defeated. You'd better get used to it because you'll be wearing it every goddamned day until the day you die."

CHAPTER 57: BRUNDAR

*I*t was ten o'clock when Brundar parked his Escalade in the club's parking lot.

Calypso was going to be so surprised. She wasn't expecting him until the early hours of the morning. He'd wanted to bring her a nice meal like he'd done yesterday, but he'd been in a rush to get to the club. Besides, nothing could top Gerard's culinary genius.

Instead, Brundar had emptied the vending machines of all the remaining pastries. Callie was going to love them for breakfast.

He smirked thinking of all the pissed off immortals who were going to find the machines empty. They would probably blame Jackson for not restocking them in a timely manner.

Perhaps he should bring her one now? A little energy boost to help her through her shift?

Taking a pastry out of the paper bag, Brundar searched his glove compartment for a clean cloth. He always kept several on hand in case he needed to clean his weapons.

He wrapped the pastry in the cloth, put it in his leather

jacket's roomy pocket, got out of his car, and locked it, activating the alarm. This wasn't the best of neighborhoods, and his brand new Escalade was too tempting of a target.

Brundar saw Donnie as soon as he rounded the corner, sitting on the sidewalk and rubbing the back of his head. A feeling of dread raised the small hairs on the back of his neck as he sprinted toward the bouncer.

"What happened?" He crouched next to him.

"I don't know. One minute I was showing Callie my comics, the next someone hit me over the back of the head. By the shape of the lump, I think it was a gun." He patted his pants pocket. "Weird, my wallet is still here. Someone must've scared the guy off."

"Where is Calypso?"

"I don't know. Maybe she went inside to get help?"

Brundar had a bad feeling. Whoever had knocked Donnie out was obviously after something other than his wallet. He ran inside, stopping by the receptionist. "Did Calypso come in?"

The girl pointed at the door. "She is taking her break outside with Donnie."

"She is not. I'm asking again. Did you see her coming in?"

"No. I thought she was still outside. What's going on?"

"Call Franco. Donnie was hit over the head and needs to be taken to the hospital. I'm going to look for Calypso."

He didn't wait for her response as he dashed out, stopping momentarily by Donnie. "Franco is coming, and he is going to take you to see a doctor. I'm going to look for Calypso."

Donnie staggered to his feet. "I'll come with you. I'm fine."

"You're not fine, and I don't need any help." Brundar sprinted to his car.

He had a good idea who had taken Calypso and where. The thing was, to get her out alive, he might need help after all. The jerk had a gun. Shawn couldn't kill Brundar, but he could incapacitate him.

Brundar needed backup.

For the second time in one day, he was going to ask his brother for a favor, and he didn't care what it was going to cost him.

To save her life, he would pay any price.

Hopefully, he wasn't too late already.

CHAPTER 58: CALLIE

*S*hawn wasn't going to kill her.

He was going to keep her locked up and make her life a living hell. Callie had read several stories about women who'd been held captive for years, rotting in some basement with no one suspecting the psychos who'd kidnapped them of anything. The difference was that in all of those cases the abductors were strangers, not ex-husbands or ex-boyfriends.

Severe cases of spousal abuse usually ended in the woman's death, not her imprisonment.

It seemed the perpetrators of the respective crimes didn't share the same psychosis.

Except for Shawn.

Either that or the stories of spouses kept under lock and key didn't make the news.

For the past several minutes, Shawn had been quiet, staring intently at the door, waiting for Brundar to show up. He was going to wait for a long time.

Thank God, Brundar was on rotation tonight. He

wouldn't even know she was missing until he came to her apartment in the early hours of the morning.

Crap. When Donnie regained consciousness, which he had most likely already done or was about to, he would sound the alarm. She had no doubt someone would call Brundar.

Would he know where to look for her?

If the roles were reversed, she would've figured it out immediately. There was only one person after her. The chances that Shawn had been the one who'd taken her were far greater than her falling victim to some random act of violence. Someone as experienced as Brundar would come to the same conclusion.

Which meant that he was either on his way or would be shortly.

God, make him call the police and not barge in here like some avenging hero.

He would, though.

The guy thought of himself as the best fighter, and maybe he was, but he wasn't fast enough to dodge a bullet fired from less than ten feet away, no matter how good he was.

She should scream for help.

No, she shouldn't.

The moment she did, Shawn would punch her again and then gag her, and the chances that someone would respond to one scream for help were slim. Shawn would hide her in the bedroom, and smile charmingly at whoever knocked on the door, telling them a story about a loud movie.

People would believe him because it was human nature to believe in what they hoped was true, and not what they feared.

Gagged, she would lose her chance to warn Brundar or plead with Shawn for mercy. Not that she harbored much hope for either, but it was better than nothing. Better than feeling completely hopeless and defeated the way Shawn was planning for her to spend the rest of her life.

Callie would welcome death with open arms rather than live like that.

CHAPTER 59: BRUNDAR

*D*riving like a bat out of hell, Brundar's mind was calm. Thanks to years of practice, he was able to slip into the zone even under the most difficult circumstances.

And these were the most disturbing he'd ever experienced.

Shawn showing up at the club meant that he'd somehow remembered their first encounter, as well as the others, and had connected the dots.

The bastard had already suspected Calypso of cheating on him, and now he had a face to put on her imaginary lover.

Well, not imaginary, but Calypso hadn't been unfaithful although she'd had every right to be. Her husband certainly hadn't refrained from it, as Brundar had witnessed in his memories.

Parking his car a few houses down the block, he removed his boots and sprinted the rest of the way barefoot. A stealth approach would give him the element of surprise. A split second difference was all he needed to disarm Shawn.

He'd expected to hear loud arguments, maybe even

I. T. LUCAS

Calypso crying, but the house was eerily quiet, and all the blinds were pulled down, blocking him from peeking inside.

Imagining the worst, Brundar's pulse quickened.

He prayed he wasn't too late.

He prayed he hadn't misjudged the situation and Calypso wasn't somewhere else altogether.

Far from a criminal mastermind, Shawn was a simple-minded thug. He wouldn't have thought to take Calypso to a motel. Besides, he needed privacy for what he intended.

But what were his intentions?

To hurt Calypso was one, that was for sure. Brundar had seen into the guy's mind. The other was to kill her lover.

He was waiting for Brundar. Which was excellent because it meant Calypso was alive. Probably gagged.

By holding her hostage, Shawn could force Brundar to submit. The jerk could actually manage to kill Brundar. The right kind of bullet, shot point blank to the heart or the brain, would end him.

It was good that backup was coming. He only hoped Anandur hadn't mobilized the entire Guardian force. He'd said he wouldn't, but he hadn't sworn on it.

Circling the house to the back, Brundar checked every window and door, but they were all locked. Not only that, they were all wired. Shawn had either activated the alarm or not, but Brundar couldn't take the chance that he had.

Not with Calypso's life on the line.

That left coming through the front door. If Shawn was waiting for him, he would be sitting in his living room and facing the door with a gun in his hand.

The question was whether he was going to shoot first and talk later or the other way around. Brundar was hoping for the second one. The guy had probably taken all of his villainous ideas from the movies, where the bad guys delivered long speeches before firing a single bullet.

A knife in each hand, Brundar kicked the door in, zeroing on his target, who was hiding behind the terrified Calypso, a gun aimed at her temple, and a second one pointing at the door.

She was tied to a fucking chair, and the only part of the coward's big body sticking from behind it was his left shoulder. Brundar could've hit it easily, but the jerk would press the trigger and kill Calypso on the spot.

It was back to the original plan—serving as a pincushion for the guy's bullets until Anandur arrived.

"You don't want to do that, Shawn." Brundar imbued his tone with as much influence as he could muster.

"None of that, asshole." Shawn pressed the trigger, hitting Brundar in one knee, and then immediately going for the other. Brundar's legs collapsed. He would've powered through the pain, but the mechanics simply were no longer there.

His knees were shattered.

It was one of the rare injuries that took weeks of regeneration instead of minutes or hours. For some reason, regrowing bones and tendons was harder than internal organs and muscle tissue.

Calypso screamed. Shawn put an end to it with a blow to her face, sending her toppling sideways together with her chair.

With Calypso out of the way and no longer providing cover for her ex, Brundar let his knives fly, both hitting the same target—Shawn's blackened heart.

The knives bounced back and clunked to the floor.

Laughing, the guy tore his shirt open, showing Brundar his makeshift armor—a large cast iron griddle strapped to his torso, protecting all of his vital organs.

Fuck, he should have aimed for the knees, same as the motherfucker who wasn't as stupid as Brundar had thought he was.

It also made sense now why he'd aimed at Brundar's knees without having any way of knowing Brundar's vital organs were less vulnerable than his joints. Shawn had assumed Brundar had come prepared the same way he had, with something to shield his heart.

The guy calmly walked around him, keeping his distance as if sensing that Brundar wasn't as incapacitated as he looked, and closed the door Brundar had left open.

Brundar tried to concentrate and effect a thrall, but the pain was too intense. He managed a weak one, only to feel it disintegrate before he was able to coalesce enough mental power to hurl it at Shawn.

Besides, the guy had somehow figured it out, probably assuming hypnosis, and was ready for it, actively resisting.

Even in peak performance, Brundar would have had a hard time thralling an actively resisting human.

"I could kill you right now, motherfucker, but I want my whore of a wife to see her lover die."

He grabbed Calypso's hair, lifting her up together with the chair she was strapped to.

Thank the merciful Fates she was still unconscious and didn't feel it.

"Wake up, bitch." He slapped her bruised cheeks, first one, and then the other.

As if yanking her by the hair wasn't enough to wake her if she could've been awakened. Brundar could hear her steady heartbeat, which meant she was first and foremost alive, but also that she was mercifully spared the pain and anguish.

"You've got the situation all wrong. I'm just a friend." Brundar was trying to stall, and he wasn't above using the misconceptions people had about him. "I'm gay. She has nothing I want. I swear."

Shawn frowned, contemplating Brundar's statement and eyeing him suspiciously.

Then he waved his gun and smiled.

"Nice try. Is that why you delivered the divorce papers in person and roughed me up? Because she has nothing you want? Is that why you are here facing death? Because she has nothing you want? I don't think so. You were thinking with your dick, buddy, not your brain. And your dick is dumb as fuck."

Hell and damnation.

Where in the name of the bloody Fates was Anandur?

CHAPTER 60: CALLIE

*C*allie came to with a start, her pain immediately forgotten as she saw Brundar on the floor with both his knees looking like they'd been blown to pieces, his pale face paler than she'd ever seen it. Shawn was standing next to her, pointing both of his guns at Brundar. He had silencers on them. No wonder none of the neighbors had called the police yet.

Or maybe they had, and help was on the way.

Not letting on that she was awake, she listened to the exchange between Brundar and Shawn. If the situation weren't as dire as it was, she would've laughed at Brundar's attempt to convince Shawn he was gay. Given his looks, it was a good try, but Shawn wasn't buying it.

She needed to come up with something else to stall.

Something that would stroke Shawn's ego. Maybe she should tell him she'd been only using Brundar, and that he meant nothing to her. She could say that she'd filed for divorce because she'd been mad about the school situation but had regretted it immediately because she missed him. Where could she ever find another man as sexy and as manly as Shawn?

Callie was about to open her mouth and start her pleading when she caught Brundar's nearly imperceptible head shake. When she closed her mouth, he closed and opened his eyes several times until she understood what he was trying to tell her.

He wanted her to pretend she was still out.

Callie closed her eyes, forcing her body to go limp and letting her head loll down.

"Say your final prayers, asshole. As soon as she wakes up, you're history."

"Don't do it, man. You don't want to spend the rest of your life in jail because of a woman, do you? She's not worth it. No woman is."

Shawn chuckled. "You're preaching to the choir. But no one betrays me and cuckolds me without paying the price. I'm not going to jail for ending your miserable life either. I'll drop your carcass in the mountains for the predators to dispose of. The bitch over here will tell no one because I'm going to keep her naked, chained to the bed, and gagged."

Callie suppressed a shiver. She had no doubt Shawn meant every word.

Brundar closed his eyes again, signaling her to keep playing possum.

"Don't you dare pass out, asshole," Shawn spat in Brundar's direction. "Or are you praying?"

"I'm praying."

"Good. Make peace with your maker, motherfucker. Pray for the Lord's forgiveness for you have sinned. God is on my side. As the cuckolded husband, it's my right and obligation to kill you and my whore of a wife. But I prefer to let her live out the rest of her life in misery."

Crap, don't let the tears fall, don't cry, dead possums don't cry...please God, if you can hear me, please help us, we don't deserve to end like this.

Callie was losing the battle against her tears. Any moment one would slide down her cheek and Shawn would kill Brundar. She scrunched her eyes, holding tight, hoping Shawn couldn't see her face because her chin was practically down to her chest.

Boom!

The door burst open, ending Callie's pretense as she instinctively jerked her head up and opened her eyes.

Her first thought was the Terminator. Her second and more logical one was that it was a guy wearing a futuristic soldier's body armor like the ones she'd seen in Sci-Fi movies.

Shawn fired at the soldier until both guns clicked on empty, but the guy kept on advancing in his slow lumbering strides, probably unable to go any faster because of the heavy suiting.

Shawn backed away, but the soldier reached with a long arm and grabbed him by the neck. A split second later, she heard a snap, and Shawn's body crumbled to the floor.

"What took you so long?" Brundar asked.

Putting both gloved hands on his helmet, the soldier pulled it off, revealing a headful of crinkly red hair.

"Anandur!" Callie called out.

He turned to her with an apologetic expression on his face. "I hope you don't mind." He tilted his head toward Shawn's body. "After seeing what he did to you and to my brother, I couldn't help myself."

"It was self-defense," she offered. Callie wasn't going to shed a single tear for that monster. Anandur had done the world a favor by getting rid of him. She would testify in any court that it was done in self-defense.

"Nope, not really. I was wearing a protective suit. But I

can't say I'm sorry I did it." Anandur removed his gloves and gently unwrapped the duct tape from Callie's wrists, causing her as little discomfort possible. A gentle giant.

"Go help Brundar, I can do the rest."

"Don't worry about him. He is going to be fine." Anandur kept unwrapping, removing the tape around her torso and upper arms.

"God, how can you say that? I don't know if your brother will ever walk again."

Brundar groaned, but Anandur's big body was blocking him from her view. "He is right, Calypso. I'll be fine. I've had worse. But it hurts like a son-of-a-bitch."

Anandur turned his head toward his brother. "Don't be a pussy. Suck it up like a man."

"Up yours."

He turned back to Callie and started working on the tape around her ankles. "I apologize for my brother and myself. That's no way to talk in front of a lady."

"I heard much worse tonight. Thank you for coming to our rescue."

He nodded, tackling the tape around her thighs.

"We need to call the police."

Anandur shook his head. "No, we don't."

"Are we going to just leave him like that? They will eventually find him and come asking questions. If we don't report it, we will look guilty."

"I'm going to make it look as if he hung himself, and we are going to clean up Brundar's blood from the floor. Case closed."

She threw him an incredulous look. "Do you think anyone would buy it?"

"Scatter the divorce papers on the floor next to where you hang him," Brundar suggested from behind Anandur's back. "They are on the coffee table."

He sounded awfully calm for someone who was in lots and lots of pain.

"All done." Anandur removed the last piece of tape and helped Callie up.

She swayed on her feet, catching herself by bracing on his bicep. He wrapped his arm around her waist, which elicited a peculiar growl from behind him.

"Cut it out, moron. The woman can barely stand."

Brundar responded with a grunt.

"I'm fine. Just a little woozy. I want to tend to Brundar." She took a couple of wobbly steps and plopped down on the floor next to him. He was lying on his back, looking as pale as a ghost. "You look terrible." She caressed his cheek, finally letting the tears flow. She'd been holding them in for so long, there was a lake of them ready to spill.

Brundar lifted his arm and wiped her tears away with gentle fingers. "You don't look so hot yourself. But you're always beautiful to me."

"Oh, that's so precious. I'm going to cry." Anandur affected a Southern belle tone and accent while hefting Shawn's body over his shoulder.

"How can he joke while carrying a dead body?"

Brundar rolled his eyes. "Don't get me started on that. In the dictionary, next to the terms inappropriate and crude, you'll find a picture of Anandur with a goofy smirk on his face."

She shook her head. "I don't get how you can joke at a time like this either."

Clasping her hand, he brought it to his lips and kissed the inside of her palm. "I'm a happy man. You're alive, I'm alive, and we get to live another day. What else could I ask for?"

The end... for now.

BRUNDAR AND CALYPSO'S STORY
CULMINATES IN BOOK 16
DARK ANGEL'S SURRENDER

Dark Angel's Surrender is Available on Amazon

Dear reader,

Thank you for joining me on the continuing adventures of the ***Children of the Gods***.

As an independent author, I rely on your support to spread the word. So if you enjoyed the story, please share your experience, and if it isn't too much trouble, I would greatly appreciate a brief review on Amazon for ***Dark Angel's Seduction***.

Love & happy reading,

Isabell

skeptical and refuses Amanda's plea to attempt Syssi's activation. But when his enemies learn of the Dormant's existence, he's forced to rush her to the safety of his keep. Inexorably drawn to Syssi, Kian wrestles with his conscience as he is tempted to explore her budding interest in the darker shades of sensuality.

2: DARK STRANGER REVEALED

While sheltered in the clan's stronghold, Syssi is unaware that Kian and Amanda are not human, and neither are the supposedly religious fanatics that are after her. She feels a powerful connection to Kian, and as he introduces her to a world of pleasure she never dared imagine, his dominant sexuality is a revelation. Considering that she's completely out of her element, Syssi feels comfortable and safe letting go with him. That is, until she begins to suspect that all is not as it seems. Piecing the puzzle together, she draws a scary, yet wrong conclusion...

3: DARK STRANGER IMMORTAL

When Kian confesses his true nature, Syssi is not as much shocked by the revelation as she is wounded by what she perceives as his callous plans for her.

If she doesn't turn, he'll be forced to erase her memories and let her go. His family's safety demands secrecy – no one in the mortal world is allowed to know that immortals exist.

Resigned to the cruel reality that even if she stays on to never again leave the keep, she'll get old while Kian won't, Syssi is determined to enjoy what little time she has with him, one day at a time.

Can Kian let go of the mortal woman he loves? Will Syssi turn? And if she does, will she survive the dangerous transition?

4: DARK ENEMY TAKEN

Dalhu can't believe his luck when he stumbles upon the beautiful immortal professor. Presented with a once in a lifetime opportunity to grab an immortal female for himself, he kidnaps her and runs. If he ever gets caught, either by her people or his, his life is forfeit. But for a chance of a loving mate and a family of his own, Dalhu is prepared to do everything in his power to win Amanda's heart, and that includes leaving the Doom brotherhood and his old life behind.

Amanda soon discovers that there is more to the handsome Doomer than his dark past and a hulking, sexy body. But succumbing to her enemy's seduction, or worse, developing feelings for a ruthless killer is out of the question. No man is worth life on the run, not even the one and only immortal male she could claim as her own...

Her clan and her research must come first...

5: DARK ENEMY CAPTIVE

When the rescue team returns with Amanda and the chained Dalhu to the keep, Amanda is not as thrilled to be back as she thought she'd be. Between Kian's contempt for her and Dalhu's imprisonment, Amanda's budding relationship with Dalhu seems doomed. Things start to look up when Annani offers her help, and together with Syssi they resolve to find a way for Amanda to be with Dalhu. But will she still want him when she realizes that he is responsible for her nephew's murder? Could she? Will she take the easy way out and choose Andrew instead?

6: DARK ENEMY REDEEMED

Amanda suspects that something fishy is going on onboard the Anna. But when her investigation of the peculiar all-female Russian crew fails to uncover anything other than more speculation, she decides it's time to stop playing detective and face her real problem —a man she shouldn't want but can't live without.

6.5: MY DARK AMAZON

When Michael and Kri fight off a gang of humans, Michael gets stabbed. The injury to his immortal body recovers fast, but the one to his ego takes longer, putting a strain on his relationship with Kri.

7: DARK WARRIOR MINE

When Andrew is forced to retire from active duty, he believes that all he has to look forward to is a boring desk job. His glory days in special ops are over. But as it turns out, his thrill ride has just begun. Andrew discovers not only that immortals exist and have been manipulating global affairs since antiquity, but that he and his sister are rare possessors of the immortal genes.

Problem is, Andrew might be too old to attempt the activation process. His sister, who is fourteen years his junior, barely made it through the transition, so the odds of him coming out of it alive, let alone immortal, are slim.

But fate may force his hand.

Helping a friend find his long-lost daughter, Andrew finds a woman who's worth taking the risk for. Nathalie might be a Dormant, but the only way to find out for sure requires fangs and venom.

8: Dark Warrior's Promise

Andrew and Nathalie's love flourishes, but the secrets they keep from each other taint their relationship with doubts and suspicions. In the meantime, Sebastian and his men are getting bolder, and the storm that's brewing will shift the balance of power in the millennia-old conflict between Annani's clan and its enemies.

9: Dark Warrior's Destiny

The new ghost in Nathalie's head remembers who he was in life, providing Andrew and her with indisputable proof that he is real and not a figment of her imagination.

Convinced that she is a Dormant, Andrew decides to go forward with his transition immediately after the rescue mission at the Doomers' HQ.

Fearing for his life, Nathalie pleads with him to reconsider. She'd rather spend the rest of her mortal days with Andrew than risk what they have for the fickle promise of immortality.

While the clan gets ready for battle, Carol gets help from an unlikely ally. Sebastian's second-in-command can no longer ignore the torment she suffers at the hands of his commander and offers to help her, but only if she agrees to his terms.

10: Dark Warrior's Legacy

Andrew's acclimation to his post-transition body isn't easy. His senses are sharper, he's bigger, stronger, and hungrier. Nathalie fears that the changes in the man she loves are more than physical. Measuring up to this new version of him is going to be a challenge.

Carol and Robert are disillusioned with each other. They are not destined mates, and love is not on the horizon. When Robert's three months are up, he might be left with nothing to show for his sacrifice.

Lana contacts Anandur with disturbing news; the yacht and its human cargo are in Mexico. Kian must find a way to apprehend Alex and rescue the women on board without causing an international incident.

11: Dark Guardian Found

What would you do if you stopped aging?

Eva runs. The ex-DEA agent doesn't know what caused her strange mutation, only that if discovered, she'll be dissected like a lab rat. What Eva doesn't know, though, is that she's a descendant of the gods, and that she is not alone. The man who rocked her world in one life-changing encounter over thirty years ago is an immortal as well.

To keep his people's existence secret, Bhathian was forced to turn his back on the only woman who ever captured his heart, but he's never forgotten and never stopped looking for her.

12: Dark Guardian Craved

Cautious after a lifetime of disappointments, Eva is mistrustful of Bhathian's professed feelings of love. She accepts him as a lover and a confidant but not as a life partner.

Jackson suspects that Tessa is his true love mate, but unless she overcomes her fears, he might never find out.

Carol gets an offer she can't refuse—a chance to prove that there is more to her than meets the eye. Robert believes she's about to commit a deadly mistake, but when he tries to dissuade her, she tells him to leave.

13: Dark Guardian's Mate

Prepare for the heart-warming culmination of Eva and Bhathian's story!

14: Dark Angel's Obsession

The cold and stoic warrior is an enigma even to those closest to him. His secrets are about to unravel...

15: Dark Angel's Seduction

Brundar is fighting a losing battle. Calypso is slowly chipping away his icy armor from the outside, while his need for her is melting it from the inside.

He can't allow it to happen. Calypso is a human with none of the Dormant indicators. There is no way he can keep her for more than a few weeks.

16: Dark Angel's Surrender

Get ready for the heart pounding conclusion to Brundar and Calypso's story.

Callie still couldn't wrap her head around it, nor could she summon even a smidgen of sorrow or regret. After all, she had some memories with him that weren't horrible. She should've felt something. But there was nothing, not even shock. Not even horror at what had transpired over the last couple of hours.

Maybe it was a typical response for survivors--feeling euphoric for the simple reason that they were alive. Especially when that survival was nothing short of miraculous.

Brundar's cold hand closed around hers, reminding her that they weren't out of the woods yet. Her injuries were superficial, and the most she had to worry about was some scarring. But, despite his and Anandur's reassurances, Brundar might never walk again.

If he ended up crippled because of her, she would never forgive herself for getting him involved in her crap.

"Are you okay, sweetling? Are you in pain?" Brundar asked.

Her injuries were nothing compared to his, and yet he was concerned about her. God, she loved this man. The thing was, if she told him that, he would run off, or crawl away as was the case.

Hey, maybe this was the perfect opportunity to spring it on him.

17: Dark Operative: A Shadow of Death

As a brilliant strategist and the only human entrusted with the secret of immortals' existence, Turner is both an asset and a liability to the clan. His request to attempt transition into immortality as an alternative to cancer treatments cannot be denied without risking the clan's exposure. On the other hand, approving it means risking his premature death. In both scenarios, the clan will lose a valuable ally.

When the decision is left to the clan's physician, Turner makes plans to manipulate her by taking advantage of her interest in him.

Will Bridget fall for the cold, calculated operative? Or will Turner fall into his own trap?

18: Dark Operative: A Glimmer of Hope

As Turner and Bridget's relationship deepens, living together seems like the right move, but to make it work both need to make concessions.

Bridget is realistic and keeps her expectations low. Turner could never be the truelove mate she yearns for, but he is as good as she's going to get. Other than his emotional limitations, he's perfect in every way.

Turner's hard shell is starting to show cracks. He wants immortality, he wants to be part of the clan, and he wants Bridget, but he doesn't want to cause her pain.

His options are either abandon his quest for immortality and give Bridget his few remaining decades, or abandon Bridget by going for the transition and most likely dying. His rational mind dictates that he chooses the former, but his gut pulls him toward the latter. Which one is he going to trust?

19: Dark Operative: The Dawn of Love

Get ready for the exciting finale of Bridget and Turner's story!

20: Dark Survivor Awakened

This was a strange new world she had awakened to.

Her memory loss must have been catastrophic because almost nothing was familiar. The language was foreign to her, with only a few words bearing some similarity to the language she thought in. Still, a full moon cycle had passed since her awakening, and little by little she was gaining basic understanding of it--only a few words and phrases, but she was learning more each day.

A week or so ago, a little girl on the street had tugged on her mother's sleeve and pointed at her. "Look, Mama, Wonder Woman!"

The mother smiled apologetically, saying something in the language these people spoke, then scurried away with the child looking behind her shoulder and grinning.

When it happened again with another child on the same day, it was settled.

Wonder Woman must have been the name of someone important in this strange world she had awoken to, and since both times it had been said with a smile it must have been a good one.

Wonder had a nice ring to it.

She just wished she knew what it meant.

21: DARK SURVIVOR ECHOES OF LOVE

Wonder's journey continues in *Dark Survivor Echoes of Love*.

22: DARK SURVIVOR REUNITED

The exciting finale of Wonder and Anandur's story.

23: DARK WIDOW'S SECRET

Vivian and her daughter share a powerful telepathic connection, so when Ella can't be reached by conventional or psychic means, her mother fears the worst.

Help arrives from an unexpected source when Vivian gets a call from the young doctor she met at a psychic convention. Turns out Julian belongs to a private organization specializing in retrieving missing girls.

As Julian's clan mobilizes its considerable resources to rescue the daughter, Magnus is charged with keeping the gorgeous young mother safe.

Worry for Ella and the secrets Vivian and Magnus keep from each other should be enough to prevent the sparks of attraction from kindling a blaze of desire. Except, these pesky sparks have a mind of their own.

24: DARK WIDOW'S CURSE

A simple rescue operation turns into mission impossible when the Russian mafia gets involved. Bad things are supposed to come in threes, but in Vivian's case, it seems like there is no limit to bad luck. Her family and everyone who gets close to her is affected by her curse.

Will Magnus and his people prove her wrong?

25: DARK WIDOW'S BLESSING

The thrilling finale of the Dark Widow trilogy!

26: DARK DREAM'S TEMPTATION

Julian has known Ella is the one for him from the moment he saw her picture, but when he finally frees her from captivity, she seems indifferent to him. Could he have been mistaken?

Ella's rescue should've ended that chapter in her life, but it seems like the road back to normalcy has just begun and it's full of obstacles. Between the pitying looks she gets and her mother's attempts to get her into therapy, Ella feels like she's typecast as a victim, when nothing could be further from the truth. She's a tough survivor, and she's going to prove it.

Strangely, the only one who seems to understand is Logan, who keeps popping up in her dreams. But then, he's a figment of her imagination—or is he?

27: DARK DREAM'S UNRAVELING

While trying to figure out a way around Logan's silencing compulsion, Ella concocts an ambitious plan. What if instead of trying to keep him out of her dreams, she could pretend to like him and lure him into a trap?

Catching Navuh's son would be a major boon for the clan, as well as for Ella. She will have her revenge, turning the tables on another scumbag out to get her.

28: DARK DREAM'S TRAP

The trap is set, but who is the hunter and who is the prey? Find out in this heart-pounding conclusion to the *Dark Dream* trilogy.

29: DARK PRINCE'S ENIGMA

As the son of the most dangerous male on the planet, Lokan lives by three rules:

Don't trust a soul.

Don't show emotions.

And don't get attached.

Will one extraordinary woman make him break all three?

30: DARK PRINCE'S DILEMMA

Will Kian decide that the benefits of trusting Lokan outweigh the risks?

Will Lokan betray his father and brothers for the greater good of his people?

Are Carol and Lokan true-love mates, or is one of them playing the other?

So many questions, the path ahead is anything but clear.

31: DARK PRINCE'S AGENDA

While Turner and Kian work out the details of Areana's rescue plan, Carol and Lokan's tumultuous relationship hits another snag. Is it a sign of things to come?

32 : DARK QUEEN'S QUEST

A former beauty queen, a retired undercover agent, and a successful model, Mey is not the typical damsel in distress. But when her sister drops off the radar and then someone starts following her around, she panics.

Following a vague clue that Kalugal might be in New York, Kian sends a team headed by Yamanu to search for him.

As Mey and Yamanu's paths cross, he offers her his help and protection, but will that be all?

33: DARK QUEEN'S KNIGHT

As the only member of his clan with a godlike power over human minds, Yamanu has been shielding his people for centuries, but that power comes at a steep price. When Mey enters his life, he's faced with the most difficult choice.

The safety of his clan or a future with his fated mate.

34: DARK QUEEN'S ARMY

As Mey anxiously waits for her transition to begin and for Yamanu to test whether his godlike powers are gone, the clan sets out to solve two mysteries:

Where is Jin, and is she there voluntarily?

Where is Kalugal, and what is he up to?

35: Dark Spy Conscripted

Jin possesses a unique paranormal ability. Just by touching someone, she can insert a mental hook into their psyche and tie a string of her consciousness to it, creating a tether. That doesn't make her a spy, though, not unless her talent is discovered by those seeking to exploit it.

36: Dark Spy's Mission

Jin's first spying mission is supposed to be easy. Walk into the club, touch Kalugal to tether her consciousness to him, and walk out.

Except, they should have known better.

37: Dark Spy's Resolution

The best-laid plans often go awry...

38: Dark Overlord New Horizon

Jacki has two talents that set her apart from the rest of the human race.

She has unpredictable glimpses of other people's futures, and she is immune to mind manipulation.

Unfortunately, both talents are pretty useless for finding a job other than the one she had in the government's paranormal division.

It seemed like a sweet deal, until she found out that the director planned on producing super babies by compelling the recruits into pairing up. When an opportunity to escape the program presented itself, she took it, only to find out that humans are not at the top of the food chain.

Immortals are real, and at the very top of the hierarchy is Kalugal, the most powerful, arrogant, and sexiest male she has ever met.

With one look, he sets her blood on fire, but Jacki is not a fool. A man like him will never think of her as anything more than a tasty snack, while she will never settle for anything less than his heart.

39: Dark Overlord's Wife

Jacki is still clinging to her all-or-nothing policy, but Kalugal is chipping away at her resistance. Perhaps it's time to ease up on her convictions. A little less than all is still much better than nothing, and a couple of decades with a demigod is probably worth more than a lifetime with a mere mortal.

40: Dark Overlord's Clan

As Jacki and Kalugal prepare to celebrate their union, Kian takes every precaution to safeguard his people. Except, Kalugal and his men are not his only potential adversaries, and compulsion is not the only power he should fear.

41: Dark Choices The Quandary

When Rufsur and Edna meet, the attraction is as unexpected as it is undeniable. Except, she's the clan's judge and councilwoman, and he's Kalugal's second-in-command. Will loyalty and duty to their people keep them apart?

42: Dark Choices Paradigm Shift

Edna and Rufsur are miserable without each other, and their two-week separation seems like an eternity. Long-distance relationships are difficult, but for immortal couples they are impossible. Unless one of them is willing to leave everything behind for the other, things are just going to get worse. Except, the cost of compromise is far greater than giving up their comfortable lives and hard-earned positions. The future of their people is on the line.

TRY THE SERIES ON

AUDIBLE

2 FREE audiobooks with your new Audible subscription!

THE PERFECT MATCH SERIES

PERFECT MATCH 1: VAMPIRE'S CONSORT

When Gabriel's company is ready to start beta testing, he invites his old crush to inspect its medical safety protocol.

Curious about the revolutionary technology of the *Perfect Match Virtual Fantasy-Fulfillment studios*, Brenna agrees.

Neither expects to end up partnering for its first fully immersive test run.

PERFECT MATCH 2: KING'S CHOSEN

When Lisa's nutty friends get her a gift certificate to *Perfect Match Virtual Fantasy Studios*, she has no intentions of using it. But since the only way to get a refund is if no partner can be found for her, she makes sure to request a fantasy so girly and over the top that no sane guy will pick it up.

Except, someone does.

Warning: This fantasy contains a hot, domineering crown prince, sweet insta-love, steamy love scenes painted with light shades of gray, a wedding, and a HEA in both the virtual and real worlds.

Intended for mature audience.

Perfect Match 3: Captain's Conquest

Working as a Starbucks barista, Alicia fends off flirting all day long, but none of the guys are as charming and sexy as Gregg. His frequent visits are the highlight of her day, but since he's never asked her out, she assumes he's taken. Besides, between a day job and a budding music career, she has no time to start a new relationship.

That is until Gregg makes her an offer she can't refuse—a gift certificate to the virtual fantasy fulfillment service everyone is talking about. As a huge Star Trek fan, Alicia has a perfect match in mind—the captain of the Starship Enterprise.

FOR EXCLUSIVE PEEKS AT UPCOMING RELEASES & A FREE COMPANION BOOK

Join my *VIP Club* and gain access to the VIP portal at

ITLUCAS.COM

<u>CLICK HERE TO JOIN</u>

(OR GO TO: http://eepurl.com/blMTpD)

INCLUDED IN YOUR FREE MEMBERSHIP:

- **FREE** CHILDREN OF THE GODS COMPANION BOOK **1**
- **FREE** NARRATION OF GODDESS'S CHOICE—BOOK **1** IN THE CHILDREN OF THE GODS ORIGINS SERIES.
- PREVIEW CHAPTERS OF UPCOMING RELEASES.
- AND OTHER EXCLUSIVE CONTENT OFFERED ONLY TO MY **VIP**S.

Printed in Great Britain
by Amazon

55778535R00200